ONE LIKE AWAY

BECCA FALL

ISBN: 979-8-9987464-0-6

Cover design by Yummy Books

Editing by Emily Keyes at The Romance Genre Specialist

Editing and proofreading by Emily Lawrence at Lawrence Editing

To everyone who feels like they have no idea what they're doing with their lives. I can relate.

1

MACEY

The Chicago airport was chaos. Rolling suitcases, last-minute gate changes, and people walking at the speed of molasses directly in front of me. I dodged a man who had come to a complete stop in the middle of the walkway, causing me to spill the remainder of my cold coffee onto my shoes.

One day, I'd experience air travel without feeling like a contestant on *Survivor*. At least I'd be home soon enough, where I could stretch out on my couch and eat snacks that weren't individually wrapped in crinkly plastic.

If you had asked me where I'd visit on my first trip to California, I would have answered Los Angeles, San Francisco, or even Disneyland. Not Fort Bragg. Honestly, I had never heard of the city until two weeks ago, when an email from their public relations team appeared in my work inbox.

Such was the life of a travel writer—I didn't get to pick my press trips. Hopefully, in the future, I'd have the ability to be selective. For now, I was a bottom-tier blogger, meaning I didn't often get invitations to events like the Whale Fest in Fort Bragg. And when I did receive one, it was either unpaid or they expected me to cover the costs of travel. In this economy? Definitely not.

There were worse places I could have been sent on a press trip. For example, a remote island without any cell service. In front of the Eiffel Tower, forced to watch couples younger than me get engaged. Antarctica in the middle of a penguin march. Say what you will, but I didn't believe those birds were as nice as they looked.

My hand tightened around the strap of my backpack as I followed the signs for baggage claim, but then, I spotted *her*.

A woman, gliding toward the airport lounge.

Full-on gliding. Not weaving around suitcases or getting shoulder-checked by an overly ambitious businessman. She wore a crisp white blouse, perfectly tailored trousers, and heels that looked both expensive and non-lethal—a rare combination. Her hair was styled in some effortlessly chic way that made me hyper-aware of the fact that a few minutes ago, I had used the airport hand dryer to fix my bangs.

The woman stepped up to the lounge entrance, nodded at the attendant like they were old friends, and disappeared inside, swallowed by a world of complimentary drinks and whisper-quiet luxury. I imagined her settling into a plush armchair, ordering an espresso martini without hesitation, and opening a hardcover book. After all, a woman with a hardcover book at the airport had her life together.

One day, that would be me. One day, I'd strut into an airport lounge with the confidence of someone who wasn't actively sweating under the weight of her own luggage. I'd skip the espresso martini and chug a Diet Coke out of habit, but best believe I'd try every available snack.

That would signify my career as a successful travel blogger. I'd own my own blog. Cover events bigger than whale migration.

Have my people call other people's people. Minions would clammer to do my dirty laundry.

For now, though, I was here—Chicago O'Hare, in all its unhinged glory—standing next to a guy loudly FaceTiming his mother about how TSA took his snow globe.

I snapped a quick selfie and sent it to the group chat that had blown up while I was in the air.

The Burrow Bitches

> Kira: Yay you're home!
>
> Ariadne: Let's have dinner soon so you can tell us about the trip!
>
> Britney: did you tell the whales I love them?

My three best friends never failed to make me smile, even when I was a sweaty, disgusting mess who had just spent the weekend chasing whales and topped it off with a whale-themed 5K. At least I enjoyed running.

My phone vibrated with an incoming call from Kira, my roommate and oldest friend.

"Hi." I tucked my phone between my cheek and shoulder, fishing through my purse for some gum. "I'm still at the airport, but I'm bringing home a Biscoff cookie and a bag of pretzels."

Kira cheered. "I'm honored that you saved me your elite airline snacks."

"Just call me your economy sugar momma."

"We'll workshop the name," said Kira. "Do you need me to come get you from the airport?"

"How?" I laughed. "Neither of us has cars."

Who needed a car in Chicago when you had two working feet, a CTA pass, and the sheer determination to power-walk faster than traffic?

"Well, no, but I could show up in an Uber and pretend to pick you up that way."

While I was new to out-of-state assignments, she had yet to offer to meet me at the airport.

"What's really going on, Kira?"

She sighed. "Nothing, I swear. I just forgot how quiet the apartment is without you."

"Are you calling me loud?"

"Well, I—"

"Oh, *shit*."

I had just decided to stop staring at the airport lounge like a raccoon locked out of a restaurant when suddenly someone emerged. It wasn't the beautiful, perfect woman from earlier. No, it was someone much worse.

I could almost see the confusion on Kira's face. The way her lips turned down and her brown eyes narrowed.

"What's shit?"

"Noah Hansley is here."

Oh, God, he wasn't alone either.

Seconds later, the perfect woman exited the lounge and flagged Noah down to ask him for a selfie. I attempted to hide behind a pole as I watched the whole incident go down. Unfortunately, the woman was immune to Noah's charms.

My neck cracked in two places when I peered around the pole to watch them. Should I visit a chiropractor about that? Wasn't twenty-four too young to need the services of a chiropractor?

"What is that Instagram bad boy wannabe doing there?" Kira asked.

"No idea." Probably relaxing and drinking martinis before boarding his first-class flight. "Listen, I gotta go, but I'll see you at home, okay?"

Noah Hansley was the last person I expected to see at the

airport, but I shouldn't be surprised. The thought of him relaxing in classy airport lounges while I suffered in public areas made my eye twitch. It wasn't fair.

Must be nice to be a tall, pretty boy who could get anything he wanted. Maybe it wasn't so much the face as it was his million followers on Instagram.

Not that I kept track of his follower count. It frustrated me that all influencers had to do was show up at an event, snap a few selfies, and share a clever caption.

Meanwhile, I spent countless hours researching and writing long, in-depth articles. How was I rewarded? With smaller corporate checks and fewer press trip invites.

Noah had made it very clear that he didn't like me. Which, honestly, didn't bother me. The problem was that he didn't respect me. When we met a year ago, we completely hit it off and even talked about doing a collaboration. I had DM'd him some ideas, which he never responded to. He ghosted me completely.

For a young woman trying to build her career, it was frustrating to be denied a basic level of respect from a man showered in it for just existing.

Noah's adoring fans on social media may love him, but he was an asshole. Most of his fans were into the smooth, didn't-give-a-fuck-about-anything bad boy image. I didn't get it.

The last thing I wanted to do was try to play nice with Noah. We usually ignored each other, so if he knew I was here, that was what he would—

Oh, he was looking in this direction. It was fine. He'd look away any minute and go back to pretending I was lesser than him.

Except he didn't.

I blinked once. Then twice. Pretty sure my vision faded for a moment there, but when it became clear again, it was Noah's bright green eyes I was looking at. So bright they were almost yellow. Like a warm spring day.

He took one step forward in my direction. On instinct, I dropped the remainder of my coffee cup into the trash and bolted toward baggage claim.

Not taking that risk.

Once I was safe in my new haven—baggage claim 7—I leaned against the wall and waited for my polka dot luggage to come swirling down. Unlocking my phone, I tried to catch up on all the social media posts I'd neglected while working this weekend.

I was grateful that I was invited—whale-y grateful, if you will —but I was so exhausted. Between writing about whales, spending long hours by the sea trying to capture the perfect video, and running, I hardly stopped moving all weekend.

I opened Instagram. I ignored my notifications, aka fifteen memes sent from Britney when she was supposed to be study-ing, and mindlessly scrolled through my favorite travel bloggers. Clever captions, cute selfies, and gorgeous sceneries. Rinse and repeat.

Don't do it, Macey.

Don't even think about doing it.

...I'm gonna do it.

Against my will, my fingers typed in Noah's handle: *@noahhans*.

Was it cool now to shorten last names? *@MaceyMon* could be my new handle. No, that was lame. Maybe I could shorten my first name, but then I'd sound like a weapon.

Hating myself more with every passing minute, I Instagram-stalked Noah Hansley. I didn't know him that well—we'd only ever had one civilized conversation—but he knew how to make a good feed of photos and videos.

Technically speaking, his photos could use some work. They

were choppy and in need of color editing. But his followers cared more about the subject than the quality of the photos. I could see why. Noah was...*hot*. Unfairly so.

Toffee-colored hair complemented his green eyes, and the strands were short yet wavy. He had a sharp jawline, with sculpted cheekbones that drew your gaze all the way up to his dark eyebrows. In every photo, he looked comfortable. Cocky. Like he was the center of attention and he knew it. His build was athletic but more like a runner than a weightlifter.

I bet I could outrun him.

I froze on an old photo of him in front of Chicago's most famous landmark, the Bean. There, in the background corner, was a younger me. My hair was a lot shorter back then—I'd let it grow to the longest it had ever been since, mid-back, and while it had been a pain to keep it dyed blonde, I loved it.

"Is that your boyfriend?" a middle-aged woman with a narrow nose, one she clearly was good at inserting into other people's business, asked. She craned her neck to look closer at my phone. "He's very handsome."

"No," I said, leaning away from her. "And he's not that handsome."

I accidentally bumped into the teenager next to me, and her glare sent me wheeling in the other direction. Back into the older woman. God, teenagers were terrifying.

The teen shamelessly looked at my phone. "No, he's hot. I'd date him."

"He is way too old for you," I said. "Stick with the frat bros for now, okay? It's a rite of passage."

Noah was only three years older than me, but still.

"You're not dating him, then?" The older woman seemed horrified by this reality.

"Nope."

The last time I dated someone considered an influencer, it

ended in disaster. It was best to stay far, far away from men with a checkmark next to their names on social media.

My comment didn't faze the teen queen, who pulled out her phone to ask, "What's his handle? I'm going to follow him."

The woman on the right did the same, except at a slower pace. "Oh, me too!"

I face-palmed. Gaining Noah followers was not part of my goal for today.

When the woman said, "Sorry, I can't read that small font," and reached for my phone, I tugged it back. She had a strong grip, but I grew up with a cell phone and had stronger fingers.

I told her his handle and pulled my phone out of her grasp. Only to accidentally double tap the photo on the screen. *Shit.*

I just liked Noah's photo from a year ago. Permanent proof that I was online stalking him. What should I do? Let it be? Unlike it and hope the notification disappeared? Unlike it and like his most recent photo instead?

I let the like remain and prayed he got so many notifications he wouldn't notice. We didn't even follow each other on social media. He probably wouldn't recognize my profile anyways.

Yep, it would be fine.

If things went my way, I'd never see Noah Hansley again.

2

NOAH

A special kind of existential dread set in when you realized everyone else had grabbed their bags, and you were still standing there like an abandoned puppy at the pound.

Patience wasn't one of my virtues, I'd admit.

The baggage carousel hummed to life once again, and I surged forward, hoping mine would appear. I was afraid I'd missed it. After my flight from Los Angeles, I had to stop by the airport lounge to collect the credit card I had forgotten a few days earlier.

A familiar head of blonde hair also crept closer to the carousel. Of course Macey Monroe would be one of the few people still waiting for her luggage.

We'd attended a few of the same events in the past—restaurant openings, local festivals, holiday celebrations—and the way she looked at me each time was painfully familiar. It was the same way people look at someone they don't respect.

Macey's attitude represented all the assumptions the world made about me: that someone with good looks fell into being an influencer and never learned how to exercise their brain.

They were right about the first half.

I hated social media. Hated the anonymity it gave bullies, hated the insecurity issues it gave everyone, and hated the way it turned life into a game of competition. But I had fallen into it, and it was challenging to claw your way out of a lucrative opportunity when someone in your life depended on you.

Macey lifted a blue-and-yellow suitcase off the carousel. *Fuck.* Not that this was a competition, but she had definitely just won.

Before I could berate myself for taking too long in the lounge, causing me to miss my luggage, I saw my black suitcase making its lap around the carousel. By the time I grabbed it, Macey had disappeared.

Outside, the sky had gone full Chicago February—gray, growling, and cold enough to slap. The wind sliced through my jacket like it had a personal vendetta. A few sunny days in LA had nearly tricked me into forgetting just how rude winter could be back home.

I stopped by the taxi stand and pulled out my phone, because apparently staring into the void is frowned upon in public. Scrolling felt like the lesser evil. Yeah, I hated social media, but it still paid the bills. I uploaded a story announcing my safe landing, then watched it struggle to post over the airport's sad excuse for Wi-Fi.

Honestly, a small part of me missed airplane mode. Something about being unreachable at 30,000 feet made it easier to imagine a version of my life where I didn't chronicle every second of it for strangers online. If I left this path behind, though, what was left? Who would I even be? A college dropout with a skincare routine strong enough to carry a personality?

The ironic part was I had options. Too many. My savings bought me freedom, sure, but also paralysis. It was like being handed a menu with a hundred items, none of which looked appetizing. Damned if you do, damned if you scroll through job listings at 2:00 a.m. wondering if goat yoga instructor could be a real career.

Only a few photos on my feed updated. A picture of my little sister, Daphne, studying at the library with her friends. A gym workout routine from another Chicago influencer I followed. And a shared post of a whale.

Wait, what?

I squinted. It wasn't just a whale—it was *Macey's* photo of a whale. Shared by a lifestyle influencer I vaguely knew. Of course it had the perfect golden-hour lighting, that moody travel-blogger filter, and just the right amount of poetic nonsense in the caption. I had to give her credit: the girl knew how to take a photo.

Too bad she only posted them to her personal accounts instead of pairing them with the snooze-fest articles she wrote for *Roamer's Digest*. Then again, maybe I was the only one who found them boring. Not that I read them often. Just sometimes. When I couldn't sleep.

"I knew I should've taken Kira up on her offer," a voice grumbled behind me. "Stupid Chicago taxis."

I recognized that voice. My eyes shut as I sighed.

Macey. Of course.

She stood behind me in the taxi queue, her breath puffing out in annoyed little clouds.

"If you hate them so much, call an Uber," I said, not bothering to turn around.

She made an exasperated sound. "I would, if there were any available."

"Then walk."

"Do you want me to get frostbite?"

I turned around to look at her. Macey's long, icy blonde hair was tied into a braid down her back. That was where the Elsa cosplay ended, considering she wore a pink sweater and black sweatpants. Definitely not warm enough for a night like tonight. Two notebooks stuck out of her purse, and she shoved them back in.

"I don't *not* want you to get frostbite." I shrugged.

Macey rolled her eyes and ignored me, scrolling through her phone instead. I should go back to minding my own business, but this was more entertaining. Instead of filtering through Instagram, she was favoriting photos in her album. Whales, whales, and—a whale-themed 5K?

A laugh bubbled out of me, and I reached for her phone. Ignoring her "Hey!" of protest, I zoomed in to the photo.

"So you really spent your weekend playing with whales?" I chuckled.

"It's called Whale Fest." She reached for her phone, but I held it above her head as I looked at the picture. "And it's a beautiful celebration of whale migration."

Oh my God. This wasn't just any picture of a whale-themed 5K. As if the concept wasn't ridiculous enough, Macey was pictured in the race *dressed as a whale*. She wore all gray and a giant hat that looked like the head of a whale, jaws open and all.

This didn't align with the Macey I knew. She was supposed to be a corporate doll who wrote drab articles about events that were actually exciting. A driven woman with an unbeatable work ethic. Someone who succeeded at blending into the crowd, except for in this picture.

I hadn't laughed this hard in what felt like years. Pretty sure tears were forming at the corners of my eyes. "Why are you the only person dressed like a whale?"

"Because at a turkey trot on Thanksgiving, everyone dresses like a turkey." She pursed her lips and crossed her arms. "I thought everyone would dress as a whale for a whale 5k."

I didn't run on Thanksgiving. The holiday was for stuffing

your face full of food, not working out. Never trust people who run on Thanksgiving.

"What a horrible thought that was." I was still laughing, but guilt bit into me when she looked embarrassed. I handed her the phone back. "I'd like to stay far away from your mind, Monroe."

"No problem," she sniffed. "You're not invited."

Macey pocketed the phone and stretched, lifting her arms above her head and exposing a small strip of skin above her sweatpants. Goose bumps scattered across her skin. I blinked and looked away.

"Where's your jacket?" I asked. Her sweater clearly didn't provide much cover from the wind.

"Whales don't get cold," she answered. "They're warm-blooded and can survive in frigid waters."

I couldn't believe I was doing this. If Mom could see me now, she'd call me a gentleman. That was far from reality, but still, I pulled off one of my jackets and handed it to her. "Unlike whales, you don't have blubber."

Hesitation flashed through her face, and she stood unmoving. I insisted, "Take the jacket."

She did, zipped it up gently, and offered me her thanks. It would be funny how much she swam in the jacket, if it weren't cute.

The silence stretched between us. I was never very good at quiet—I always had a playlist or podcast in the background—but Macey seemed comfortable in it. The slow murmur of the crowd around the taxi stand was enough to keep me from going insane, and rationally, I knew I could put on my headphones and play music at full blast. But I didn't want to.

I glanced frequently at Macey, trying to get a glimpse into her mind. Her face was impenetrable, like the security at concerts I tried and failed to sneak into as a kid.

When she started to put an earphone in one ear, I finally thought *fuck it* and asked, "So are we finally going to talk about it?"

Her hand, with fingernails painted light blue, froze halfway to her ear. "Talk about what?"

"Why do you think you're better than me?"

Macey looked at me half-startled, a touch of pink creeping up underneath the collar of my jacket. "I don't think that."

I crossed my arms. "Your every action says otherwise."

When I first met Macey at a world showcase held at the Bean, I was immediately captivated. It had been a year, but I could still see her the way she was that day, standing in the middle of a crowd, completely unaware of the chaos around her and inside my chest. When she spoke, her voice carried a warmth that seemed to wrap itself around everyone.

Too bad she hadn't directed that warmth in my direction since. It was like once she understood what being an influencer meant, she stopped caring.

"Between us, Hansley, you're the one who thinks you're better than me." She shoved the earphones into her purse. "Considering you're the one who disrespects me and my time."

I frowned for a moment. "I don't know what you're talking about."

"Really?" A sharp edge caught into the smooth current of her voice. "Has every interaction with me been so insignificant that you immediately forgot it?"

"Better to be forgotten than treated unfairly."

Macey furrowed her brow. "I guess you're just too important to spend time with a measly magazine writer such as myself. God forbid your fans witness you treating me better than trash."

Memories barreled over me like splintered steel, sharp and painful. *I* was the one who treated *her* like trash? The audacity of her to say that to me when she was the one who wanted to feud with influencers because of some internalized prejudice.

"Maybe I would give you the time of day if you ever wanted it."

The next gust of wind whipped at my cheeks. Macey chewed at her bottom lip and asked, "What's that supposed to mean?"

"You're the one who treats me like trash, Monroe." I stepped close enough so that I could tower over her and smell the sunscreen on her cheeks. Coconut. "Every time I see you, you look at me like you wish an anvil would fall on my head."

"And ruin your perfect, Botox-sculpted influencer face?" She lifted a hand to her cheek in mock surprise. "I'd never."

I'd never used Botox. Every part of me was natural.

"Is that what it comes down to?" My voice lost the playfulness from earlier. The girl in front of me was suddenly a lot more serious than the one who showed up to a 5k dressed like a whale. "You think you're better than me because you're some corporate writer and I'm an influencer."

There was a gasp from somewhere in the crowd. I hadn't noticed until now, but a circle had formed around us. People finding entertainment in our argument. This scene would send my manager into a panic, but it was too late to simmer down now.

To people not in the industry, writers and influencers were very similar. We both got invited to the same events. We both got paid to promote brands and people.

The difference never seemed clearer to me. Writers liked to hide behind the screen and show specific, perfected pieces of themselves. Influencers put it all out there—we weren't allowed the space to cower.

"Don't put words in my mouth," she gritted through her teeth.

Macey was the perfect example of someone who showed

limited parts of herself. She was a talented writer and photographer who polished her favorite words and hid behind the ones that didn't fit.

"Does it make you upset that influencers like me can be successful?" I felt like I was poking a bear in a cage now, waiting for it to snap its jaws at me. "You ever think about why you're not successful, Monroe? It's because you don't put any personality into your writing."

Locals and travelers encroached on us, eager to hear more. Let them listen. At this point, I didn't care.

She poked me in my chest, then pushed. Actually pushed. I glued my feet to the ground so I didn't stumble. "Oh, and should I be like you, then? Constantly sharing shirtless selfies and basking in the likes?"

"I know you've *liked* some of those photos." Yeah, I didn't miss the like she just gave to my photo from last year. The pretty pink flush crawled from her neck to her cheeks. "Maybe you should work on being more genuine in the words you write and say."

Macey scoffed. "Excuse me if I don't want to take advice on being genuine from someone who makes a living off posting photos with their five-hundred-dollar designer jacket and jeans with rips in places physics doesn't support."

"At least I have a brand," I said. "I've learned more about you in one picture than I have through reading a year of your articles. Anyone can see you're beautiful, but no one would know you have wit and humor. Put it out there!"

What was I saying? Was I giving her advice? Insulting her? I wasn't sure anymore.

Macey didn't let my words faze her, jumping immediately into a rant. "It must be so easy to be you. An all-expense paid trip in LA? Guess I can do the bare minimum at the festival but not bother to show up to the final event. My pretty face and hot body will make up for it!"

My hands clenched into fists as frustration pounded at my head. But she wasn't done yet.

"Some of us actually have to work hard. We research, we write, we edit, and we take our own photos. Some of us haven't had easy lives and aren't used to getting whatever we want with a snap of our fingers."

I laughed, but there was nothing funny about this. Her baseless assumptions were a joke. If she had an inkling of what I'd been through, she'd never kid about it again.

We were chest to chest now. I could easily lift a finger and trace the lumps in the braid she wore. "You think I've had an easy life? You don't know the first thing about me. And I guarantee I've worked harder than you."

"Yes." She nodded frantically, like she was eager to show she agreed. "Those one million followers didn't come without a lot of pushups and green juice."

"Well." I pinched her cheek and she slapped my hand away. "Those one million followers are better than ten readers."

When she stepped back, she almost slipped on an uneven rock. "I have more than—Oh, you are such an asshole."

"And you're a judgmental princess."

"Ken doll."

"Corporate spawn."

I didn't even realize we had moved to the front of the taxi line. Macey pushed her way in front of me and flagged down the yellow taxi by the curb. We sent each other one last glare before she shoved her suitcase in the trunk. Whatever. She could have the taxi if it meant I didn't have to see her again. I was committed to putting Macey's face out of my head.

Which lasted about a day, until I saw our faces screaming at each other in a TikTok video with over two million likes.

3

MACEY

The Burrow Bitches

Britney: when i said one of us should be a social media star, this is not what i meant

Macey: OMG. I can't watch the video.

Macey: This is my worst nightmare.

Ariadne: Is that you...wearing Noah Hansley's jacket? While yelling at him?

Macey: I can explain.

Ariadne: Coffee. The Burrow Café. 8am tomorrow.

Britney: i'll be there!

Kira: Brit you work there

Nestled at the base of The Burrow, the towering corporate building in downtown Chicago, was The Burrow Café, where executives and associates alike stopped in the morning for a cup of coffee on the way up to their office. I was guilty of donating part of my salary to them twice each week. As much as I wanted to buy coffee there every day, my office did have a coffee machine.

The interior was bathed in a soft, amber glow, sunlight filtering through floor-to-ceiling windows and casting long shadows across the polished wooden floors. Above, exposed industrial pipes crisscrossed the ceiling. It always smelled like freshly ground beans here.

Local artwork adorned the walls and plush leather couches were scattered throughout. The couch in the left corner was ours. Not officially, but after a year of meeting here every Monday morning before work, the regulars knew to leave it open for us.

The whirr of the espresso machine punctuated the air as Kira and I entered, followed by the rhythmic clink of ceramic cups and saucers.

"Do you want your usual?" I asked as Kira went to claim the couch.

"Please!" she called, halfway to the other side of the room.

Kira and I had lived together for six years, but we'd known each other since we were ten. She didn't realize it at the time, but she was my first real friend. There were kids in class I'd talked to, maybe even did homework with after school, but no one I connected with.

I'd never forget meeting Kira on the monkey bars at school. I dangled from the first bar, terrified to swing forward, until I saw a smiling face at the end encouraging me to go.

We'd been best friends ever since.

And in the past six years of drinking coffee, Kira's order—

chai latte—had never changed. She liked the familiar. I preferred to keep my taste buds guessing.

"Good morning!" a beautiful barista clad in an apron adorned with a muffin logo said. Britney. "Chai latte for Kira, I know. What do you want, Macey?"

"Iced vanilla latte, please. Extra shot of espresso."

I needed it. A bundle of fear curdled inside my stomach, and I hoped espresso would kill it. Although I technically didn't do anything wrong this weekend, I was afraid my boss would use this as an opportunity to punish or even fire me.

It wasn't a secret in my office that she disliked me. Most days it felt like she was constantly breathing down my neck. It felt unfair, receiving the sharp edge of her frustration while others only saw the blunt side. But what doesn't kill you only makes you stronger, or so I'd heard.

Britney winked and started the espresso machine. "You got it."

Sometimes I thought the men of The Burrow didn't come here for its coffee so much as they did for its barista. Britney's fiery locks cascaded like molten copper down her shoulders. Her eyes, a mesmerizing shade of emerald green, always sparkled with a mischievous twinkle. Porcelain smooth complexion, with freckles dusted across her nose. And double-Ds that begged me to stare at them.

It was like she had been hand-drawn by a male artist. With a sigh, I glanced down at my body—the near-flat chest and distinct lack of freckles made me feel almost insignificant, but then I remembered all the amazing things my body could do. Run a 5k. Store all the nutrients I needed to stay healthy. Birth a literal human being, if I wanted.

I wasn't immune to insecurities, but comparing myself to other people wouldn't make them go away anytime soon.

Besides, when I thought about Britney or any of my friends,

it was never physical appearance that came to mind. I thought about Britney's tenaciousness every day, working at this café while attending law school. Kira's selflessness, volunteering every week. Ariadne's relentless positivity in difficult times. And how we wouldn't all know each other without this café.

I'd been the first to work in The Burrow, starting my job as a writer at *Roamer's Digest* a few days after graduating from the University of Illinois Chicago and then encouraged Kira to apply for a job opening in the building. She was an actuary, and I still had no idea what that meant besides numbers.

I met Ariadne, who had just started working on the second floor, during my first week. While graphic design was her passion, her day job was in IT, saving people from computer bugs and stopping them from buying suspicious gift cards for their boss. And we all hit it off immediately with the building's best barista.

"I'll be there as soon as I can." Britney handed me two cups, and I went to join Kira.

I heard Ariadne's laugh before I saw her. Short, curly brown hair filled my vision as I gave her a hug from behind. Her hands released their tight grip on her reusable to-go cup to squeeze me back. The most practical person I knew, she always brought coffee from home.

"Where are my sunglasses?" Ariadne asked, pretending to look through her backpack. "This celebrity's fame is blinding me."

"Dramatic as always." I laughed and took a sip of my latte, but internally, my heart sped up.

If I had known that conversation between Noah and me was going to be filmed and posted on social media, I would have never yelled at him like that. I still would have told him off, but I would have found another way to do it. A strongly worded letter, perhaps.

Ariadne continued, "I didn't realize you knew how to yell."

"I think the last time Macey got mad, she stole her enemy's animal crackers during nap time." Kira laughed but ceased when I glared at her.

"Very funny," I muttered. "It's rare that I lose my temper."

White sneakers pattered against the floor as Britney came running. "Don't get to the juicy parts without me!" She collapsed on the stool in front of the couch. "Okay, tell us everything. Start with the kissing."

"Kissing?" I felt like a cartoon character whose eyes popped out of their head.

Britney fluttered her eyelashes innocently. "You were wearing his clothes. I assumed something had happened."

"Definitely not." I choked on my drink, and a little bit dribbled down my chin. *Get it together, Macey.* "All that happened was we left the airport at the same time. He asked me why I think I'm better than him, and I explained to him what makes influencers so frustrating to simple plebeians like me."

My three best friends sipped their drinks and pointedly looked away.

I suddenly felt like a comedian who told a joke that didn't land. "What?"

"Well..." Kira started, tucking a lock of long, dark hair behind her ear. "You guys were insulting and complimenting each other at the same time. It was confusing."

Britney interrupted. "She means arousing."

"I do not."

"Just be careful around Noah," said Ariadne. "I'm not sure what to make of him. Remember when he went viral for getting into a fistfight with that food influencer?"

"At least you know he could fight to defend your honor," added Britney.

I faintly recalled seeing a viral video a few months ago of

him in a fistfight. "Don't worry, I have no desire to talk to him again."

Kira crossed one leg over the other. "Where did the two of you leave things?"

We didn't leave things anywhere. We had a small argument that got posted to TikTok and will blow over by the end of the day. Did I feel a little guilty about what I said? Sure, but logically, I knew I felt guilt way too easily, so I wasn't planning to do anything about it. Our insults to each other evened out. Plus, Noah took pride in being someone who wasn't fazed by the world around him, so he probably hadn't even thought of me since the argument.

My finger traced the lid of my cup. "I think we'll go back to ignoring each other at the next press event."

"Why? He's hot. You're hot. The hookup would be hot," Britney argued, wiggling her eyebrows suggestively. "Let me live vicariously through you. I need this."

"Well, because *you* need it…" I said with an eye roll.

"Now you're getting it." Britney hummed, then hurried to her feet when a customer approached the counter. "I've got to go, but listen, Noah's a ten and so are you. Do with that what you will."

"I have to go, too." Ariadne shoved her reusable cup into her backpack, then swung it over her shoulders. "I have to help a vice president who doesn't know how to reset his computer password."

Kira and I joined her, taking the rest of our coffees into the elevator. "Two dollars that his password includes a birthdate," she whispered to me.

I shook Kira's hand as Ariadne laughed, used to our frequent betting. Typically, we bet a few dollars at a time, and the winning dollars always went to our shared fund for utilities. It was my favorite game.

When the elevator opened, Ariadne stepped out and said, "It's his daughter's birthdate."

"Yes!" Kira fist-bumped as I sighed. It might be my favorite game, but I wasn't very good at it.

I settled into my desk and pulled up my notes from this weekend's event. So many details, so little time. I had started writing my article on the flight home from California last night, but then I crashed after the second paragraph. My vision for this article included a recap and a list of reasons why people need to visit Fort Bragg during Whale Fest.

Did I decide to glance at Noah's content from the festival he attended in LA? I did. But the decision was out of spite. He posted a handful of Stories, a series of photos, and one video. It was shocking how little he posted about an event. I wondered if he was getting lazy after years as an influencer.

Noah was a lifestyle influencer—meaning he posted a little about a lot of things. Local and national events, restaurants, gym workouts, daily routines, to name a few. His good looks helped him get away with posting so many different things. To me, it seemed like even though he influenced well, he didn't *actually* know what he was doing.

Victoria, my boss, entered the office, an Hermès bag hanging off her shoulder. She zoomed toward me and the fear reappeared in my stomach. I was nervous it might come up my throat at any moment along with my coffee and bagel.

Her cropped brown hair looked freshly cut, and as always, her makeup was flawless. She drew her cat eyes sharp enough to kill me, if she wanted. Which based on the look on her face, she did. "What is this?" She flashed her phone, which was playing the video of me and Noah on repeat. *Shit.*

"Um..." *Deny, Macey, deny!* No, she had a video in her hands. That wouldn't work. "Me enthusiastically interacting with a famous influencer?" Honestly, I was surprised Victoria even used TikTok.

"You just consider yourself lucky you weren't wearing any *Roamer's Digest* swag in this video." No swag was worn that day at all, unless you counted a whale costume. "Or else you'd be out of this office like *that*." She snapped her fingers.

My throat felt thick when I tried to swallow. "I'm sorry, but it's really not fair that a random person shared a private moment of me on the Internet."

"Life's not fair, Macey," she said. "Your article better be worth it. Send it to me by the end of the day."

She turned to go, but I foolishly stopped her. "What about my photos?" I held up my Canon. "I got some great shots of the whales, and I thought we could use them in the article."

It took standing by the ocean for four straight hours, but dang it, I got those photos.

Victoria didn't bother giving me a second glance. "I'll take a look."

That was what she said every time. And every time, she rejected them.

My chair rolled backward when I crumbled into it. I stuffed my head between my arms for a minute, leaning against the desk, trying to get a hold of myself. *I won't cry. Big, scary bosses don't deserve my tears.* At forty-four, Victoria was twenty years older than me, and she had no trouble beating down my self-confidence.

Usually, I took it in stride. Everyone in the office walked on eggshells, aware that she could snap at any moment. One of the few things that kept me going after a particularly bad day was Victoria's implication that she was training me to rise in rankings. But the pace of the training was at snail's speed and full of little-to-no constructive criticism.

I allowed myself a few shaky breaths, then moved forward.

The first thing I did on Monday mornings was check my column's analytics. I pulled up my dashboard, intending to compare week-over-week analytics, and I nearly fell out of my chair.

It was a glitch. There was no other explanation.

Because somehow, my page views shot up by 5,000 percent over the last day.

Who did I go to about a glitch like this? I'd draft an email right now. *Dear Google CEO, wtf is this?*

I quickly scanned which articles attracted the interest, and that reaffirmed there was a problem. The majority of the views weren't for my articles, they were for the *About Macey* page on the *Roamer's Digest* website.

Once I confirmed that no nudes of mine had been leaked, it was back to confusion. Why would thousands of people suddenly be interested in…

No. It couldn't be.

A single viral video couldn't have brought all these people to me.

Right?

Someone dropped into the seat next to me. I glanced over at Calculator Cal. I didn't know much about him except he owned his own tutoring business as a side hustle, had luscious hair, and used a blinged-out pink calculator.

Calculator Cal shoved his phone in my face. "Did you see this?"

"Technically, yes." I pushed the phone away. "I'm too scared of the comments to watch it, though."

"Scared?" He laughed. "Girl, people love you."

My heart stopped. Then it kicked up to a fast tempo, like I was in the middle of a marathon. "Really?"

"Really. Let me read you some of my favorite comments." He cleared his throat before taking on high-pitched impressions. *"She's right, influencers get anything they want,* and *Whale girl spits nothing but facts,* and my favorite, *Glad Noah finally found someone who puts him in his place."* Calculator Cal gasped like we were two teenagers in a gossip session. "Are you dating Noah Hansley?"

"Of course not!" I squeezed my coffee cup so hard the top flew off. "I don't know how that can be the impression anyone gets from that video. Did you miss the part where I called him an asshole?"

And he called me a judgmental princess.

"Did you forget the part where you also said he had a pretty face and hot body?"

Did caffeine heighten or worsen anxiety? Too late. I downed the rest of the topless latte. "We only complimented the physical stuff. That doesn't mean anything."

I hated how gentle Calculator Cal's voice was when he said, "He did say you were beautiful and witty. And he let you wear his jacket when he was obviously freezing."

"...he was?"

"Whoever took this video has amazing camera quality. I mean, you can literally see the goose bumps on his arms."

Guilt, the filthy traitor, grew stronger in my chest. I yelled at him while wearing his jacket? I never returned that jacket, either. It was buried somewhere in the bottom of my carry-on, which I inevitably won't unpack for another week.

"I need to get back to work," I hinted.

"Fine, fine." He pushed out of the chair, then lowered his voice. "But you always complain about how Victoria closes doors for you instead of opening them. This looks like a new door that she doesn't have the key to. Knock, knock, bitch. Time to open it."

Once Calculator Cal was gone, I pulled out my phone and opened Instagram. I hadn't checked it since stalking Noah's posts in California, and I didn't want to set any expectations now.

Fifteen thousand new followers.

The phone slipped out of my hand and onto the floor. Whispering a prayer to the gods of phone screens that it didn't shatter, I picked it back up and double-checked the number. Yep, my follower count doubled overnight.

I had never bothered to focus on social media. All I did was post the photos Victoria never let me attach to my articles, and I shared links to those articles. But now, people were leaving comments about how good my photos were. About how pretty I looked during a recent girls' trip to Charleston. About how they wanted to read my column.

And read it they would.

Knock, knock, bitch.

4

NOAH

I woke up to the sound of my phone vibrating nonstop. Typically, I silenced it before going to bed, but I couldn't be trusted to accomplish much after an exhausting flight home. I rolled across the bed, reaching one arm out from under the duvet to pull my phone off the charger. The most recent text was from my cousin.

> Nathan: Is that video online really you?

My sister blasted me with texts, too.

> Daphne: Why is there a video of you trending on TikTok??
>
> Daphne: Who is this girl?
>
> Daphne: I wanna meet her

I was about to respond and ask what she was talking about when another text from Ezra, my manager, came in.

> Ezra: Call me ASAP

What is happening?

Still half-asleep, I clicked play on the video Nathan sent me. It was one and a half minutes of clear footage of Macey and me arguing at the airport. *Shit.* I had noticed a few people listening in, but the size of the crowd was well above a few. It had hundreds of thousands of views already.

God, of course the argument had to be with Macey. She knew how to rile me up enough that I blacked out my surroundings. A problem, considering I always needed to care about what people saw when they looked at me.

She was a nuisance that I had planned to avoid for the rest of our lives, but the persuasive part of me screamed its protest. I wanted to argue more. I wanted to prove that everything she said was wrong. I wanted to see her defend herself.

Macey Monroe. How good was she at hiding things under the surface?

If my manager wanted a phone call, I'd need coffee to keep up. My ankle throbbed as I hobbled to the kitchen and switched on the coffeemaker, but icing it could wait.

Once drops of coffee started to fill the pot, I called Ezra, who immediately answered.

"Who the fuck is that girl in the video with you?"

Ezra had been in social media management for far longer than I had an Instagram account, but he always said he could never be an influencer himself. That warm greeting again exemplified why.

"Good morning, Ezra," I said patiently, pouring a cup of coffee into my mug that said *#1 brother*.

Ezra's Boston accent really came through when he was fired up. "You know, this morning did not start off good. I woke up to a viral video of one of my clients yelling at a pretty girl."

"She yelled at me first."

I could almost see Ezra pulling at his black-and-blue striped hair.

"Semantics." He brushed it off. "The point is I thought that video was going to be the worst thing to happen to us this week. This month, even. But in a rare turn of events, I was wrong."

When was the last time I went grocery shopping? All I had was eggs, eggs, and...more eggs.

Eggs for breakfast, it was.

"What are you talking about?" I asked, pulling the carton out of the fridge.

"Noah, we've got brands lining up for deals this morning. Since you're the rep for VelocityGear, I was thinking you and the girl could get matching outfits or something."

The egg cracked beneath my hand when I tapped it against the counter. "Huh?"

"Oh! I haven't even told you the best part yet." If social media management didn't work for Ezra in the long run, he should consider a career switch to theater. So dramatic.

"Which is?"

"Opal Serenity, a brand-new five-star resort in Aruba, reached out and wants you there for the resort opening next week."

I put Ezra on speakerphone, exchanging the bowl on the counter for my phone. I held the bowl close to my chest with one arm, the other hand whisking the eggs in it.

While I'd been to a few hotel openings before, they were nothing as luxurious or expensive as a resort in Aruba. "Seriously? That's huge."

"Sure is," he said, then his voice lowered. "There is one catch, though."

Of course it was too good to be true.

"What?"

"They want you to attend with the girl from the video."

"Macey?" The bowl fell out of my arms, scattering eggs across my kitchen and my feet. "Absolutely not. I won't go."

Ezra sighed for the second time in this conversation. "I don't recommend that. You know how you've been moaning about wanting to take a three-month social media break to road trip the country with your sister? Which, by the way, I also don't recommend."

"I don't think *moaning* is the word I'd use, but yeah."

"Noah, this deal is huge. It's the equivalent to what you usually make in three months," said Ezra. "This is your ticket to a stress-free social media break, my friend."

Now *that* caught my attention. I leaned against the counter, egg catastrophe forgotten, and grabbed a nearby journal and pen.

"Tell me what we'd have to do."

The door to the bar creaked when I pushed it open, revealing a dimly lit room with the scent of roasted peanuts and the tang of well-aged whiskey. Soft jazz music drifted from a jukebox in the corner, scratchy tunes that warmed my brain as I shut the door behind me. The sign hanging from the ceiling displayed the bar name: Rose Buds.

Faded posters and vintage stickers adorned the walls, as well as signatures and hand-written notes. Guests scattered across tables and chairs, plus a few booths against the wall. A bizarre mix of people: young beatnik-looking artists, aged businessmen, a group of girls on a post-work happy hour adventure, and a few dudes who were admiring said group of girls.

And then there was me.

When I had DM'd Macey on Instagram and asked to meet for a drink, I'd expected we would go to a hotel bar or a craft cocktail bar. Hell, I'd take Chili's over whatever this was. Macey had an eclectic taste in bars. Not bad, because I could get used to the vibe. Just...weird.

I was both surprised and relieved she had agreed to see me. Despite my determination to play it calm and cool, I wasn't sure what to expect. *Is she mad about the TikTok? Will she bring it up? Are we going to end up having a sequel argument?*

Macey waved at me from a table designed for two.

Here we go.

She dressed more casually than I've ever seen her, whale outfit excluded. Black long-sleeved top and tight denim jeans. I had never been much of a leg man before, but I suddenly found myself with a new appreciation for them.

"Hansley," she greeted when I sat across from her.

"Macey." I forced a smile, knowing I had to be on my most charming behavior tonight. "How are you?"

She eyed me carefully. There was a splash of color on her eyelids that wasn't normally there. Sparkly. "I'm good. I was surprised to see your message."

"I'm surprised you come here," I commented, my wrist dragging over a sticky spot on the table, "on purpose."

Macey, un-offended, laughed and sipped her drink. "Once you have one of Bear's cocktails, you'll see why."

"Bear?"

The burly bartender lifted his arm in a wave, and the bear tattoo on his forearm caught the light. "Ah. I get it now."

I stood to order, but Macey stopped me. My hand suddenly felt like it was on fire, even though she only lightly grazed it with her fingertips. "No," she said. "Bear knows what you want."

"How does Bear know what I want?" The bartender shook a mysterious concoction, which I assumed was meant for me. "He doesn't even know me."

Macey shrugged. "Don't ask questions. Besides"—she slyly

peeked up at me beneath dark lashes—"he probably just looked at what drinks you hold in your selfies. Hopefully, it's nothing lethal."

My breath caught somewhere in my chest. "Lethal?"

"He's pretty protective of me. That TikTok video may have made you public enemy number one."

Here was my opening. Time to set the record straight. "I had no idea that someone recorded us."

"I didn't think you did," she said with a neutral face. "It sucks, but it's done. I guess next time we should fight in private."

"Listen, Macey...I went too far with some of the things I said. I don't think you're an unsuccessful corporate pawn."

Macey pulled her hand into her lap. "Technically, the word you said was *spawn*. Corporate spawn. Like I'm a demon who crawled out of hell or something."

"Well, I've heard you're a fast runner."

She stared deadpan back at me.

I winced. Not a good start to my apology. "Yeah. Too far. I'm sorry."

I thought she would egg me on further and request I grovel on my knees, but she did something even more shocking. She accepted it.

"It's okay. I'm sorry for my comments, too." She twirled the ice in the glass with her straw. "You were right. My articles are dull. But it's not my fault. My boss has me edit them so much it takes all the personality out of them."

Bear, a middle-aged man with a thick beard, dropped off a glass with a chipped edge. He placed a tiny white napkin below it and a red straw inside. Based on the color, it looked like a whiskey drink with a few add-ins. He clapped Macey on the shoulder before returning to the bar.

I grabbed the glass between my hands and gave it a whiff. "Have you tried explaining that to your boss?"

She laughed, and it evoked a strange feeling in my chest. Could smelling alcohol lead to heartburn? I'd Google it later. "More times than I can count. It's not that easy."

As soon as I sipped the drink, I noticed a hint of sweetness, perhaps from a touch of honey, that softened the whiskey's bite. Then a subtle hint of spice that tingled on the tongue. It tasted like liquid gold, sweet and indulgent.

"Holy shit." I greedily drank more. "This is the best drink I've ever had."

"Told you so," she said.

I pushed the glass to her. "Here, try it."

"No, thanks," she declined. "But you're welcome to try mine."

I took a sip of the offered glass. Equal parts sweet and tart. "It tastes like a flavored lemonade," I said as I passed it back to her.

"It is," she said lightly. "I don't drink alcohol. That's why we come here. Best cocktails and mocktails in town."

Interesting. Most people in our age range—especially those who worked press events, where alcohol was served by the bucket—drank. It was rare to find someone who didn't. Not that it bothered me. I thought it was cool that people could have a good time without getting drunk. And I secretly hoped that Daphne was one of those cool people. Even though based on her 2:00 a.m. private Instagram Stories, she wasn't.

Which was also fine, as long as she made good decisions.

"Is there a reason?" It wasn't any of my business to prod, but I was curious.

She shrugged one shoulder. "I've tried it a few times, but I don't like how it makes me feel."

"I get that."

Macey pulled her black-and-white purse off the chair and stood up. "Well, this has been—"

I stood up straighter, instinctively reaching out. Ready to grab her if needed. "Are you leaving?"

"I thought that's why you wanted to meet." She sounded confused. "To apologize and clear the air."

The group of girls a few tables over waved at her and pointed to their empty chair. Macey waved back at them and lifted one finger to signal that she'd be there in a second.

Absolutely not.

"You know those girls?" I asked.

"They're my best friends," she said. "They're here to make sure you don't murder me."

My jaw dropped. "Murder you? You're the one who suggested this place. I think you could get murdered here perfectly fine without me."

"You're the one who wanted to talk."

"Exactly." I pointed at her seat. "There's more I have to say. Sit down." She cocked an unamused brow, and I amended, "Sit down, please."

Macey sat. "What did you want to talk about, then?"

Very direct. I could work with that.

"I have an offer," I said, then launched into a full-blown explanation of the Opal Serenity resort in Aruba. How few people the resort was inviting to celebrate their grand opening. That they wanted us both to attend—Macey could cover the event for *Roamer's Digest*, and I'd share it on social channels.

Macey's attention was studious, like a scholar examining a textbook. Intense. It shouldn't add extra pressure to know she was really listening to me, but it did.

Once I finished my prepared speech, I took another sip of Bear's cocktail. "So what do you think?"

"I think that sounds like an amazing opportunity," she said.

Perfect. I could picture the check already. Then the deactivation of my social media account for three months. I'd use that time to figure a way to get out of this career forever and—

"But you should take someone else."

Wait.

I leaned over the table. "You're saying you don't want to go? To Aruba? For free? With me?"

My voice went embarrassingly higher with each question. Anyone would be crazy to turn down the offer. If there was one thing that bound the human race together, it was our love for free things.

"Correct," she confirmed. "I'm not going on some press trip as your plus-one."

The whiskey soured in my stomach. "You wouldn't be my plus-one. We're both being invited as part of the press team."

"Thanks for the offer." Macey stood for real this time, taking what remained of her drink. "But my answer is no."

I watched her walk to the group of girls in the corner, feeling confused beyond belief. I wasn't sure what hurt more: that the check I needed was still far away or that Macey had just rejected me.

5

MACEY

The Burrow Bitches

> Ariadne: I was just looking up photos of Aruba.
> How did I not know it was so gorgeous?

> Macey: I already said no.

> Kira: The beaches look really nice though

> Britney: you know what would look even nicer?
> seeing noah shirtless on that beach

> Macey: Yeah, but then I'd have to be with Noah
> on the beach.

> Ariadne: Oh darn, being on the beach in
> Aruba....

> Kira: For free...

> Britney: woe is macey

It was approximately 1:00 a.m. when I finished the article.

Technically, I finished the article days ago. Then Victoria emailed me a long list of changes I needed to make that she expected back by this morning. It's like she thought I was a robot who didn't need sleep to function.

The new article followed the pattern of everything I'd written for *Roamer's Digest*. What started off as a funny, quirky, and full of whale-pun work of art had turned into a dry, 2000-word article about the history of whales in Fort Bragg. Not saying people didn't care about whale facts, but what they cared about more was what it felt like to attend the Whale Fest.

Everyone wanted to live vicariously through others' experiences. It was physically impossible to experience everything in this lifetime—I wanted to hike Mt. Everest's base camp, swim with sharks in Australia, and touch down on the moon—but all those things wouldn't happen for me. That was why writers were so important. We could pretend we were them for thirty seconds and transport ourselves to any corner of the world.

The last time I tried to explain this to my boss, she laughed and sent someone in my place to the local dessert bar opening. As someone who loves sweets, that crushed my soul. Ever since, I'd kept my head down and did whatever she told me.

When I graduated college, I thought I was so lucky to land the dream job immediately. My mother had been even more excited than me. When I told her I got the job, she sent me a bouquet of flowers so big, I had to buy a new vase for them.

The reason for Lora Monroe's flowers was less about me getting the job than it was the job itself. She had always dreamed of working for a magazine. Granted, the ways of work had changed since she was young—less print media, more online coverage—but the mechanics were the same.

She never had the chance to pursue that dream, though. Mom and Dad were high school sweethearts who had an oopsie baby—aka me—at sixteen. They struggled to take care of me, and while I always thought they did great, Mom chose a stable, less stressful job over her dream magazine job.

I knew my parents were worried I lacked things growing up. Maybe I never had the shiniest toy or the newest phone, but I recognized that the love they poured into me at a young age was worth so much more. They gave up so much for me. I wanted to repay them in any way I could.

But now I was beginning to wonder if there really was something like a "dream job." It felt like we were all suffering during the hours of 9-5 so that we could afford to live our lives from 5-9. Rinse and repeat, and you have a typical week.

"What are you still doing awake?" Kira padded through our shared living space to the kitchen. "Still thinking about Noah's proposal?"

"Proposal is a strong word. I'm working," I answered. "Hey, if you're making a snack, can I have some?"

Kira returned with a pint of cookie dough ice cream and two spoons. "Don't distract me with ice cream talk. You didn't tell us much about Noah's suggestion the other day."

"I didn't?"

"I think you were too busy complaining about how annoying he is."

I spooned a large amount of ice cream into my mouth. Sweet, sweet calories.

When Noah had first DM'd me and asked to meet up, I almost sent him to spam, convinced it was a bot. Then I saw the blue checkmark and realized that yes, it was the real Noah Hansley asking me out.

Not that it was a date.

My first instinct was to delete the message and move on. But when I realized he might have more intel on the video than me, I thought it would be a good idea to meet up. Just so I could learn what he knew.

I never expected a resort in Aruba to have contacted him about hosting us as members of the press team.

"He is annoying," I said as I stabbed a chunk of cookie dough. "Though I suppose him telling me about the press trip invite makes him a little less annoying."

And a little bit nice.

Twirling the spoon between her fingers, Kira said, "I'm still surprised you turned him down. Weren't you just telling me about opening new doors in your career?"

I dropped my spoon on the stained coffee table and curled my knees under myself on the couch. "Yes, but I only want to open them if they're my door to open. Not Noah Hansley's."

Even though the invite had made me feel a little special. And maybe, just maybe, I took a little satisfaction watching him flounder when I turned him down.

"Fair." Kira shimmied the fluffy throw blanket off the top of the couch and covered both of us with it. "But you don't have to open doors alone. Sometimes, the door is so heavy you have to go through it with someone else."

I huddled under the blanket. "We're not going to Narnia."

Kira cracked a smile, all perfect, shiny teeth. "I was scrolling through his posts..."

I groaned and pulled the blanket over my head. I could make a home under here. Warm and cozy, with ice cream only steps away.

"He's got that bad boy persona, but I bet there's more under the surface. Also, he's hot."

I lowered the blanket beneath my eyes.

She looked at me and said, "And you know that means a lot coming from me."

"I'm still not going."

Kira pulled the blanket down, exposing the rest of my face. "Macey, not all influencers are like your ex."

Ugh, just thinking about *that* situation sent a spiral of anger through me. Considering I was a writer for an online magazine and my ex was a famous local influencer, I should have known from the start that getting involved romantically could impact my professional future.

There was nothing that threw me off my game more than attending events for work and running into the boy who cheated on me.

Our relationship only lasted six months before I found out that he was dating two other girls. Guess he thought our circles were too far apart for me to ever figure it out. When I caught him in bed with one of them, I broke it off immediately. Later, he said I should feel lucky that he had even been with me. That he did me a *favor* and helped me get followers.

Never mind the fact I didn't care about followers. All I wanted to do was write and maybe publish some photos. It would be nice to share that passion with someone special, but I learned quickly that influencers only viewed relationships as transactions. And that they'd only ever view a relationship with me as something below them.

"I'm not sure about that," I said, blinking away the pinpricks behind my eyes.

Thankfully, Kira didn't press. "Why are you working so late, anyways?"

The bright screen of my laptop sat on the coffee table, mocking me. "Victoria tore my article apart. I had to redo it before the morning."

"God, she's the worst." Kira resealed the pint and headed for the kitchen. From there, she yelled, "I know you think your destiny is to stick it out and suffer or whatever, but remember when you wanted to start your travel blog? Maybe this is your chance!"

I had considered starting a blog a few times over the last two years. Each time, I managed to convince myself that things at my job would get better. Not to mention, it could be seen as a conflict of interest.

If I had my own blog, I could share any article I wanted. Put as much personality and whale puns in them as possible. My photos would accompany my words. I'd be in charge of my schedule and would attend whatever press events I wanted. It would be a lot of work, but wasn't I already working all the time anyways?

But...

My column with *Roamer's Digest* just increased its viewership. My mom was going to freak out when I told her. A raise was inevitably coming soon. It'd be a bad idea to pivot now that I had the eyes I'd been seeking for years.

"It's just something to think about." Kira waved on the way back to her room. "Good night."

It was too bad people saw me as either the girl from the video or Macey Monroe from *Roamer's Digest*, instead of just Macey.

The next morning, Britney already had a shot of espresso ready for me when I walked into The Burrow Café. She was a saint. An angel in the human flesh. I was going to give her a best friend of the year plaque. No, a *trophy*.

She was busy making someone else's cappuccino but flashed a smile at me when I approached the counter. "Kira told me you didn't sleep much. You need it."

I took a sip and cringed at the taste. People who drank straight espresso were another level of human. I was but a mere mortal who enjoyed milk and sugar with a side of espresso. "Thank you."

Britney handed an intern his cappuccino and joined me, a matching shot of espresso in her hand. "Cheers." We clinked our cups together.

"You look more exhausted than I feel." I eyed the bags under her eyes.

"Exams are coming up," she explained. "Once those are over, I'll sleep for a week."

A second-year law student, Britney was preparing to practice intellectual property law one day. "Let me know if I can help."

"Know anything about civil procedure?"

"I know 'Stop, in the name of the law!'"

Britney laughed and shut her eyes. "That has nothing to do with...You know what, I'll call you if I need someone to review flashcards with me."

"Now that"—I checked the time on my phone—"I can do. I have a meeting with Victoria in ten, but I'll call you later."

My soul cried when I took another sip of the espresso, but the tired part of my brain sang with pleasure. In the elevator, I prayed to all the grammar gods that my middle-of-the-night brain functioned normally and I didn't accidentally mix up *their*, *there*, and *they're*.

I had emailed the article to Victoria at 1:13 a.m. and passed out on the couch after. My neck hated me for it.

I'd always believed that people were good and prone to mistakes. Things happened: sometimes you forgot to restock the coffee, you tipped over salt that was difficult to clean, you locked someone out of the apartment (sorry, Kira).

But everyone was capable of rising above those mistakes. An apology could take you very far. The problem was when people refused to apologize for their actions.

I didn't think Victoria had ever apologized for anything.

In the office, I dropped off my lunch in the kitchen—peanut butter and jelly sandwich because I was too exhausted to pack anything else—and headed straight for Victoria's office. She was finishing a call and gestured for me to step inside.

Her office reminded me of something I'd seen in a movie. Giant windows offered sweeping views of the Chicago River, designer furniture like a sleek glass desk elevated the space, and there was a sound system in the corner. Why? I couldn't tell you.

I took a seat on a plush leather chair and crossed one leg over the other. Victoria hung up the phone and spun around in her chair. "Macey, thank you for revising the article."

She was...thanking me? Alarms wailed inside my head.

"Of course," I said with a smile, even though I was dying inside.

"I have your assignment for the next week." Victoria handed me a one-sheeter with information about an upcoming event. My interest piqued.

If she thanked me for the new article, that must mean she liked it. The article, plus my photos, hopefully proved to Victoria that I was ready for more press trips. Bigger events. I was ready to cover the most exclusive events, like the—

Groundbreaking of a new parking garage?

Excuse me? I skimmed the rest of the overview. Yep, she wanted me to witness history as city officials took turns awkwardly shoveling dirt while dressed in business casual.

"You want me to write about a garage groundbreaking?" I asked. "This doesn't even seem worthy of an article on the site."

"It doesn't have to be long." Victoria shrugged, already turning her attention away from me and back to her computer.

My body froze with shock. What was happening here?

"But...why?" Aware that I sounded like a petulant child, I straightened my shoulders and forced myself to add confidence to my voice. "I thought I proved myself worthy for bigger assignments after Whale Fest."

Victoria paused whatever she was doing on her computer to

eye me. "After Whale Fest? You mean, when you embarrassed the company in a viral video?"

I wouldn't say embarrassed was the right word, especially when it drew readers to my page.

"Macey, I think maybe you aren't as far along in your development as I had hoped. Think of this as back to basics. Just for a little bit."

Back to basics?

No way. I hadn't hustled these past two years just to be assigned to something an intern could do with their eyes closed.

But how did I counter her point without appearing rude or ungrateful?

The words flew out of my mouth.

"Actually, I was personally invited to cover the opening of Opal Serenity, a resort in Aruba."

Personally may have been an exaggeration, but, well...close enough.

Victoria's eyebrows shot up, and a strange sense of satisfaction overcame me. "Really?"

I nodded, pretty sure I could see wheels turning in her mind.

After consideration, Victoria nodded. "You've never been scouted specifically for an event before, so I'll agree to it. Email me the details."

Oh my God. It was going to happen. I was going to attend a press trip all the way in Aruba.

"Of course." I jumped up, tucking my notebook under my arm. "Thank you, Victoria."

Thanks for nothing, the sassy part of my brain said. At least I had a good filter in a corporate work environment.

Victoria didn't say anything as I left her office. I shut the door quietly, making eye contact with Calculator Cal, who got up from his desk to join me in my walk down the hall.

"Did you take my advice?" he whispered as I filled up my water bottle at the fountain.

"Maybe," I said with a grin. Even though I had to fight for a better opportunity, I knew this would be a chance to prove myself and hopefully scrub the video from Victoria's mind.

"I knew it." He smirked. "Knock, knock."

A snort escaped me. "Goodbye for now."

When I returned to my desk, a fist pump or two escaped my body. A few people at their desks gave me the side-eye, but my spirit wasn't affected. I had to text my friends. I had to call my parents.

I had to—damn it, I had to get the details from Noah.

6

NOAH/MACEY

Noah

One of my favorite hobbies was one that my manager Ezra said he wouldn't hesitate to fire me over if I ever shared publicly. That seemed over the top, considering it was building LEGOs, not murdering puppies.

Ezra thought I was starting to lose the "bad boy" image we worked hard to create and posting about LEGOs would shatter it completely. I told him it would add some layers to the image, but he threw an onion at the wall and said the vegetable needed to be more layered than me.

Another thing I hated about social media: once you showed a different side of yourself, people lost interest. Maybe bad boys weren't supposed to like LEGOs, but I found it fun. LEGOs sparked my passion for architecture when I was a kid. Who would have thought a stocking stuffer would change my life?

Even now, I could easily spend nights building the newest set (and spending a portion of my paycheck on it—seriously, why were they so expensive?).

Besides, hot people built LEGOs.

I was working on the roof of a three-story LEGO building

when someone pounded on my door. I abandoned the set on the carpet to answer.

Arms immediately surrounded my torso.

"Noah!" Daphne stuck to me like a sloth would a tree.

On instinct, my arms wrapped around her. Internally, my brain was still trying to compute what was happening. It was spring break. When I invited my sister to Chicago, like I did her freshman year, she had snickered and said, "I have friends, you know."

Panicked, I double-checked there were no other twenty-year-olds waiting down the hall.

"What happened to New York?"

In lieu of an answer, Daphne tightened her arms around me. Okay. Okay. This was the hardest part of being a caretaker. What would Mom do?

She wouldn't say anything. She'd just let Daphne get the feelings out. So that's what I did. Just two siblings, hugging it out in the middle of the sixteenth floor.

There was a suitcase at Daphne's feet. Suspicion stirred like a cat from a nap, but I swung open my apartment door and ushered her inside.

She paused in the entryway. "Your place is a mess."

Mess was a strong word considering it could have been a lot worse, but her point stood. There was an avalanche of clothes cascading from my overflowing laundry basket in the corner. Dishes from last night needed to be washed. Unfolded blankets and pillows covered the couch. A stack of books on the coffee table sat entirely out of place.

"I would have cleaned if I were expecting company."

"No, you wouldn't have," she said. "Not if it was me."

I snorted as I started folding the blankets on the couch. She was right. "No, I wouldn't have."

I didn't need to impress Daphne, and we'd lived together the majority of my life. She knew every habit of mine, good and bad, and she loved me anyways.

My little sister held a lot of those same habits. From the little things, like our granola obsession, to the big things, like visiting our mother's grave every December, we acted the same. Funny, considering if someone were to stop us on the street, they probably wouldn't have guessed we were siblings.

Daphne took after Mom. She had Mom's curly dark brown hair and hazel eyes, along with a heart-shaped face and two dimples on both sides of her mouth. Her smile was wide, covering her face, and it appeared now when she sat next to me on the couch.

Meanwhile, I took after Dad's appearance, though the only reason I knew that was because of old photos. There was a box of photos Mom kept hidden under the bed: from their wedding day, their honeymoon cruise, happy days outside in the park. I didn't find them until after the funeral.

Six years ago, I had just finished my junior year of college at Cornell when Mom died in a car crash. With an absent, out-of-the-picture Dad since day one, that left Daphne and me on our own.

Technically, we had an aunt and uncle—my cousin Nathan's parents—but he emancipated when he was seventeen. He said he already raised himself so may as well make it official. Considering I hardly talked to my aunt and uncle, I took Nathan's side.

Cornell was dead to me once I moved back home to St. Louis. I couldn't go back to college and leave Daphne to a foster system. She was fourteen, so she only needed a guardian for four years. Even though I was twenty-one at the time, I became her guardian. I wasn't sure how good a job I did, but she graduated high school and got a scholarship to her local college.

So I could have been worse.

Although I once dreamed of returning to Cornell to finish

my architecture degree, it never happened. We lived off the money I made doing various part-time jobs, Daphne posting ridiculous photos online of me every day. Soon the page took off, and so did influencer deals. Why would I go back to college when there were two rents and tuition to pay? Daphne insisted she'd take out loans, but I wouldn't let her. A part of me was disappointed I never finished what I started, but there were other priorities in place.

I probably would have stayed in St. Louis to make sure she was okay, but in her loving words, I needed to, "Move out and get a girlfriend or something, Noah, you're pathetic."

While I didn't succeed in getting a girlfriend, I liked to think I wasn't pathetic. A pitiful state wasn't the reason for my single-ness so much as was my belief in the people-to-follower correla-tion. People, like Instagram followers, will drop or dislike you for no reason. I preferred to openly accept followers but keep the people behind the account far away.

Daphne was happy to be here now, I was sure. But some-thing was wrong. I could tell by the way her body pulled taut like the strings on a violin.

I debated digging into the issue, asking again what happened to New York, but she didn't look ready to discuss it. I'd give her some time to decompress, but then I needed answers.

So I said the three words everyone in the world wants to hear the most. "Pizza on me."

She perked up. "Deep dish?"

"Obviously."

We gathered our things in silence, Daphne pulling out a purse from the inside of her luggage. It was early for dinner, but the two of us could always eat. Always.

Daphne's hand, clad with rings on each finger, held a spare LEGO that had been cast aside. "You're such a nerd. How do all these girls on the Internet think you're so cool?"

I snatched it out of her hands and placed it back in the box. "Don't make me order you anchovies."

She gasped so dramatically her bun loosened, a few curls knocking against her face. "I thought you loved me."

I wrapped an arm around her shoulders. "I mean, there are worse—" When I opened the door, I froze. "What the fuck?"

Macey Monroe stood on the other side.

Of my door.

To my apartment.

"Um..." Her hand, which had been floating in the air, close to a knock, faltered. "I was in the neighborhood?"

Chestnut eyes widened to the size of dinner plates.

"Again, what the fuck?" I repeated, aware that Daphne was giving me a weird look. "No. Better question, *how* the fuck?"

She mindlessly played with the button-up sweater she was wearing. "I don't think *how the fuck* is a real question."

"Macey."

"I mean, *how the fuck* implies how did you do something or—"

I let go of Daphne to pinch the bridge of my nose. "Let's start with how you know where I live."

Between my fingers, I saw Macey's expression relax. "I asked your manager for your address. He responded in twenty-nine seconds."

Fucking Ezra.

"Why are you talking to Ezra?"

"Oh." She glanced at Daphne as if the presence of my sister would impact her answer. "Well, I really needed to talk to you about something, and you didn't respond to my DM. I got a little impatient, so I thought I'd ask him for your address."

Realization lit in Daphne's eyes. "You're the girl from the video."

That stupid video. Days later, it was still haunting me. Ezra had made it his new hobby to screenshot and send me the growing number of views as well as his favorite comments. Which, of course, were all about how cool Macey was.

Macey smiled and held out a hand. "Regrettably. I'm Macey."

"I'm Daphne. Noah's sister."

"I didn't know you had a sister." Macey glanced at me.

Daphne smirked, crossing her arms. "He doesn't like to brag."

Macey giggled. My eyes caught for a second on the swoop of her eyelashes. I pointedly looked away. *Focus, Noah.* "What are you doing here?"

She pressed her lips together, then rocked onto the tips of her toes like she was trying to shake off nerves. "I wanted to ask you if your offer for Aruba still stood."

I blinked, my brain struggling to catch up. Of all the things I expected her to say, that wasn't one of them. Daphne let out a low, suspicious hum, her gaze flickering between us.

"If so, I'd love to go with you," said Macey, almost shyly.

My stomach twisted. Not unpleasantly, but almost with... nerves? That was unusual. I didn't ever get nervous. I must have eaten something bad earlier.

This would be the longest stretch of time we'd ever spent together. What if we got into another argument, the kind that would make great TikTok fodder for some bystander recording on their phone? The last thing I needed was another viral clip of us bickering in public.

But we'd started to move past the bickering. We were professionals. We could handle being good-natured colleagues for the long weekend in Aruba.

I had a sneaking suspicion that any job—hell, even covering a paint-drying competition—would be more fun with Macey. Her presence crackled with the kind of energy that turned even the most routine moments into something worth remembering.

I cleared my throat, forcing myself to play it cool. "Of course. I'll let them know. You can write a few articles, and I'll come up with a few social campaigns."

"Maybe we can collaborate on some posts," she said, tucking a strand of hair behind her ear. "If you want."

I barely had time to process the suggestion before Daphne cut in.

"Are you hungry?" she asked, way too casually.

I froze, my attention snapping down to my sister. What was she up to?

Macey hesitated for a second, then nodded. "Yeah, I could eat."

Macey

Mariano's overflowed with people, the line stretching out the door. What started off as a hole-in-the-wall pizza joint had transformed into a fan favorite. It had only opened a few months ago. How did it get so popular?

Memories of attending the opening and writing an article about their life-changing pizza came to mind.

Right.

Magazine writers like me made it popular.

As a travel writer, I preferred to, you guessed it, travel. But that wasn't always possible. We were a Chicago-based magazine, so I covered a lot of events in the city: restaurant openings, store pop-ups, festivals, whatever. I didn't mind it, though, especially when it involved sampling food. Writers weren't exactly rolling in dough. However, we were great at making pizza puns.

Noah, Daphne, and I pushed through the crowd and lucked our way into a corner table. The long red-and-white checkered tablecloth hid my clammy palms, my body's response to nerves.

There was no reason to be nervous, I knew, but I was well out of my comfort zone.

Maybe I'd be less nervous if Noah weren't acting weird. It was like a switch flipped in his head the moment we walked inside. He was still Noah but more...uppity. Like he and his fancy clothing labels were too cool to be here. Ironic considering it was him and his sister who decided on the location.

It was exactly the image he portrayed online: rebellious and cool. An image I had recently begun to realize wasn't entirely real.

I wondered if he'd try to act this way in Aruba. I wasn't sure how well I'd survive being around Mr. Cool every time we walked into a new room together.

A young waiter in a crisp white button-up and black apron stopped beside our table, pen poised over his notepad. Daphne didn't hesitate. "Sausage and mushroom pizza. Side salad."

I resisted the urge to gag. *Mushrooms.* I absolutely despised the fungi that snuck itself into the category of vegetable and ruined perfectly good pizza. But I didn't want to be that person and complicate the order.

Just as the waiter started to jot it down, Noah spoke up. "No mushrooms."

Daphne frowned at him. "What? We always get mushrooms."

"Macey doesn't like mushrooms," Noah said simply.

The waiter, who seemed too busy to care about their sibling argument, tucked his notepad into his pocket and walked away.

I leaned forward. "How did you know that?"

"You posted something dramatic about a pizza place in Avondale that tried to push their 'Fun Guy Special' on you."

Huh. I remembered that day, though I'm pretty sure that happened what, eight months ago? Maybe Noah just really had a vested interest in pizza joints.

Unsure of how to respond, I turned to the other Hansley sibling. "So, Daphne, what brings you to Chicago?"

Noah sipped his water eagerly.

Daphne seemed like a sweet girl. Young, confident. By the suitcase in the door, I guessed she was staying with Noah for a few days. She chewed on the edge of her cuticles before she answered.

"Spring break," she said. "I thought I'd come hang out with my favorite brother."

Noah set down his glass. "I'm your only brother."

"My point stands."

I laughed as the familiar pang of envy pricked me. Sometimes, I wished I had siblings. Sure, it was nice not having to share my things with anyone or spend my youth in petty arguments, but it would be nice to have someone to relate to. Someone who stuck by your side no matter what.

I had my friends, but it wasn't quite the same.

"Where do you go to school?" I asked, folding a napkin onto my lap.

"St. Louis Community College," Daphne answered. "I'm transferring to another university soon, though."

"That's great," I said. Noah's eyes narrowed at me, like he wasn't sure if I was being sincere or not. "Noah, I didn't know you were from St. Louis."

He had the air—read: arrogance—of someone from an elite Los Angeles neighborhood. I would have never guessed he was from Missouri.

"He is." Daphne answered for him. "Though it's been a few years since he's lived there."

Mentally, I tried to calculate when he could have moved to Chicago. After high school? After university? I turned to the man I knew very few trivia facts about. "Did you also go to SLCC?"

Once again, Daphne stepped in. "No, he went to—"

"I didn't finish college," Noah finished, voice stony. A little threatening. Maybe a different person would have cowered beneath it, but it made me push harder.

"That's okay too," I attempted to reassure him. "You technically don't need a degree to—"

Noah suddenly stood. His wooden chair rocked back before all four legs fell to the ground. "I'm going to order garlic bread."

I mean, I loved carbs as much as the next person, but that was rude. It didn't matter to me if he went to college or not. Sometimes I wish I hadn't. I'd probably be paying off these student loans until I retired.

I wished someone had told me that there were alternate paths in life. Despite what my high school academic advisor preached, you weren't required to go to a good school and get a good degree in order to get a good job. It was okay to take a different road, even if it was narrower.

Noah's shoulders were stiff as he leaned against the counter. Behind the counter held a glimpse of the bustling kitchen: pizza chefs rolled out thick dough, layering it generously with cheese and chunky tomato sauce.

As Noah chatted with the waiter, I found myself drawn to his thick forearms. I could almost picture his workout routine: a long morning run, followed by bicep curls as everyone in the gym stared in awe.

Just then, a pretty college-aged girl approached Noah with a smile. He stepped into a selfie with her, and I blinked, feeling uneasy. Daphne stared at me knowingly, a grin on her face as she played with the straw wrapper. When I made eye contact with her, she threw it, and the paper bounced off my forehead.

"Hey." I unconsciously rubbed my temple. "We're not on that level of friendship yet."

She reached across the table to grab the wrapper. "Noah's a

little sensitive when it comes to his degree. Or lack of, technically. Which is dumb considering how smart he is."

I nodded, arranging my fork and knife next to my plate. Though I'd probably go full savage and not bother with culinary items during the meal. "Seriously, it doesn't matter—"

Daphne prattled on like I hadn't opened my mouth. "I mean, it's not his fault he had to drop out of Cornell to take care of me."

My fork slipped between my fingers and clanged when it hit the ground.

Noah went to Cornell.

Noah dropped out of Cornell.

And he took care of his younger sister, which implied that there was no one else to do it.

I ducked below the table to grab the fork, but I let myself linger longer than needed. Just so I could let my face make a series of surprised reactions without anyone seeing. When I came back up, Daphne was chewing on her cuticle again.

"I probably shouldn't have said that." She sounded stressed. "Can you not tell him I said that?"

I only had enough brain power to mumble an agreement before Noah returned with a basket of garlic bread. He held it in front of me, waiting for me to take a piece. When I didn't, he placed two on my plate.

Noah, with his one million followers and perfected online presence, was a Cornell dropout. I wondered why he never went back to school. *One million followers, Macey. He's probably rich.* I guess you didn't need to finish college if you had that many followers and a constant stream of brand deals.

I felt a little bad as I bit into the garlic bread. Maybe I should be a little less judgmental.

"So," Daphne drawled. "Can I go to Aruba, too?"

"No," Noah answered. "You'll be back at school next week."

Daphne stole the bread from his hands in retaliation. He rolled his eyes and gave me a look of *Can you believe this?*

The waiter returned with a tray full of colorful drinks and different types of coffee.

"Oh, we didn't order those," Daphne said.

"The manager sent them. They're on the house." He set them down on the table. "Your food will be out shortly."

This wasn't the first time I had been offered something for free—it usually came in exchange for the hope of a positive article. This probably happened to Noah all the time, considering he was way more recognizable than me.

Noah and Daphne reached for a glass.

"Macey, it's free!" Daphne said when I didn't touch anything.

I grabbed hold of my water. "There's a very fine line as to which things I can accept for free and which ones I can't."

"What does that mean?"

"My contract with *Roamer's Digest* is pretty strict," I explained. "If I'm hired to cover an event, I can accept free gifts as long as they're disclosed in my article. If I'm not writing about it, I usually turn down free gifts because it could turn into a conflict of interest."

"So you're not going to take the free drinks because you don't want them to think you're going to write about them. But you get to go to Aruba for free, and in exchange you write a few articles?" Daphne asked.

That was the simplest way to explain it. There were a million other technicalities that went into contracts: spending limits, hours of work spent on the event, disclosure agreements, taxes, and more.

"Basically," I answered.

Noah continued to sip from one of the free sodas, so I assumed there weren't any qualms for him.

"Maybe I should change my major." Daphne ruminated as

she stirred the orange liquid in her glass. "I don't think nurses get to go to Aruba for free."

The waiter brought the pizza then and set it in the center of the table. Noah sliced it, and I ignored the frown on his face. I gave Daphne my full attention as she rattled on about majors and minors, and why did finals count so much toward your grade, anyways?

"Well," I said through a mouthful of cheesy goodness. "Enjoy spring breaks while you still can. I think it's nice you planned to visit your brother."

I didn't realize I had stepped onto a landmine until it exploded. The full force of it hit Noah's face, as he stared at Daphne, who pointedly looked away from the disaster.

An unplanned visit, then.

"I missed him," Daphne said, then admitted, "Also my friends told me it would be best if I didn't go to New York with them."

"What?" Noah exploded. "Why?"

"It makes sense," she said in a small voice. "We wanted to do different things. And they wanted to stay in these expensive, five-star hotels—"

"*Daphne.*" Noah covered his face with his hands. "We've been over this. If you need money, just come to me."

"And as I've told you, I don't want to spend my life depending on you—"

"You're twenty years old. You're not in any way dependent on me—"

"I am," Daphne said decisively. "And it stops now."

Suddenly, I felt very out of place. The wallpaper behind them became fascinating to me. Black-and-white swirls spiraling into the abyss. If I stared too long, I swore they moved.

Moving. *Great idea.* I should move. Relocate. Flee the

premises and let the two Hansley siblings duke it out without me.

I shifted toward the edge of my seat, but Daphne stopped me with an arm. "Macey, what do you think?"

From Noah's glare, I gathered I shouldn't have any opinions on the matter. Unfortunately for everyone involved, I did.

"Based on the limited knowledge I have of this situation"—I met Noah's eyes—"I think it's understandable that you'd want to be independent and handle things yourself."

Daphne nodded, satisfied. Noah, on the other hand, looked like he was mentally drafting my obituary.

"But," I continued, hoping I could hop out of the grave he was ready to dig, "it's also okay to accept help from other people, too. I wish I had someone like Noah in my corner when I was in college."

Noah's glare shifted from murderous to mildly offended. "You make it sound like I'm a rare Pokémon."

Daphne smirked. "A charitable, overprotective Pokémon."

Noah groaned, dragging a hand down his face. "I swear—"

But Daphne was already humming the Pokémon theme song under her breath.

Noah tilted his head an inch, and I had a bizarre urge to run a hand through his hair. Check if it was as soft as it looked. He looked not at all like an Instagram bad boy. Just an older brother. A lot of concern. A little vulnerability. Watching me quietly.

"True friends would have met you in the middle," I added.

Daphne nodded. "I know. Chicago's better anyways."

Noah tried to force salad on my plate, but I waved him away. Only carbs for me tonight. "Now that, I agree with."

For the remainder of dinner, I focused all my attention on Daphne, trying to ignore the way her not-so-bad older brother was staring at me like he had just learned something that tilted his world on its axis.

7

MACEY

The Burrow Bitches

Britney: hey remember that one time someone invited me to go to aruba?

Kira: No.

Ariadne: That never happened.

Britney: i was just thinking, i could be macey's plus one...

Macey: That's not how it works. Also, shouldn't you be studying?

Britney: if i don't know the material by now, i never will

Not even a brisk Chicago morning could stop me from a good photography session. Clear skies. Trees in bloom. Open view of the horizon. Today's golden hour was prime for a sunrise photoshoot. I flipped through the photos I took with my Canon, mentally noting my favorite pictures and deleting the amateur-looking ones.

My tripod and coffee cup sat on the crushed limestone next to me. A yawn escaped my jaw as I chugged the rest of the coffee. I could almost feel the caffeine swimming through my veins.

Yes, I was aware that wasn't how caffeine worked. No, I couldn't be bothered to research how caffeine impacted our brains.

Coffee gave me something to look forward to on these god-awful early mornings. Not that I had anyone to blame but myself. It was my choice to practice my photography skills and expand my portfolio while most sane people were asleep.

Aruba was only a few days away, and I had written a shot list. At the top? Sunrises and sunsets. I could picture it now—a beautiful beach-front resort with a pink-and-red sky backdrop. The most unrealistic part of that dream wasn't the pictures themselves. It was the fact that Victoria wouldn't take a second glance at them.

Truthfully, I was a little in over my head here. I'd attended multiple press events and covered hotel openings before but never one with this much luxury. Never an international press event. And never one with so many big names on the guest list. Like Noah.

This was out of my comfort zone. Britney intervened last night, lending me a few outfits to pack. *Fake it*, she had whispered as she handed me a short red dress with more cleavage than I was used to showing.

Faking it, I could do. Just ask my ex-boyfriend.

A rustle in the trees down the trail had me throwing my tripod to the side of the road. The Lakefront Trail attracted runners and cyclists alike, either of whom might run over it. A good tripod cost more than an *I'm so sorry, here, have an energy bar*.

Still, I held the camera up to my eye once more. Maybe I needed to get my eyes checked because it almost looked like the waves of toffee hair on the runner around the corner were Noah's. My finger fluttered over the trigger, tempted to capture the moment. His features were always lighter than the clothes he wore. Gray hoodie. Black pants. Large headphones that covered his ears. I couldn't decide if he looked more like a runner mid-race or a bank robber.

Nah, I'd glanced at the inside of Noah's apartment. He had no need to rob a bank.

Note to self: don't let Noah see the inside of my apartment. Or rather, the thrifted couches and second-hand art that hung in my room.

As he turned the corner, I made the snap decision to take the picture. The top of his hoodie was peppered with beads of sweat, and his eyebrows lifted when he saw me behind the camera.

Okay, I definitely needed to get my eyes checked because I couldn't help the way I slowly drank in the image of him. My eyes caught on definitive parts of him. Tan skin. The white-and-black ankle socks. The softness of his eyes despite the smirk on his face.

"First my apartment, now my trail?" Noah slowed down, then paused in front of where I sat on the ground, dressed in an old University of Illinois Chicago sweatshirt and yoga pants. Not exactly the picture of an elegant Aruba tourist. My ass was already damp with morning dew, and I shifted uncomfortably. "You stalking me, Macey?"

I scoffed. "Why would I do that? You post more online than I want to know."

"So Internet stalking has turned into real-life stalking?" His tone was a familiar teasing, but there was a new faint sparkle in his eyes, a warmth that matched the rising sun.

Noah glanced behind me, where the early rays of the sun

pierced the horizon. The shimmering expanse of a lake on one side and the lush greenery of the parks on the other flanked us.

Subtly, I removed the lens from the camera and returned it to its case. A frown tugged at my lips, but I focused on my task.

I wasn't sure what Noah and I were currently. Definitely not stalker and target. Rivals? Acquaintances that you wave to in passing on the street? He allowed me to crash dinner with his sister last week and wouldn't let me chip in to pay the bill. I supposed wherever we stood now was better than arguing with each other in line for a taxi.

"No, let me guess." He lifted a finger to his mouth in contemplation. "You work for the paparazzi on the weekends."

The zipper to my camera bag almost tore under my hand. "Bold of you to assume I'd spend my free days photographing you."

He laughed, but his eyes were pensive. Watching me carefully. "Why don't you show me your camera roll, then?"

My pulse flickered. As I tried to get it under control, I folded the tripod. "Maybe I'm trying to help you." Damn it, this piece of metal never bent to my will. "Your pictures aren't very good."

Noah reached for the tripod, and without a second thought, I handed it to him. "Not sure if I'd agree with that. They get plenty of likes and saves."

I didn't want to think about who was saving his shirtless selfies.

The metal of my tripod bent under Noah's hands like it was water tipping out of a kettle. *Well, I loosened it for him.*

"That's due to the subject, not the technical quality," I grumbled as I accepted the folded tripod.

Whatever I expected in retaliation from Noah, it wasn't silence. Once the contents of my bag were packed, I stood to his level. Well, as close to his level as I could get considering he was a head taller than me.

From this angle, the lake surface next to us was like glass, reflecting the pastel colors of dawn—soft pinks, purples, and oranges.

That same soft pink covered the top of Noah's ears.

Was Noah...flustered? I would have thought that a half-hearted compliment would be a drop in the sea of praise he received each day.

Instead of latching onto my words, he breezed over them entirely. He took a step forward, his left ankle shaking as he did. A flash of pain bolted across his face as he exhaled.

"Noah, what's wrong with your ankle?"

"Nothing," he grunted. "I just need to run home and put some ice on it."

I gently pushed at his shoulders, ushering him to the bench on the side of the trail. "Running is the last thing you should be doing. Especially on hard terrain like this." When he relented and sat down, I squatted in front of him. "Let me look."

"What?" He moved his ankle out of my reach and asked hesitantly, "Why?"

"Because you're in pain."

"It's not that bad."

In lieu of a response, I poked his ankle. He hissed a breath between his teeth, eyes fluttering shut.

"Did you hurt it during another fight?"

I wasn't the only person Noah had gone viral for fighting with, though I'd only seen a few quick clips of the famous fight he had last year with a food blogger.

He stayed unnervingly still as I wrapped my hand around his ankle and lifted it carefully to examine. I could have sworn he wasn't even breathing—until he broke the silence with, "No. I've only been in one fight. It just looks like a million, thanks to the magic of online editing."

I raised an eyebrow, barely suppressing a smirk. "Well, at least you won."

Noah gave a half-hearted shrug. "I guess. But the stuff people said about it was bullshit. Everyone made it sound like I was some kind of scary wild animal."

"I wonder why they would say that." I chuckled.

He rolled his eyes, then rubbed the back of his neck awkwardly. "I did throw a few punches, okay? But it wasn't for the reasons people thought. A food blogger was running his mouth about this guy Kenny, a genuine dude who was trying to get into food influencing. And this jerk called Kenny a 'fat wannabe' and said he'd never make it in the industry. So yeah, I lost it a little."

I blinked, surprised by the turn of events. "Wait—so you *weren't* the bad guy?"

"Sorry to disappoint you," he said. "I was just defending Kenny's honor."

"Why didn't you tell people that?"

"It's hard to sell the bad boy angle when the truth is you were sticking up for a shy guy," Noah said, a wry grin pulling at his lips.

"On the contrary, I think that makes you seem pretty badass."

I focused on my task. The back of his ankle was swollen along the Achilles tendon. I wasn't an expert on injuries, but I knew enough to understand Noah shouldn't be running on this.

One thing I was an expert on? Shoes. Specifically, good running shoes.

The sneaker had seen better days. The once-bright fabric was now a dull, weathered shade, scuffed and stained with remnants of past runs. The sole had been worn down to an uneven, threadbare state. Tread? Nonexistent. Laces? Frayed. How was Noah running with these? I didn't know.

"You need new shoes."

Noah placed his elbows on his thighs, looking down at me. It suddenly occurred to me how intimate the position could look to a stranger—Noah on the bench, me on my knees in front of him. I rolled to the side, reaching for my bag.

"These are Nikes," he said.

I laughed as my hand blindly searched the bottom layer of my bag. Pretty sure there was a corner of crushed Cheez-Its and peanuts in there. Gross. "Obviously. But they're worn out. They're not giving you any kind of support anymore."

"And you're a Nike expert because...?"

"Because I worked in a running shoe store for two years."

My first job, actually. Not to mention, I'd been running since I was sixteen.

"Huh," was all he said. But once I slipped off his sock, he jolted. "If you wanted me to take off my clothes, all you had to do was ask."

Noah's words were flirtatious, but his tone was quiet, hesitant. Like he was trying to use a flirty remark as a shield, instead of addressing my help.

I started to wrap my spare KT tape around his ankle. Good thing I was a running nerd and always had supplies on me. As I did so, the ends of his hairs stuck up. I ignored it, asking, "If not a fight, then what happened to your ankle?"

"Achilles tendonitis," he answered, wiping a bead of sweat off his brow. "I'm a glutton for running injuries, apparently."

"Oh?" I tightened the wrap, and he squeezed the edge of the bench with one hand. "What other injuries?"

"Tendonitis, knee sprains, stress fracture," Noah rattled off like he was collecting injuries as one would souvenirs.

I hummed, cutting the edge of the tape and finishing the wrap. "Have you ever considered that you get so many injuries because you don't give yourself time to rest in between?"

"No."

Eye roll.

I was thankful I didn't have to look him in the eye when I said, "I have asthma."

"...Okay?"

Right, so I wasn't great at connecting the dots for people. "What I mean to say is that I love running. But this disease that I've had since I was a kid gets in the way sometimes. That doesn't mean I stop running. It just means I learned how to live with it, even if it means taking breaks."

And it meant that I always carried an inhaler with me. Even now, it was tucked into the corner of my bag. Another one stayed in the fanny pack I took running. Sometimes the most unexpected thing set me off, but I knew how to manage my asthma now.

"Yeah. I see what you're saying."

Lifting his ankle, I inspected my work. Damn. I should be a nurse in my next life. He reached for his sock, but I beat him to it, stretching it over the wrap and fitting it snugly against his skin. He willingly accepted my help with the shoe, and I took my time lacing it up again.

I finished the bow, then gently placed his foot back on the ground. His breath shuddered and the artery in his neck pulsed with a tattered rhythm.

"Noah." The signals of his body gave me a boost of self-confidence. "Do I make you nervous?"

No response.

I placed one hand on each of his knees, rising up on my own knees to force eye contact. "You know, everything you post online makes everyone think you're this scary bad boy." Leaning forward, close enough to see the flickers of yellow in his eyes, I said, "I don't think that's true at all. Do you?"

Constellations of freckles shimmered around his nose. I wished I had a permanent marker to connect them all.

Who would have thought that one of the most notorious bad boys of Instagram would be frantic with nerves, near shaking under my touch? I thought he was the king of game, but in this moment, he had very little. I'd never seen Noah Hansley speechless before. It was endearing.

He looked at me with awe. With confusion, too.

"I know what a man like you wants." I leaned in an inch closer, keeping my hands solidly on his knees, and whispered seductively, "What you *need*." Noah wasn't breathing. I waited a second and said, "New shoes."

A smile cracked the frozen expression on his face, and I moved away. On the bench next to him, I held out a hand expectantly. "Give me your phone."

Noah found his voice again and asked, "Why?"

"I'm giving you my number," I said, pleased when he handed me his unlocked phone. "I need to approve the next set of shoes you buy."

He leaned back into the bench. "I can Google shoes, you know."

"Or you can ask me." I typed away at his phone, saving my number. I paused on his background; it was a picture of him and Daphne, standing side to side in the middle of a field. "You and your sister are really close."

"Yeah." He swallowed. "It's been the two of us for a while."

"She mentioned something about that."

I expected him to be upset that I knew, but instead, he let out a small laugh. "Yeah, she's not a very good secret keeper."

"It's a secret, then?"

"Of course not." His eyes—no longer laced with nerves—peered at me. "I just don't advertise it to the world, that's all."

"I'm not the world."

His expression warmed. "No, you're not."

Noah examined me, a thoughtful expression on his face. It was the first time I had seen that look, and it made me uncomfortable. Like he had already let his image drop and now leaned in entirely to this version of himself, the one who was more boyish and sweeter than anyone could have assumed, considering it was typically hidden beneath a layer of swagger.

I cleared my throat, anxious to change the subject. "Anyways, we should talk about Aruba. Are you packed?"

Disappointment flickered across his expression, there and then gone. It must have been a fluke. There was no way Noah would want to sit on a bench in the cold, discussing family and health problems with me.

"I'm more of a throw a bunch of clothes in a bag in the morning kind of guy," he said.

It was a fact universally acknowledged that for every woman who wrote a detailed packing list, there was a man who would throw a handful of clean underwear into a bag at the last minute and call it done.

"Can't relate," I said. "It took twenty minutes to decide which bathing suits to bring."

He chuckled. "Which ones made the cut?"

"You'll have to see," I said with a small smile.

Noah's phone vibrated in my hands. I glanced down, checking the familiar notification. "Oh perfect, your Uber's here."

He looked confused. "I didn't order an Uber."

"I did"—I shoved his phone into his hands and pulled him up by the elbow—"on your behalf."

"What the hell, Macey?"

No amount of protesting could hide the way he leaned most of his weight onto his right leg.

Throwing on my backpack and holding my reusable water

bottle in one hand, I nudged him toward the trail exit. "The Uber will only wait five minutes before you're charged. C'mon, I know a shortcut."

"I shouldn't be paying for an Uber at all," Noah protested, followed by another push to his shoulder blades. "How are you this strong? You're like five feet tall."

"Five-three. Show those three inches some respect."

We walked through a path of trees to the nearest exit. It took exactly four minutes, so Noah should be thanking me for saving him a late fee. We could have made it in three, but Noah must be in more pain than he originally let on. That, coupled with adjusting to a new wrap, made him slower than usual.

In the distance, a sleek black car honked at us. I waved at the driver and felt a little like a divorced parent dropping their kid off.

"There's your ride," I said.

"You're not coming?"

"Unfortunately for you, we don't live together."

He flushed again. Teasing him was really more entertaining than it should be. "No, but he can drop you off at your apartment."

Pass. I knew I shouldn't be embarrassed about where I lived or the apartment itself—Kira and I had turned it into a comfortable home—but compared to his, it was tiny. I didn't need to make it any more obvious that as a large influencer, he made considerably more money than me.

"It's fine," I insisted. "It's not too far a walk back to my place."

Actually, it was. Thankfully, Chicago public transport would get me there fast.

Noah blinked a few times, his eyes casting down. He was debating how much he wanted to reveal, watching me from beneath long lashes. My heart hammered in my chest.

"What?" I asked.

"No one...no one's taken care of me in a long time," he finally admitted. "Thank you."

Satisfaction and pride flushed through me. I didn't think I was particularly good at taking care of people—the only person I'd ever taken care of was myself—but maybe there was a part of me buried deep down that instinctively knew how.

The Uber driver beeped again.

"You better go," I said. He waved a hand goodbye.

Later that night, when Noah posted the photo I took of him and gave me photo credits, I smiled for a full minute.

8

NOAH

When Nathan showed up at the crack of dawn in his Bentley, I struggled to believe he was doing me a favor by driving me to the airport. Don't get me wrong, we were family, but it was never something for nothing with my cousin. When we were fourteen, he once covered for me when I was out past curfew, and in return, he made me do all his chores for the entire summer.

But whenever I needed him, he'd been there. When Daphne started college, and I was ready to leave St. Louis, Nathan offered me his spare bedroom until I got a place of my own.

While I trusted him with my life, Nathan knew how to play people like they were dolls on strings. His IQ was insanely high and the dude had emotional intelligence too. A dangerous combination. He could take one look at someone and figure out how to manipulate them. According to him, 99 percent of the time it came down to money, power, or sex. All that's to say is I kept a wall of caution between us.

Also, who the fuck drove a Bentley here?

True to what I told Macey, I set my alarm for thirty minutes earlier than originally intended so I could pack my bags. And by pack, I meant throwing a variety of clean clothes and bathing suits into a duffel bag and suitcase.

Hopefully, by the time I saw her, she'd have forgotten the embarrassing way I acted during our last encounter. She complimented me, and I froze. She wrapped my ankle, and I froze harder. She ordered an Uber and took care of me, and I was damn near ready to cry.

I didn't even know the last time I cried.

I had my sister, Nathan, and a large circle of acquaintances. People who I bumped into at events around town, people who I ran 10ks with on occasion, and people who were dying for the opportunity to tag me in an Instagram photo.

For a while, I had Kyle, the only other Chicago influencer I actually liked. We stuck together during press events and chatted a fair amount via DMs. He was easy to get along with, probably because we had a lot in common. We hadn't talked in a while, though.

My circle hadn't always been surface level. Back in college, I participated in clubs. I ran track for a bit. Debate team too, though I tried to keep that one a secret. Point was, I knew how to cultivate friendships. But after Mom passed, I gave up on them. I didn't have the time, energy, or desire for relationships.

Nathan glanced at me from behind the steering wheel. "You're deep in thought."

"It's been known to happen," I said lightly.

"Not frequently."

"Fuck you, too."

The corner of Nathan's mouth tilted up. He was only a year older than me but enjoyed taking on the older and wiser than thou appearance. His black hair curtained green eyes and dark brows. The wind from the window blew at his collared shirt, revealing the top of a tattoo on his chest.

At a quick glance, he was the same cousin I had grown up

with: playing soccer in the backyard on sunny days, burning marshmallows by the fire in the winter, collecting bugs in jars to terrify Daphne. It wasn't until I took a second look at him that I could recognize the ways he'd changed: less patience, more intimidation. Like he walked on a fine edge and could tip over at any point.

We were similar in the ways that mattered, but at times it was blatantly obvious we had taken different paths in life. I didn't even understand what he did for a living. One hundred percent chance it was something with cybersecurity. Fifty percent chance it was illegal. All I knew was he spent a few years down on his luck, like me and Daphne, but recently, it made him a lot of money.

Nathan shifted his hands on the wheel. "Thanks for inviting me to be your plus-one, by the way."

"Like you couldn't easily afford a trip to Aruba," I scoffed.

"Will Macey be there?"

Tension burned through my body, starting in the ankle that still bothered me and trailing all the way up into my jaw. "Macey?"

"The girl from the video," he clarified. "I looked into her after admiring the way she tore into you."

Nathan was a powerful guy, with a lot of resources at his disposal. I had no doubt that looking into her could mean much more than the typical Instagram stalking. Did he offer to drive me to the airport to try to get closer to her?

The question struck me without permission, visceral and uncomfortable. Then I remembered Nathan didn't "do relationships." The realization should calm me, but it only made me spiral more.

Was Macey a relationship-only kind of girl, or did she want something casual?

"Yes," I answered.

"She's pretty," he remarked casually, turning on his blinker as we approached the airport. "Good for you."

"What is that supposed to mean?"

"It means I can't remember the last time you dated a girl," he said. "Maybe you should take her out before someone else does."

Someone else? Did Nathan know something I didn't?

He pulled into a spot in front of the drop-off gate, and I readily pushed open the door. "It's not like that." I seethed as I pulled my bag out from the trunk.

Nathan winked, totally unbothered from the driver's seat. "Sure it isn't. Have fun in Aruba."

I dropped off my luggage with the attendant outside and checked my texts.

Macey: I'll be there in five.

Instead of heading inside the airport, I decided to wait for her outside. It might be full circle, to have a decent interaction outside the airport instead of a fight. As I waited, I scrolled through my email and skimmed the latest update from Opal Serenity.

We're so excited to welcome you and your girlfriend, Macey, tonight! At reception, you'll find...

I frantically reread the sentence.

Girlfriend.

No, no, no. This wasn't happening. Macey and I weren't dating. How did they even come to that conclusion when the only recent time we'd been seen in public together ended with an argument?

Maybe I could call the PR contact on the email and clear up the misunderstanding. I was sure she'd already spoken with Ezra—

Fucking Ezra.

My manager had recently proclaimed himself a "Noah and Macey shipper," so this must have been his way of pushing his agenda. It was too late to walk it back now without making me and Macey look like frauds.

I rubbed a hand over my face but dropped it once I saw Macey get out of the car in front of me. How was I going to tell her that Opal Serenity thought she was my girlfriend, and there wasn't anything we could do about it?

In my defense, I did try to tell her a few times.

First, as we went through security. But then I got dinged for an electronic in my pocket and had to be pulled aside.

Second, when we waited to board. Macey must have had a double shot of espresso before arriving because I could hardly get a word in before I gave up completely.

"I've never flown first class," Macey commented as we boarded the aircraft.

I'd never heard of ArubaAir before, but through the plexiglass, the plane had seemed standard. Safe. Opal Serenity was a five-star resort; I was sure we'd travel there on a nice plane.

As we climbed over the rickety bridge into the aircraft, I realized how wrong I was.

First class, as it turned out, was no different than the rest of the aircraft. The only difference was a curtain that separated a handful of seats from the others. A general feeling of neglect emerged from each part of the plane: outdated, uncomfortable-looking seats, and stale air.

The line moved slowly as the people ahead of us stopped to shove their oversized carry-ons into the small overhead compartments.

"You should have checked this," I scolded a middle-aged man with a suitcase that hardly fit in the compartment. Between the two of us, we were able to jam it in.

Macey and I settled into our seats, then she was the one scolding me. "Not everyone has the extra cash to afford to check in luggage, Noah. He's not flying first class."

"Then he should have packed less."

The plane was so tiny that there were only two seats on each side of the aisle. Our seats were so close together, our arms constantly brushed. I scooted closer to the window to try to gain some distance. Said window was scratched and smudged, reducing visibility.

Macey clicked her seat belt closed and sighed. "I bet you're the guy who leans his seat all the way back."

"I pay good money for plane seats," I defended. "Hell yes, I lean them back." There was no other way to get comfortable.

"Technically, you didn't pay any money for these seats."

"Neither did you."

She nodded solemnly. "Exactly. And that is why we will not be leaning our seats back."

We'd see about that.

I flagged down the nearest flight attendant, a woman with a bun at the top of her head. "Excuse me, could I get a coffee?"

She pursed her lips. "Oh, we don't serve coffee on this flight."

"A beer, then."

"We don't serve alcohol on this flight, either."

I rubbed my temples and tried to ignore the inner urge to bang my head on the seat in front of me. "Water?"

The flight attendant nodded. "That we have."

As she walked down the aisle, Macey giggled, which also brought me closer to that urge. "What?" I snapped.

"You're such a diva."

"I'm a diva for asking for a drink?"

Macey rolled her eyes and focused on the backpack in her lap. "No, you're a diva for not waiting until they come around with the drink cart to ask."

"Something tells me they don't do that here." My lip curled when my hand skirted over a rip in the seat. "Not a great first first-class experience for you."

She pulled a book from her bag and dropped it on her lap. "It's fine. Besides, I'm sure you'll post a photo that makes our experience look much better than reality."

"Hey, you're the one who liked three of my photos the other day." The flood of heat I felt knowing she spent free time looking at my photos was totally unnecessary. I blamed the inadequate air conditioning on this plane. "Does this mean you *like* me now?"

She flushed. "Don't be ridiculous. Social media isn't real."

"I don't know," I said. "You're the one doing all the liking."

"Say what you will, but you're the one who's tagging me in photos."

Minutes after she texted me the running photo, I posted it online before I could chicken out. Yes, I tagged her. It was only fair. "I looked good in it. You're welcome for the photo cred, by the way."

"It did get me more followers," she admitted as she opened the book. "Not that it matters."

"It's okay if it does matter."

Macey considered it; I could tell by the way her finger froze on the corner of the page. Eyes that should be roaming the printed words stayed in one place. After a few seconds, she answered, "Maybe it would be important if I had my own blog, but as a cog in the machine that is *Roamer's Digest*, it doesn't."

A cog in the machine. I always hated how corporate terms sounded so robotic. At least let your employees have some personality in the ways they describe themselves.

"Do you want your own blog?"

"I'm a writer for a magazine," she said, deflecting with ease. "That would be a conflict of interest."

She dove nose-first into the book, intent on ignoring me for the rest of the flight. I laughed when I saw the title: *A History of Whale Migration.* Guess her costume spurred a newfound love of whales.

The discussion about the girlfriend and boyfriend situation could wait until we landed.

It was a long flight, though, and there was no built-in entertainment system. How was I going to survive without my favorite hobby of monitoring the plane's location on the map?

I gained a few minutes of entertainment from watching people on the flight. You always saw the same people on airplanes. There was the nervous flier, who repeatedly checked the safety card; the sleepy flier with an eye mask and ear plugs; and the health enthusiast, who brought their own snacks onto the flight.

Once the air kicked on more strongly, it was a bearable temperature. Not for Macey, though. She immediately dug through her backpack to find a sweater and shoved her arms into it.

I did a double take.

Wait a damn minute.

"Is that my jacket?"

Macey blinked and glanced down at the jacket, looking just as surprised as I did. "Oh, yeah, it is. I almost forgot you gave it to me the last time we were at the airport." She started to pull her left arm out. "Here, take it back."

"No, it's fine. You can keep it." At Macey's raised brow, I amended, "Until the end of the weekend. In case you get cold again."

"Right." She tucked her head down into the book again, but I thought I caught a smile on her face. "Thanks."

I looked at her hands, poking out of the sleeves of my jacket, distantly aware of how domestic this entire situation was. There was a fine white scar on her index finger I'd never noticed before. Small hands. Mine would wrap around them easily.

I shook myself out of the thought and looked down at my own hands, safe and far away from hers.

This sudden sense of domesticity wasn't real. We were just two people who were going to be forced to pretend to date for a few days. I didn't need *real* domesticity with anyone. I especially didn't need anyone else close to me. I just...ached a bit sometimes. That was all.

Ready for a nap, I leaned my chair fully back, ignoring Macey's glare. Moments later, I slipped into a restful dream of whales and whale costumes.

"That's funny," Macey commented as we stepped into the cool blast of baggage claim at Aruba International Airport. "They put our names together."

She pointed to a private driver waiting for us, holding a sign that said *Noah & Macey.*

"Because they think we're dating."

"*What?*"

Maybe I shouldn't have ripped the Band-Aid off like that.

"There's no way they think that," said Macey, pacing in small circles. "Why would they?"

I pulled up the email on my phone and held it out. She clamped a hand over her mouth as she read it, but I could have sworn I heard a muffled *sonofabitch* escape through her fingers.

After a few frenzied breaths, Macey dropped her hand. "We have to set the record straight."

"No, we don't," I said. "It would make both of us look bad if we showed up to an all-inclusive resort's press event only to say *just kidding, we're not actually a couple.*"

Her eyes narrowed. "What are you saying? We should let them think we're dating?"

"That's exactly what I'm saying."

She blinked, utterly appalled. "No way."

I smirked. "So you want to be the one to explain to the PR team that we scammed them into giving us a free vacation?"

"But we didn't scam them. It's just an innocent misunderstanding!" Macey let out a strangled noise. She jabbed a finger toward me. "How are we supposed to sell this?"

"They already believe it," I said. "We just have to do enough to make them continue believing it."

She stared blankly back at me. God, she was acting like I'd suggested we take up synchronized swimming. Surely getting along with me for a few days couldn't be that hard, could it?

"Fine," she grumbled. "Fine, we'll figure it out."

My suitcase appeared first on the carousel, and we waited for Macey's bag to follow. But after a few minutes, in which Macey switched from chewing her nails to tapping her foot, it never did. The same few suitcases made their rounds, Macey's long forgotten. I watched her braid, undo, and re-braid her hair three times before she gave up.

With a deep sigh, Macey drawled, "I'm going to the lost luggage counter."

There wasn't an invitation there, but I followed anyway. This section of the airport was shockingly quiet. Apparently, we were the only ones to have bad luck today.

After a long conversation that culminated with a *We're sorry, we have no idea where your luggage went, please enjoy this free drink coupon,* it became clear that Macey wouldn't have her bag tonight. They assured us that it would be delivered to the resort as soon as it was found, which could be as early as tomorrow morning. Or as late as the end of the grand opening. Or never. Yikes.

I thought Macey might let loose with a lecture or at least a death glare—I know I would have—but instead, she gritted her teeth, smiled like a saint in a bad mood, and said, "Thank you. Have a nice day."

Really? It took so little for her to insult me and call me a Ken doll, but the idiots who lost her luggage were off the hook.

"I never realized how polite you are to everyone," I murmured as we searched for our driver again. He was tall and lanky, so I wasn't sure how he disappeared so easily. "Except me."

"It's not the customer service rep's fault," she said. "People are good. They just make mistakes sometimes. The rep apologized. Besides, I packed my inhaler and an outfit into my carry-on, so as long as I get my luggage in the morning, it'll be okay."

Inhaler. I had almost forgotten what she had shared with me on the bench, too focused on the pain in my ankle and her soft touches. Thank God she had her inhaler with her or else I'd make us skip the opening event to go to the pharmacy.

"Interesting," I said with a shake of my head.

"What?"

"You tend to see the best in people. I never noticed it before."

I pushed down any hurt I felt at being the exception, not the rule.

"And that's bad because..."

Because people were the worst. There were a few exceptions, but generally, people treated others terribly. Just turn on the news at night. And when people weren't the worst, that was when you had to be careful. It was in those instances that you were at risk of having someone close to you leave.

Macey tightened the straps of her backpack and waved at our driver, who had been snacking on yucca chips in the corner. We trailed behind him like two kids following their dad.

"People do bad things," said Macey through a hardened mouth. "It doesn't mean they're intrinsically bad."

"I usually don't stick around to find out."

The warm Aruba air hit as we walked out of the automatic doors of the airport. We trailed through a parking lot until arriving at a small white van that would take us to Opal Serenity.

I opened the back door for Macey. Because that's what fake boyfriends do. And real ones, I guess.

She hummed as she got comfortable in the back seat. "I don't think that's true," she said. "A man who drops out of Cornell to take care of his sister doesn't sound like a flaky person to me."

The car roared to life, and we pulled out of the parking spot. Fortunately, the driver couldn't seem to care less about our conversation. Or he wasn't fluent in English. "Maybe you need to get your ears checked, Scribbles."

"Scribbles?"

I shrugged. "You're always scribbling down notes in your notebook."

"There's nothing wrong with old-fashioned notebooks. Especially when it'll help me make this weekend a great trip. Minus the fake dating thing." Macey flipped to a to-do list in her notebook. Pictures to take, people to talk to, articles to write. "My column is spiking, and if I can get my boss to let me publish what I want, I think I can walk out of this as a mid-tier travel writer, at least." She checked off the first item: fly to Aruba. "I'm sure everything else will go smoothly."

Which would, inevitably, jinx a million other things into going wrong, but I wisely kept my mouth shut.

9

MACEY

The Burrow Bitches

Macey: IS THIS TOO MUCH BOOB

Ariadne: Yes but I like it

Kira: Maybe yes for a professional event

Britney: no

Britney: give the people what they want

We spent the rest of the car ride in silence, me mourning my lost luggage and Noah scrolling through Instagram. Soon the driver made his final turn. The resort grounds unfurled in front of us, and the only adjective that came to mind was *lavish*. It was massive, sprawling across well-groomed lawns and lush land-scaping. Not to mention, direct access to a beach with crystal-clear turquoise waters.

Hundreds of lanterns dangled from the trees, swaying gently

in the breeze. No doubt it turned into a rom-com set after dark. Calming music filtered through speakers and blended in perfectly with the sounds of the waves. Next to me, Noah's eyes were bright and wide.

When we pulled up to the front, a valet attendant appeared to collect our luggage. Well, Noah's luggage. I swung on my backpack and met Noah's eyes over the hood of the car. We must be thinking the same thing: *holy shit*. I took a deep inhale. It smelled delicious here, like freshly baked bread and flowers all in one.

Noah handed over his luggage to the attendant, who smiled and pointed to the doors. "Check-in is that way."

We thanked the attendant.

"Wow." Noah sounded how I felt. In awe. "Look at that caryatid."

I squinted at him. "What?"

"The sculpted female figure over there," he said like I should obviously know this.

"Uh-huh. And that's the first thing you notice why?"

"Because it's pretty and functional!" He grinned, clearly proud of his architectural crush.

"Right, because that's what I'm looking for in life: beauty and structural support."

Smooth jazz played quietly as we entered the main building. It was impeccably clean and decorated for the grand opening in a few days. A balloon arch of metallic tones framed the walkway, which was clad with a red carpet. What were we, celebrities?

Oh my God. Maybe some celebrities would be attending. I craned my neck around the corner, hoping to catch a glimpse of Brad Pitt, but there was only a group of people on their phones. Influencers. Noah would probably ditch me in a few minutes to go hang out with his kind.

A tall blonde woman dressed in all black greeted us by the

reception. "Good evening and welcome to Opal Serenity! Can I have your names for check-in, please?"

"Macey Monroe," said Noah. "And I'm Noah Hansley."

"Pleasure to meet you, Macey and Noah. We're so excited to host you this weekend." She handed us a few slips of paper to fill out and sign. It was a list of commitments and terms we'd agreed to already via email.

"My name is Jennifer. I'm on the public relations team heading the grand opening." She stapled both of our papers together and flashed a smile. "Feel free to contact me if you need anything this weekend."

She passed a business card across the counter, which Noah pocketed.

After clicking on the keyboard for a few seconds, she pulled out a set of key cards. "You can check into your suite now."

Suite?

As in...singular?

"Suites," I clarified, waiting to see her reaction. Next to me, Noah tensed.

"Yes, suite." Jennifer smiled, blissfully unaware that she was gift-wrapping another problem for me with a bow. As if my missing luggage wasn't enough, the universe decided to double down on our fake dating disaster. Apparently, misery came with a complimentary side of a singular suite. "It does have a living room and bedroom, though."

I glanced at Noah, hoping he'd pitch in as well, but he was looking as frozen as he did on the bench the other day. I was on my own here. "Is there any chance of a second suite?"

She blinked a few times, seeming confused. "My apologies, ma'am, we assumed that you and your boyfriend would want to stay together."

Yep, that confirmed it. I was going to have to share a room with Noah for three days. What if he snored like my father did on our family vacations? Or, worse, what if he didn't snore at all, and I had to suffer through the awareness of his presence in silent darkness?

My face must have looked unhinged because panic flashed across Jennifer's eyes. She practically dove into the safety of her computer screen, probably praying I'd vanish like a pop-up ad. "I would offer a second suite, but I'm afraid all of our rooms are booked for the press event. Is that a problem?"

Before I could respond, Noah slung an arm over my shoulders. "Not a problem at all."

Jennifer beamed at him, her smile practically sparkling. Great. Now I looked like the selfish, diva girlfriend. She slid two matching key cards and itineraries across the counter. Normally, I'd pay close attention to the details, but it was hard to focus when Noah's warm arm was draped around me like it belonged there.

Out of the corner of my eye, I caught a glimpse of his forearm —the subtle flex of muscle, the way his skin seemed to glow under the lobby lights. That damn forearm. When had forearms become so hot? The heat of his thumb brushing against my shoulder sent a shiver down my spine, and for a moment, I forgot all about Jennifer and the problems she brought me.

In the elevator, I glared at Noah until he let go of me. "Not a problem?"

"I didn't want to cause a scene." He eyed me. "Besides, wouldn't a couple want to sleep in the same suite? You already raised a red flag."

Point made.

When the elevator opened on the fourth floor, we didn't have to walk far until we reached the room. *Our* room. Frustration festered in me, on the cusp of bubbling over, and then the door swung open.

My breath caught in my throat, and all feelings of anger dissolved. For a fleeting second, I wondered if this was even real life. How was I, low-tier travel writer Macey Monroe, standing in a suite that looked like it was ripped straight out of a luxury magazine?

The polished marble floors gleamed under soft, golden light, and the scent of fresh lilies mixed with the faint tang of ocean air from the balcony. An absurdly spacious living room held a couch, two reclining chairs, and a coffee table. To the left was a dining nook with a small kitchen table set for two. On top was a vase of flowers and a variety of Opal Serenity themed swag: magnets, drinking glasses, coffee mugs, and stickers. Tucked under the vase was a tiny white envelope.

My eyes followed the wall until they stumbled upon the best part of the suite: a sliding glass door that opened to the balcony. The view overlooked the ocean, waves crashing against a large bundle of rocks.

Amazing. Flawless. Beautiful.

I was almost out of adjectives to describe this moment until one ruined them all—*disaster*.

Noah cleared his throat and held out the envelope, now opened.

Noah and Macey,

We are thrilled to welcome you to the grand opening of Opal Serenity here in Aruba. Your chemistry and newly found love is what we want our guests to experience during a romantic getaway or a honeymoon here. We hope that you can find relaxation and passion this weekend.

Please join us for a welcome ceremony at 6:00 p.m. tonight.

Your friends,

Opal Serenity

I read it once, then twice, before dropping the letter onto the plush white carpet. Words stuck out in my mind like drops of honey: chemistry, romantic, passion.

I pressed my palms to my eyes. "Why is this happening to us?"

They must have seen the video of us yelling at each other, but why would that lead them to assume we were in love? They should assume the opposite. Despite the screams inside my head, I picked up on the absolute silence from Noah.

I removed one hand to glance at him. "How are you so calm right now? From now until we leave, we have to convince them we're in love."

"It's only three days."

I faltered, having just realized something else. Something that would dramatically impact the rest of our stay and work at Opal Serenity.

"I guess," I said, but my voice sounded watery. "They only want me here because they think I'm your girlfriend."

I saw concern hidden in his yellow-green irises, in the way his brows pinched ever-so-slightly. It should be comforting, but it only made me more upset. The last thing I wanted from anyone, especially Noah, was pity. "Macey, that's not true."

I stood so suddenly I almost knocked over the coffee table. "I need to get ready for the welcome ceremony. As the girlfriend in this fake relationship, I think it's only fair that I get the bedroom."

Then I bolted before he could respond and—more importantly—before he could see the tears that threatened to leak out of my eyes.

"Do you think it's too—"
"Short?"

"No—"

"Tight?"

"N—"

"Boob-y?"

"*Red*," I snapped. "Too red. But thanks for telling me how you really feel."

When traveling, I always followed the cardinal rule: carry a spare outfit in your carry-on. Unfortunately, this outfit was one of Britney's dresses. I hadn't thought twice about it at the moment, fully confident that my luggage would make it with me to Aruba. That was what happened when you got too comfortable, though—something inevitably went wrong.

Noah shrugged. "What can I say? I'm an honest boyfriend."

I tucked my key and tube of lipstick into a black clutch, side-eyeing him. Of course he was the picture of ease and confidence tonight. White button-down tucked into black, form-fitting dress pants. His classic leather jacket was folded over the dining chair, where I assumed it would stay tonight. "An honest *fake* boyfriend," I corrected.

After collapsing onto the king-size bed and avoiding a complete breakdown by the narrowest of margins, I got ready for the welcome ceremony in the bathroom. Besides the dress, I only had spare mascara and red lipstick in my carry-on bag. My hair was still messy from the plane ride, so I attempted to finger-comb it, only to give up and pin it to the back of my head.

There was no dress code for the welcome ceremony, but panic had already settled in. What if it was secretly a black-tie event? What if everyone showed up in Louboutins and all I had was two-year-old kitten heels?

"Well," I muttered, giving my reflection one last doubtful glance. "Good thing they invited me for my pretty words and not my wardrobe."

I turned to leave the suite, but Noah's hand closed over mine, gently tugging me back. When I glanced at him, his gaze was already trailing down to where our fingers intertwined. Before, when I'd asked for his opinion, I'd barely noticed his eyes on me, too focused on the uncomfortable dress riding up my thighs, but now, his eyes moved upward, pausing for a heartbeat too long on the neckline of the dress. His Adam's apple bobbed, and for a moment, something dark and smoldering flickered in his expression—desire, unmistakable and raw.

"Your words are pretty," he said, his voice low and deliberate, "but you're even prettier." It wasn't a compliment; it was a fact, delivered with absolute certainty.

Then, like he'd realized he was holding fire, he dropped my hand, the absence of his touch sharper than I expected. His fingers brushed the door handle, but not before he added with a small, almost-gruff smile, "Red suits you."

I hoped he meant it because that same shade of red flamed my cheeks all the way down to the welcome ceremony.

The ceremony was held in the ballroom. Soft, live music set the tone, with a quartet playing classics. Resort staff welcomed guests with warm smiles and fresh flower bracelets. Elegantly branded gift bags handed to us contained press releases, photos, and small gourmet treats.

Thick white drapes, chic furniture, and floral arrangements decorated the ballroom. String lights added a warm glow as the event extended into the evening. Stations were set up along the walls with samples of the resort's culinary offerings, from seafood to sandwiches.

There had to be around a hundred people here. Everyone bustled around, glasses of champagne in their hands, greeting each other with hugs and smiles.

"I'll be right back," Noah whispered. I didn't expect him to return, sure he'd find a familiar group of people to hang out with for the night.

I took one deep breath and reminded myself who I was. It didn't matter if I was considered the most unimportant person here or not. I'd attended events like this alone countless times. The trick was to find someone, or a small group, who also looked like they didn't know many people. Introduce yourself, tell a few jokes, then invite others to join in the fun. Soon enough, you had a group of like-minded individuals to hang out with all evening.

A duo of girls in the corner caught my eye. They looked nice and easy to chat with. I inserted myself into their conversation, introducing myself with a handshake. They were warm and receptive. Two bloggers from Florida who focused on luxury travel.

"That's so cool," I said after they told me about their blogs. "How does it feel to live the dream life?"

The taller of the two laughed. "It comes with its own set of challenges, but it's really rewarding."

"So much better than working for someone else," the other girl added.

For a second, I toyed with the idea of working for myself. To not have to wake up miserable at the thought of going into the office and seeing what mood Victoria was in that day.

It wasn't realistic for me, though.

"What's your writing process like?" I asked, then listened as they dived into the details of schedules, daily word count goals, and editing tips.

Some of it sounded familiar, but I mentally took notes on the rest. How they organized their trips, the nerves that came with pitching brands instead of being assigned a topic. I admired their passion.

"Everything okay here?" Noah wrapped an arm around my shoulder, tucking me into his side. He turned his face down toward mine. "For you."

He held out a champagne glass.

Even though he was my fake boyfriend now, he forgot this important fact about me. Good thing there wasn't much of an audience here to witness this blunder. "I don't drink—"

"It's sparkling grape juice."

Oh.

"Thank you." I accepted the glass and took a small sip. Bubbly and sweet. "Where did you get this?"

The waiters around the ballroom only carried trays of champagne, and the tables in the room only contained food. I would know, as the tiny brownies in the corner were calling my name.

"Bartender," Noah said dismissively, then addressed the two bloggers. "Hi, I'm Noah. Macey's boyfriend."

Immediately the two girls fawned over us, saying how we were such a cute power couple. The compliments reddened my cheeks—I really hoped my luggage with foundation appeared tomorrow—and I leaned further into Noah's side. How was he always so warm?

The three of us chatted for a few minutes, and they invited us to Florida sometime. Nice gesture, but I'd probably never see Noah after this weekend, let alone travel to Florida with him.

"Oh, look, it's our best friend Jennifer." Noah pulled me toward the public relations team, who each had giant smiles on their faces.

The rest of the night blurred into a mix of lively conversations and sampling everything from quesillos to pastries that looked too fancy to actually enjoy. I was pleasantly surprised by how warm and welcoming everyone was. But Noah? Noah was a different kind of magnetic.

He moved through the room with an effortless confidence as if he owned the space. Every person he passed lit up, eager to share a laugh or pose for a photo. He greeted everyone like they were old friends, making each interaction feel personal and genuine.

I could tell people were excited to chat with him, not just because of who he was, but because of how easily he made them feel seen. He made being around him feel like a privilege—no wonder everyone was clamoring for a selfie or a spot in his next Story.

I felt a sudden pang of thirst as my glass emptied, and after mentally adding sparkling grape juice to my grocery list, I excused myself from Noah's side and the lively group of influencers we were chatting with.

At the bar, I flagged down the bartender's attention. "Could I have another sparkling grape juice, please?"

"We don't serve that here." The bartender glanced at my glass and then back at me. "But we have champagne, soda products, and water."

"Really? Then how..." I frowned as my hands played with the damp napkin under the glass. "Never mind. Thank you."

They didn't serve sparkling grape juice here.

Yet I just had a glass of one.

Noah had said...

Leaning against the edge of the bar, I let out a small laugh, the realization hitting me. Noah must have purchased it from the on-site convenience store.

He picked up on my amusement as soon as I returned to the group. "What's so funny?"

"Nothing," I lied. "Let's go try the brownies."

10

NOAH

My body ached when I woke up the next morning, and I immediately regretted not fighting for the bed. Here I was, limping toward the kitchen and rubbing at my back like I was an eighty-year-old man. This ankle was the real problem. I'd rested it for days and still no improvement.

I poured a glass of water and searched for the itinerary, which was buried in the mess of papers on the kitchen table. We'd only been here one night, and the table looked as packed as the one in my apartment after chucking a week's worth of forgotten mail onto it.

When we left the opening ceremony yesterday, a bunch of vendors shoved flyers and packets into our faces. Macey took them all with a smile, while I declined each. Now brochures for restaurants, activities, and photography services cluttered our space.

Before I could find the itinerary, there was a knock at the door.

Suddenly glad I woke up early and put on a shirt, I greeted the resort employee at the door. He held a large tray filled with dishes in the palm of his hand.

"Good morning, sir," he said, looking far more pleasant than someone should in the morning. "I'm here to drop off breakfast and luggage. Your suitcase arrived a few minutes ago."

That would make Macey's morning.

When we checked in yesterday, after the disaster of learning we were sharing a suite, we filled in breakfast forms for our three mornings here. Veggie omelet for me, French toast for Macey. She had also ordered four different coffee options, and as the waiter set up the dining table, I was thankful she did. Extra photo content.

"Thank you." When the waiter finished, I held the door open for him as he exited the suite.

I pounded on the bedroom door. "It's time to wake up, Scribbles!" I heard a grunt of frustration on the other side, muffled by a pillow. "Your luggage is here."

Immediately the sounds of frustration turned into excitement. Macey threw open the door and rushed out to hug the suitcase. Her hair was messy, frizzy on the top but as long as ever. Only a robe covered her body, and one side playfully fell off her shoulder.

Kneeling next to the suitcase, she whispered, "I knew you would come."

"I never left," I drawled.

"I was talking to my suitcase."

Once I removed the covers of the dishes, the smell of honey and chocolate filled the air. "Macey." I distracted myself by taking photos of the breakfast spread. "Why are you wearing a robe?"

The distraction didn't work as she grabbed her phone and joined me. "I didn't have any other clothes, so I slept naked."

My phone fell out of my hands and into the vanilla latte. Fuck. I pulled it out and dried it on a dishtowel.

But my feverish brain only cared about one thing.

Macey Monroe.

Slept naked.

All night.

Only a wall separating her from me.

I shouldn't be so invested in this new piece of information, but it was all I could do not to picture the scenario in my head. Soft skin, painted by the sun's early morning rays. Ruffled sheets. Warm hands as they dragged over my naked chest, all the way down to—

Nope. Where did that come from?

Obviously, I knew Macey was attractive. That *I* was attracted to her. Studious, deep eyes that challenged me. The way she always smelled like coconut. An ass for days.

Lust, attraction—that was all familiar stuff. But I had no frame of reference for the tender ache in the pit of my stomach.

"Noah!" Macey sighed, helping to clean up the mess. "Don't ruin the other drinks."

A few minutes later, we thumbed through the brochures on the table as we ate our breakfast. Macey had decided she was comfortable sitting across from me in nothing but the aforementioned robe, and she was currently pouring an obscene amount of syrup and strawberry preserves onto her French toast.

"Do you want any bread with that sugar?" I asked, halfway through my omelet.

She showed me the spears of her fork. "What's the point of French toast if you don't douse it in toppings?"

"To enjoy the toast itself," I said dryly.

"Not everyone likes to eat egg whites and lean protein all the time, Noah."

Macey was going on and on about the ranking of different French toast toppings, but it turned into white noise as I finally pulled out the itinerary from its place underneath a bundle of ads.

Friday, March 12

1:00 p.m. – 6:00 p.m.: Guest Arrival

6:00 p.m. – 8:00 p.m.: Welcome Ceremony

Saturday, March 13

9:00 a.m. – 10:00 a.m.: Breakfast via room service

10:00 a.m. – 11:30 a.m.: Couples massage

11:30 a.m. – 1:30 p.m.: Poolside lunch

1:30 p.m. – 3:00 p.m.: Free time

3:00 p.m. – 5:00 p.m.: Tour and executive interview opportunities

5:00 p.m. – 6:00 p.m.: Cocktails in the lounge

6:00 p.m. – 10:00 p.m.: Dinner and sunset cruise

Sunday, March 14

9:00 a.m. – 11:00 a.m.: Breakfast available in the lounge or via room service

11:00 a.m. – 12:00 p.m.: Tour of the gardens

12:00 p.m. – 2:00 p.m.: Cooking class

2:00 p.m. – 6:00 p.m.: Free time

6:00 p.m. – 8:00 p.m.: Dinner and send-off

Monday, March 15

9:00 a.m. – 10:00 a.m.: Breakfast via room service before guests depart

I slid the itinerary across the table to Macey, who lifted it to her face with her free hand. "Oh my God." She shoved her plate to the side so she could bury her head in her arms on the table.

"What's wrong?"

"I just realized we're going to have to post content of us together in Aruba." Macey sighed. "Everyone's going to think we're dating."

I collected her emptied plate and dropped it on top of mine. "Everyone already thinks that."

"No," she corrected. "Everyone at the resort thinks we're dating. But soon everyone in the world is going to think we're dating once you post about it."

It wasn't like I was going to Photoshop us kissing on the beach. "Don't worry, I know how to manipulate photos well enough. I would never post something you're not comfortable with."

"I'm surprised you aren't more worried. What if all your fangirls think you're taken now?"

I hadn't considered that. Probably because it didn't matter. "I don't have fangirls."

"Whatever you say." Macey stood and tucked the chairs under the table. "Wrap your ankle today."

"What?"

"You're limping, Noah. I know it must be hurting."

"I don't have anything to wrap it with."

Macey's eyes flickered to her suitcase then back to me. "I brought some tape. Good thing my luggage didn't end up in whatever Bermuda Triangle all lost bags disappear to."

She unzipped her suitcase, and I wondered if she had an injury I didn't know about. "Here you go."

I barely caught the small bundle of tape she threw at me.

"I thought you might need it."

And that answered that question. She brought it for me. But why?

Macey excused herself to go get ready as I started the annoying process of wrapping my ankle. When she returned, seeming pleased with the result, I couldn't stop the warm feeling that zipped through me.

The spa was tucked between swaying palm trees, its entrance framed by a cascading waterfall that trickled into a turquoise pond. The air smelled of coconut oil and something flowery, and the soft sound of wind chimes blended with the lull of waves in the distance.

We stepped inside, and a woman in a crisp linen uniform greeted us, then handed us cool towels. We hadn't even started; what did we need towels for?

"Welcome to your couple's massage experience," the spa attendant said with a smile. "Macey and Noah, right?"

"That's right," said Macey, who was wiping down her hands and forearms with the towel.

"We have you booked in for massages with Leoni and Penny. Before you begin, would you like to choose your aromatherapy oil? We have vanilla orchid, sandalwood, or island coconut." She held up three small glass bottles.

"Ooh." Macey took the vanilla orchid bottle and gave it a sniff. "This one, please."

The attendant turned to me. "And for you, sir?"

I glanced at Macey. "Coconut."

"Great choices." She gestured toward the open couches. "Please have a seat. Your masseuses will be with you shortly."

It was hard not to feel calm in this environment. The *drip, drip, drip* of the fake fountain, the fruit-infused water cups, the comfortable couches. No wonder self-care was so trendy. I could take a nap right here.

Macey leaned sideways to whisper in my ear, "You should tell the masseuse about your ankle."

"Why would I do that?"

She shrugged. "Maybe they can work out some of the kinks."

I take everything back. Any sense of calm evaded me. Now that I was hyperaware of my environment, I felt like all eyes in the room were on us. There were other couples in the waiting area, and I swore they glanced at us every few seconds.

Were they onto us? Were we not passing as a couple?

A uniformed woman holding a clipboard appeared at the end of the hall. "Macey and Noah."

We stood to follow her, and in a moment of instinct, I grabbed Macey's hand. She looked startled at me but didn't let go. Hands clasped, we followed the woman down the hall to a dim room with two massage beds.

Outside the room, Macey and I came to a stop, made eye contact, looked at our hands, and let go like our hands were on fire. I felt like I was on fire.

We stared at each other, waiting for the other to step into the intimate room.

"You guys can come in," the woman said as she dropped the clipboard on the side table. "I'm Penny. My colleague Leoni and I will be your masseuses. Please take some time to fill out this sheet with any prior injuries and areas of focus. We'll be back in a few minutes. You can leave your clothes on the table."

Oh.

Oh, no.

The masseuse closed the door behind us. Panic coated Macey's eyes as she glanced down at her linen shorts and white shirt. "Can they not massage us in this?" she whispered.

"Have you ever had a massage?" I whispered back. "They need bare skin."

We were supposed to be dating, which meant we were supposed to be comfortable with undressing in front of each other. Although I might have gotten tiny flashes over breakfast this morning—a collarbone here, a wrist there—I didn't think either of us was ready to fully disrobe.

She made a circle motion with her finger. "Fine. Turn around."

I turned around. There was some shuffling and the sound of fabric falling to the ground. For the second time today, Macey was naked in my presence. I heard a pumping sound, only for it to be the sound of my heart racing.

How sick was it that I was tempted to turn around? I never would betray Macey's trust like that, and the last thing I wanted was to make her uncomfortable. It was better this way, staring at the tiny water bottles by the wall instead of the woman who I wanted to kiss. As a starting point.

She is your fake girlfriend, Noah. You'll probably never see her after this weekend. Get your shit together.

Besides, she'd made it clear that she was not interested in me in that way. I'd never forget the horror in her eyes at her realization we'd have to pretend to date. I couldn't imagine her reaction to me asking her out on a *real* date.

"Okay, I'm getting under the sheets."

I heard Macey crawl into the massage bed.

"You can undress now. I promise not to look."

I spared a glance over my shoulder, where Macey was lying face down on the massage bed. The only thing she could see right now was the floor. I undressed quickly and climbed into my own bed. "I'm done, too."

I stretched lazily on the massage table, the linen cool against my skin. Beside me, Macey lay unnaturally still.

"What's wrong?" I asked.

Macey shifted so her temple was pressed against the head-rest. "I've never done this before."

"I would be a little insulted if you've already had a couples massage with a fake boyfriend."

"No, I've never had a massage before."

I propped myself up slightly, trying to keep my amusement in check. Even more important, keep my eyes in check. At the bottom of my vision was the soft skin of Macey's collarbone. "Really?"

"Nope." She huffed. "I don't know, the idea of a stranger kneading me like bread always sounded weird."

I smirked. "You do realize that's the appeal, right?"

She shot me a look. "Is it? Or is the appeal signing up to get publicly humiliated when they find out my back is just one giant knot?"

"That sounds like a very specific kink. I'm not against it, though." Her fingers tightened around the linen, and I sighed deeply. "Don't overthink it, Scribbles."

"I'm not overthinking," she said. "I'm just mentally preparing. What if I can't relax? What if I tense up so much they have to call in reinforcements?"

I chuckled. "That would be a first. I highly doubt you have that much tension."

She peeked at me, narrowing her eyes. "Maybe I didn't, until I was forced to spend all this time with you and—"

The moment the masseuses walked in, all serene smiles and effortless grace, Macey practically flung her face back into the headrest. I turned my head away just in time to compose myself. Barely.

"Are we ready to begin?" one of the masseuses asked in a calm, melodic voice.

Macey made a noise that might've been a yes.

I said, "Oh, I definitely am."

Macey's hand twitched like she wanted to reach over and smack me.

Soft island music played through hidden speakers, blending with the rustling palm trees outside. The masseuses poured warm oil into their hands, the scent of coconut and vanilla orchid filling the air. The second the first stroke of pressure rolled over my shoulders, I let out a deep exhale.

"See?" I said, voice melting into relaxation. "Not so bad, right?"

Macey made a noise, the sound of someone slipping into pure bliss.

I grinned. "Is that a yes?"

"Shut up," she murmured, but there was no bite to it.

The masseuse's hands moved expertly over my back, kneading tension I hadn't even realized I was carrying. I sank deeper into the table, letting the steady pressure work through each muscle.

Then, from beside me, I heard another little sound—soft, almost surprised.

"That definitely wasn't a noise of de-stress."

Macey retaliated, "I am *not* making noises."

"Mm." I cracked one eye open, watching her out of the corner of my vision. "Whatever you say."

We slipped into comfortable silence, luxuriating in the massage. I was about ready for a nap when I heard it—a small, barely there squeak from the massage table next to me.

I turned my head slightly, just enough to catch Macey's face. Her eyes were squeezed shut, her lips pressed together like she was trying very hard to will herself into serenity.

Another shift of the masseuse's hands, and her body gave the slightest twitch.

I withheld a laugh. "Was that—"

"It was nothing," she said quickly, voice tight, her fingers gripping the edges of the table like she was bracing for impact.

I raised a brow. "Are you ticklish?"

"No," she shot back, too fast, too defensive. Which, of course, meant *yes*.

I rolled my head back onto the headrest. As if this massage couldn't get any better.

The masseuse, still calm and professional, kept working her way down Macey's legs. The second her hands glided over her foot again, Macey lost it. A full-body twitch, followed by a burst of barely contained laughter, muffled by a hand over her mouth.

I watched in delight. "You are ticklish."

"I am *not*." Macey gasped, sounding desperate. "It's just my muscles reacting."

"Yeah. Reacting like a kid getting poked in the ribs."

She glared at me, eyes narrowed, cheeks flushed, right before another stroke of the masseuse's hands sent her into another helpless giggle—followed by a sudden flail of her leg.

It took me a second to process what happened, but when the masseuse let out a soft "Oh!" and Macey practically launched herself upright in horror, I was the one losing it.

"Oh no," she stammered, turning to look at the masseuse she'd just kicked. "I am so sorry! I didn't mean to—oh no, this is mortifying."

I shook with laughter. "No, this is incredible."

Macey held the sheet against her chest, but she didn't let that stop her from glaring at me. "I hate you."

The masseuse, the true MVP in all this, just gave a small, amused smile. "It's okay, miss. This happens sometimes."

"Does it?" I asked slyly. "Because I feel like it doesn't."

Macey peeked at me again, eyes still sharp despite her obvious humiliation. "I will kick you next."

"Worth it."

She let out another muffled groan, but I caught the way her lips twitched. And when the masseuse very carefully avoided that spot for the rest of the session, I had to fight back another laugh.

11

NOAH/MACEY

Noah

By the pool, we had time to do nothing. Unfortunately for us, that meant catching up with work. I was editing video footage from this morning as Macey frantically typed on her laptop next to me.

I glimpsed yet another look at Macey out of the corner of my eye. One navy blue bikini was enough to send me to an early grave. I didn't know what was appropriate for a fake boyfriend to say or do, so I settled onto my own lounge chair, and she did the same. We were close enough that I could smell the coconut sunscreen on her skin, mixed with the vanilla orchid oil from the massage.

Macey lifted her head from her laptop. "Sometimes I don't understand how Victoria graduated with an English degree. She used the wrong version of *your* versus *you are* again."

"Victoria?"

"My boss." She shut her laptop and placed it into her bag. "She can be difficult to work with, but at least with her I have a path at *Roamer's Digest*."

I paused the video. "Do you guys not get along?"

"It's complicated. She's tough on everyone but only ever rude to me. I know she's made me a better writer, but sometimes I wonder if it's worth it."

"No job is worth losing your sanity. If you learned what you can learn, why stay?"

She stared at me, pensive. "You're very good at simplifying things."

"Life's complicated enough already."

"True." Macey pushed her sunglasses up to the crown of her head. "I don't know why romance books make fake dating out to be this big deal." She laughed. "All we have to do is hold hands and make moony eyes at each other."

"Moony eyes?"

"You know, like the *I-want-you-so-bad* eyes that you toss at me every few minutes."

I didn't know how to tell her that was just what happened to my eyes when I looked at her.

No idea when it happened or even how it happened. But whenever she smiled at me, all I wanted was to lean forward and capture those lips in a bruising kiss. It was more than that, though. I wanted to be the reason she smiled in the first place.

Fuck, what was happening to me? Just weeks ago, we both pretended the other didn't exist in public, and now I wanted to stake a public claim on her.

A waiter paused in front of us. "Can I get you two anything to drink?"

Macey, with her cascading braid and warm eyes, smiled at him. "Could I have a diet coke, please?"

The waiter turned expectantly at me. My eyes caught on the smile still pasted on Macey's face. "Coconut water."

After, Macey commented, "Coconut water is severely under-rated. Good choice." The waiter returned a minute later and handed us our drinks. "So what do you do when you're not posting shirtless selfies?"

"I know you claim I only post shirtless selfies," I said as I sipped at my water. I wondered if Macey's skin would taste as sweet. "But I share other content, too."

I wouldn't say I had a particular "brand" on social media other than being an attractive guy who got famous. My content was lifestyle focused, and while there wasn't a typical day in my life, my posts usually focused on gym workouts, food, and activities happening locally.

National events or press trips were included too, just less frequently. If an event wanted to cater to mid-to-late-twenties men, there was a chance I'd be on the list.

"Like your nerdy LEGO collection?"

Daphne spilled that secret to her so easily. I glanced around us, thankful there was no one in hearing distance. "Don't talk about that."

"God forbid I ruin your image," Macey said, equal parts amused and offended.

"That's all it is," I insisted. "An image."

"Really?"

I ran my tongue over the inside of my teeth. My profile had started real and authentic—it began with Daphne posting daily clips of me working out in the front yard. Later, when I moved to Chicago, I admittedly had a late-stage rebellious spurt. My content changed with my lifestyle: breaking into abandoned buildings, throwing wild parties, skipping responsibilities. That content, plus the famous food blogger fight, continually went viral.

Now I was attempting to keep up the cool guy image without actually doing any of the rebellious things.

Which was tiring, to say the least. I was sick of sharing half-truths about me. It felt like I was becoming only half a person, the other half some kind of doll stuffed with views and like count.

"Really. It might have been true once, but it doesn't reflect who I am now."

She leaned closer to me. "And who are you now?"

"An average guy who likes to build LEGOs and who has more followers than the average person."

"Who do you want to be?"

I paused. "I'm...not entirely sure."

The sun was warm on my skin, and I shut my eyes for a minute. In the near distance, waves from the ocean crashed onto rocks. In front of us, the resort pool was a destination in itself. The water was a crystalline blue, so clear that I could see the mosaic tiles at the bottom. Palm trees bordered the pool, their fronds casting playful shadows across the surface. At the edge, a waterfall tumbled over a rocky ledge, leading to a shallow wading area where children splashed and played.

Paradise.

But then the public relations team ruined the paradise.

"Don't you two look cozy!" a familiar voice trilled.

Fucking Jennifer.

"How has your day been so far?" Jennifer leaned against the palm tree that shaded our lounge chairs.

Macey lifted the Canon that had been sitting in her lap. "So great. I got some amazing pictures today."

"Great!" Jennifer clasped her hands together. "Speaking of pictures, can we get one of you two together?"

"Of course." Macey placed the camera in her tote, then turned to face Jennifer.

Jennifer let out a high-pitched giggle. "I meant, like, *together.*"

What did that mean?

Macey and I stared at each other for an indeterminate

amount of time before something lit in her eyes. "Right, of course." She cleared her throat before joining me on my lounge chair.

Her thigh pressed against mine, warm and sure. She grabbed my hand, intertwining our fingers and holding them on her lap. I let out a shaky breath and reminded myself that this was nothing but a gimmick. But my body didn't listen, leaning in closer to her. I very carefully did not show on my face what the electric touch of her so close to me did to my insides.

"You guys are the cutest." Jennifer swooned and lifted her camera to her eyes. "Smile!"

I thought that would be all, that she'd be happy with that picture and walk away. I should've known it wouldn't be that easy.

"Okay, now one of you kissing!"

Macey let out a sound that could only be described as a cross between a whine and a sigh. Neither of which did anything to appease my insides.

I grimaced. "We're not really PDA people."

"Just one kiss. It doesn't have to be anything sensual."

If she said the word *sensual* to describe me and Macey again, I'd have to excuse myself and my hand from the pool area.

"It's fine," Macey whispered under her breath. "Just one kiss. It's not a big deal."

A prickle of irritation shot up my spine. Not a big deal?

It wasn't a big deal to kiss someone who slithered unwelcome into the depths of my mind? It wasn't a big deal to kiss someone who saw beyond my fame and called me out on my bullshit? It wasn't a big deal to kiss someone who I was at present dreaming about doing way more than kissing?

Maybe it wasn't a big deal to Macey, but it was to me. And I hated it.

"Pass," I said.

"*Noah*." Macey wheeled back, looking disappointed. She turned to Jennifer. "He's just nervous."

Admittedly, I'd never felt nervous around a girl before Macey. With most girls, I was confident, but apparently, when Macey showed that she cared about me, I froze. Now that I could acknowledge we cared about each other, the nerves had relented.

Besides, I didn't get nervous in the bedroom.

Soft hands squeezed my cheeks, and Macey brought my face closer to hers. "But there's nothing to be nervous about, right, honey?"

Before I could answer, she was pressing her lips to mine. The gentle brush of her fingertips caressed my cheek, then unfolded over the angle of my jaw. They stayed there for—for however long we kissed. Hell if I knew. Time had completely escaped me. We could have stayed there for minutes, hours, days.

I should have pulled away the moment I heard the click of Jennifer's camera. But I didn't. Instead, I leaned into Macey's touch like a man lost in the desert, finding not just water but the purest oasis—something I hadn't known I craved until now, and in impossible, unmeasured amounts.

My blood thickened, moving slowly through my veins like molten honey, every sensation heightened by the warmth of her skin against mine. Yet my heart betrayed me, pounding with a rhythm that threatened to give everything away. And then, just as quickly as it had begun, Macey pulled back.

Her expression flickered for a moment, eyes wide and pink lips swollen, as her confidence in her decision simmered.

Well.

Fuck me.

Jennifer let out a sigh of envy and glanced down at the screen of her camera. "We definitely got the shot. I cannot handle you two, seriously. See you on the cruise!" She waved and strutted off to find some other poor souls to photograph.

Macey's hands, which were still on my cheeks, dropped suddenly. "Um," she stuttered.

Who's the speechless one now?

"That shouldn't have happened," I started.

Macey jerked up and reached for her tote. "You're right, it shouldn't have." She tucked a spare tendril of hair behind her ear. "I'm sorry."

"No, I didn't mean—"

"I'm going to go set my camera up for the sunset photos."

Then Macey ran off, leaving me alone with thoughts that screamed for her to come back.

Macey

I'd done an excellent job of avoiding Noah since the pool kiss. Maybe people should learn from me. I'd write and publish the 101 guide to avoiding someone in public. Only ninety-nine cents plus tax.

Even now, inside the intimate lounge, I'd managed to avoid him. Potentially not a good look considering we were supposed to be playing the role of the happy couple, but couples needed space too, right?

I leaned against the centerpiece of the lounge, a marble-topped bar illuminated by pendant lights hanging from the vaulted ceiling, and sipped at my soda water. I wasn't a relationship expert by any means, but deep down I knew couples on a short weekend trip to Aruba wouldn't want any space from each other.

Up until now, I hadn't wanted any space from Noah either. We were having a great day until I had to go and ruin it with that kiss. I should've followed Noah's lead and insisted against it, but I didn't think one kiss would have the power to change things between us.

How wrong I was.

Because that one kiss made me want to skirt my responsibilities for the rest of the weekend to continue kissing him. Which was a capital P problem as Noah's reaction had been a look of disappointment coupled with the phrase every girl wants to hear: *"That shouldn't have happened."*

Getting involved with Noah would be a guaranteed path toward heartbreak. I'd done the whole date-an-influencer thing, gotten the T-shirt, and never intended to return.

All that was left on the schedule today was the sunset cruise. Fake a few smiles, take some photos, and be the first ones off the boat.

Next to the lounge's exit, Jennifer stood with a clipboard in hand. In her other hand, a mic. She raised it to her lips, cutting through the hum of conversations to announce, "Good evening, all. I hope everyone has enjoyed their day so far. If you'll please follow me, we'll head to the pick-up point for the sunset cruise."

I glanced down at the heels I wore. God, I hoped the pick-up point wasn't far. At least my outfit was comfortable—a deep purple, silky dress with a pearl lining. Despite the risqué red dress from last night, Britney had taste, and I was grateful she let me borrow her clothes. I made a mental note to buy her those peanut butter cookies from The Velvet Whisk she liked so much.

As I exited the lounge and bumped shoulders with various strangers, a familiar hand pulled me back. Noah laced our fingers together and whispered in my ear, "I hope you're finished."

A shiver snaked down my back. "With?"

"Ignoring me."

Jennifer led us through the gardens and to a set of steps

heading toward the ocean. I slowed my pace, focusing on not tripping in these shoes. The steps were even, but I wasn't taking any chances. "I wasn't ignoring you."

Noah met my pace, never letting go of my hand. "Oh? Then please elaborate on why you haven't spoken to me since kissing me and running away."

"I was *avoiding* you," I admitted. At the end of the stairs, we walked over a series of smooth stones. "There's a difference."

Ignoring someone involved turning your head away from them in conversation and pretending they didn't exist. Avoiding someone was being very aware they existed but not wanting to alert them to your presence.

"Semantics," he hissed.

I let go of Noah's hand as we approached the boat. We had probably convinced everyone around us by now that things were hunky-dory between us, and I didn't want to make him uncomfortable. Again.

A sleek and elegant catamaran awaited us in the harbor. The pristine white exterior gleamed in the golden light of the setting sun and accents of polished teak wood added nautical charm. Small bottles of water were handed out as everyone boarded the catamaran. I could smell dinner wafting from the kitchen.

Cushioned benches lined the spacious deck. A retractable awning provided shade over part of the deck, not that we needed much cover from the sun now. Soft, ambient music played from hidden speakers as we took a seat on the edge of the bench.

Noah set his arm on the bench behind me—not touching me but close. "We both look good tonight."

I snorted. "You know, most people would say 'you look good tonight' and wait for the other person to say 'you do, too'."

"Why do that when we both know we look good?"

I rolled my eyes and turned my head down. "Noah, where's your ankle wrap?"

He brushed it off. "I'm fine."

As the boat set sail, the crew distributed hors d'oeuvres, including fresh seafood and artisan cheeses.

I shoved a piece of shrimp into my mouth. "Fine. But don't come crying to me if you're in pain later."

"Me and my ankle were doing fine before you inserted yourself into the healing process." He snapped a piece of cheese in half, crumbs falling to the floor. "Let's get drinks."

By the bar, the sky had begun to paint itself in shades of orange and pink. The tranquil water around us reflected the vibrant colors, creating a mirror image. I took a few minutes to grab photos and videos. After snapping a few, I noticed everyone else on board doing the same.

If there was one thing writers and influencers had in common, it was that we recognized a photo opportunity when we saw one.

"I'll have a Coke, please," I said to the bartender, a woman around my age with a button nose.

"Two," said Noah.

I paused, fingers drumming on the top of the bar. The bartender cracked open two Cokes and poured them into glasses with ice and slices of lemon. She handed them over, and I took them both. I thanked her and she moved on to the next guest.

At Noah's raised brow, I brought the glasses closer to my chest. "I don't care if you want to get a cocktail. It doesn't bother me."

"Good," he said and took one of the glasses from me. Our fingers brushed. Such a small touch shouldn't make me nearly keel over, but here we were. "Sometimes I want to have an alcoholic beverage, and sometimes I don't. Not everything is about you, Scribbles."

Warmth flickered to life in my chest as we walked toward the edge of the ship. Maybe things were okay between us, despite the awkward pool kiss. "I guess it will be nice not to be the only sober person by the end of the night."

We found spare seats near the railing, watching as someone insisted on initiating a game of limbo on the deck. My phone vibrated. We must not be that far away from land if I still had service.

Glass in one hand, I checked my texts.

> Mom: So proud (and jealous!) of you, Macey. A press trip in Aruba, so cool! Bring me back a souvenir and let me know what you're going to write for the magazine.

I dropped my phone back into my bag. Later, I'd respond, but right now I didn't want to think about the magazine.

"Who died?" Noah asked. "Besides that man who just died of embarrassment slipping on the deck."

"No one." True to his words, there was a man on the deck trying to brush off the fact he'd tripped over his own feet. "It was just a text from my mom."

"Really?" He waited for my nod. "Then why do you look so troubled by it?"

I tapped my foot against the floor, trying to find the best words. "Sometimes I think my mom loves my job more than I do. It had always been her dream to work at a magazine, but she and Dad had me when they were sixteen, so she never really had the chance to chase that dream. She texted to ask what I'm writing about this weekend."

"Do you?"

"Do I what?"

"Love your job," he clarified.

"Oh," I considered the question. I loved my paychecks and financial security. I loved having insurance that covered my inhalers and annual doctor's appointments. "It's a job. It's something I'm meant to do, not love."

"There's nothing else you'd rather be doing?"

"I used to want a travel blog of my own, but that's not in the cards for me right now. My column is doing really well, and I should focus on that."

Noah responded, "Maybe you should focus on doing what you love, instead of what you feel obligated to do. Even if it's scary to start something new."

"That sounds like something a rich person would say."

The words were a little scathing but not entirely untrue. I tensed, worried he would take offense, but he laughed and playfully shoved my shoulder. "You got me there. I know being an influencer isn't all bad. Brand deals pay a lot."

Must be nice.

"You must like it a lot, considering you gave up Cornell for it."

"I gave up Cornell for Daphne," he corrected me. "To take care of her after Mom died."

"Was there no one else to help?"

Noah hesitated. I worried I scared him off with my questions. "No. We never had a relationship with our father. He left after Daphne was born. Was barely in the picture before that."

I placed a comforting hand on his knee. "That's awful. I'm sorry to hear that."

"It's probably better that he stayed far away instead of hurting us from up close."

To an extent, I understood where he was coming from. But I worried he was letting that philosophy dictate his current relationships.

I cleared my throat and removed my hand from his knee. "By the way, I am sorry for not asking about the kiss. I know you didn't like it."

He looked confused, turning his attention from the small dance party that had gathered on the deck to me. I watched his eyes dip from my eyes to my lips then back up again, his own lips parting. "I liked the kiss. What I didn't like was the setting."

"What do you mean?"

"Our first kiss shouldn't have been for show like that."

His spine immediately stiffened, like he was shocked the words left his mouth. Suddenly, a spot on the horizon appealed to him much more than looking me in the eye. A shame because his eyes were so pretty by sunset. They looked like the sun over a field of freshly mowed grass.

I gave him a shy smile, one that hopefully didn't let slip how fast my heart was racing. "Our first kiss?"

That implied there would be more kisses. A fact that probably shouldn't please me as much as it did.

"No, I didn't mean..." He backtracked, stuttering over his sentence. "I mean I did, but—"

Jennifer, clad in the sleekest black dress I'd ever seen, interrupted. "There's my favorite couple!"

I was very confident she said that to every couple on the press trip at some point.

"We're taking a group picture at the front of the boat." She nudged us along. "Make sure your pretty faces are in it."

My feet walked my body to the front, but my mind was long gone, full of hazy images. Noah, pressing me against the bar. His thigh in between mine, mouth hot on my neck. Dissolving into kisses that gave way to more. Passion. Heat. Noah, Noah, Noah.

I couldn't help the part of myself that wondered how Noah would act in bed. In front of everyone, he was the cocky influencer who held fame in one hand and confidence in the other. When it was just us, he was hesitant and off-guard. Soft, even.

Would he strike the balance between soft and hard, rough in bed but down for tender cuddles after? Would he hold me through the entire night, or pin me down just to thrust—

Macey, stop the dirty thoughts.

At this rate, I'd need to jump into the ocean to cool down.

I settled for reminding myself that sex with Noah, the guy I was fake dating, would be a very bad idea.

The mood on board grew more intimate after the photo as a few stars appeared on the horizon. The crew dimmed the lights, enhancing the natural beauty of twilight. Soft lanterns and fairy lights added a magical touch.

Noah and I filtered through the crowds with a practiced ease, like we had done this a million times together. We spent a shockingly large amount of time spinning up lies to questions people had about our relationship. Like to Francesca, the woman in front of us. Big influencer from Italy. She asked, in the sweetest of accents, "How did you two meet?"

I was ready to answer the question, but Noah jumped in. Rude, considering I had a friendly spin on the how we met story. In reality, we hit it off and planned to help each other with a campaign showcasing snowy Chicago spots, only for him to ghost me weeks later. In my version of the story, we went through with it, only for him to realize he was in love with me in Millennium Park.

Noah's arm slipped around my waist, pulling me closer. "We were both covering a world showcase event about a year ago. I spotted the most beautiful girl across the street. After working up the courage to talk to her, I just knew."

"Knew what?" I asked, my voice tight with curiosity.

Noah met my gaze, his eyes softening as a gentle smile tugged at his lips. "I knew that anyone who got to be with you would be the luckiest person alive. Too bad it took us so long to get here."

"But you're both here now," Francesca said with a smile.

When Noah smiled, the freckles on his face moved. Like stars in the night sky, searching for their next home above us. And when I smiled back at him, I think they found a place to call permanent. Because that smile didn't leave his face for a long while. Based on the way my cheeks hurt, mine didn't either.

It was a while until we were alone again. I would've counted time with my pulse, but it had been fluttering out of control all night.

I should probably get that checked.

We were sailing back to land, and we were likely not far from returning to harbor. In the back of the boat, it was the two of us facing each other, proud looks on our faces. "I think we successfully fooled everyone today," I said. "Did you get any photos of us?"

Noah stared at me, confused.

"You need to post a bunch of photos tonight, remember? Jennifer thinks we're together, so she's going to expect you to post about us." I paused. "And me too, I guess."

"Right." It dawned on him, but he didn't look happy about it. Odd, considering his life consisted of photos on social media. "Scoot in for a selfie."

I did. He held his phone out in front of us, the selfie camera on. He hooked his free arm around my shoulders and flashed a smile. A real one. It would no doubt stand out against the gimmicky grins he usually posted.

After, I tried to glimpse the phone to see how the photo turned out, but Noah slipped it into his back pocket. I reached for it, but he grabbed my hand.

"Are you trying to grab my ass?" he asked, fake-scandalized. "In public?"

"Maybe I need to remind everyone here who my fake boyfriend fake belongs to."

The corner of his mouth twitched. "There's no one around us."

"Right. We are alone." I acted disappointed. "Guess there's no claim staking needed."

The reminder did something to me. Lit a new fire inside my belly, one that could only be doused by stepping closer to Noah. I suspected he felt the same heat because he stepped toward me until our chests were brushing.

He leaned in closer and I stood dangerously still, not wanting to disturb the moment. The steady waves brushing against the boat. The twinkling stars in the sky.

Logical me said *you idiot, didn't you just tell yourself this would be a bad idea?*

Horny me said *fuck it, kiss him anyways.*

Noah's nose brushed against mine, and that was it. I was a goner. If you had asked me a year ago if I would ever be desperate for a kiss from Noah Hansley, I would have died of laughter. Now I might die if he didn't kiss me.

He stepped a hair closer.

Then his ankle buckled and he tumbled overboard.

12

NOAH

The first thing I noticed when I hit the water was how much my ankle hurt, which shouldn't be my highest priority considering I'd just fallen over the railing of a boat. While about to kiss the girl I was fake dating. And my phone was in my pocket.

Fuck.

The cold water enveloped me instantly. The chill sent a jolt through my muscles, making me gasp as I sank beneath the surface. I kicked my legs frantically, bubbles swirling around me as I fought my way back up.

Breaking through the surface, I frantically inhaled all the oxygen I could. Wet hair plastered against my forehead. The boat loomed above me, and I could just make out Macey's panicked voice yelling my name.

I treaded water, keeping my head above the surface. Thankfully, I was a decent enough swimmer, as the waves catapulting from the boat would be strong enough to pull a weaker swimmer under.

"Oh my God!" Macey's head appeared over the edge of the railing, her eyes wide and panicked. "Are you okay?"

The cold had fully seeped into my bones now, making every

movement stiff and awkward. Adrenaline kept me from feeling too miserable. I spat out a mouthful of salt water. Gross.

"Yeah, I like falling overboard for fun!" A shiver coursed through my body.

Macey's hands gripped the railing as she leaned her chest over to get a closer look. Not that there was much to see—just me and the water. A match made in heaven, really. "What do I do?"

"Gee, I don't know, Macey." The boat was getting ahead of me now, so I wasn't sure if she heard me scream, "Get help!"

A panic-induced laugh escaped her, one that rang through the air. It warmed my chest for a moment before the water cooled it again.

I hoped no one was recording this.

Or, maybe if someone was, I could use this as an excuse to sign off social media for the three months that I'd be road-tripping with my sister. Write some sob story post about how embarrassed I was and that I would be off the grid for the foreseeable future, learning how to stand properly on boats.

All of this depended on me getting safely out of this water, of course.

I heard some commotion ahead from the catamaran before it stopped in the water. A few cries were made, and I started swimming again toward the boat. This was good. It gave me something to do to warm myself up.

Plus, the added bonus: my ankle had gone totally numb.

A neon orange rescue boat emerged from the side of the catamaran, and I could have cried tears of joy. Two crew members were holding lanterns and flashlights, swinging the beams through the ocean.

"Over here!" I yelled.

Yellow light spilled across my face, forcing me to blink against its harsh brightness. My muscles screamed as I swam toward the rowboat, each stroke more desperate than the last. As I neared, a hand reached down, and I gripped it tightly. The crew member pulled me in with surprising strength, his voice gruff but concerned.

"You all right, son?"

"Never been better," I replied, my teeth chattering so violently I could barely form the words.

The wind hit me like a slap as we rowed toward the catamaran, biting into my damp skin. Goose bumps erupted across my arms, and my hair stood on end as though it too was reacting to the cold.

The crew member, seemingly unfazed by my shivering state, gave me a sideways glance. "Good thing we got to you before the sharks did."

I froze, my heart skipping a beat. "What?" I scooted away from the edge of the boat, my mind racing. "There are sharks in these waters?"

The man quickly backtracked, sensing the panic building in my chest. "No, no… Of course not." His eyes flicked to the other crew member, who was trying—and failing—not to laugh. "Just messing with you."

I wasn't sure if he was lying, but I was too cold and exhausted to care. I chose to believe him, letting the false sense of relief wash over me.

A ladder appeared on the side of the boat like a beacon. I scrambled up the rungs, my legs weak, and nearly collapsed when I reached the deck.

Everyone greeted me. Seriously. Any fleeting hope that me falling overboard and returning could be brushed under the rug immediately fizzled. A small group formed around me, with people asking questions.

"What happened?"

"Are you okay?"

"Why did you jump?"

"Eliza, you can't just ask people why they jumped!"

My eyes looked for one person.

There, pushing through the crowd, was Macey. Her hair, which had been weaved flawlessly into a braid before, had come undone. A few strands were stuck to her forehead, the others cascading down her shoulders. A flush of pink coated her cheeks.

And when she saw me, wet and shivering and pathetic, she burst out laughing.

She.

Laughed.

Unimpressed glances turned in her direction, but considering she was the only one holding a blanket for me, I knew she was concerned.

I much preferred this reaction over half-hearted questions about my health.

Her laughter was a melody that had me trapped—I trudged through the deck until I was in front of her. She doubled over with laughter. "I'm sorry," she said between breaths. "But you look like a wet rat."

I cracked a smile. "That's very flattering."

"Are you okay?" she whispered just for me.

"Yeah." Freezing my ass off, but I was fine.

She handed me a small tote bag with a sly smile. "The captain gave me some extra clothes from the crew. You should probably get out of those wet clothes before you freeze."

I nodded gratefully and disappeared into the bathroom, then quickly shed my soaked slacks and button-down shirt. I stuffed them into the bag, feeling a mix of relief and awkwardness.

When I pulled on the sweatpants and the faded Jaws T-shirt, I couldn't help but chuckle. Maybe it was the ironic humor of a shark-themed shirt after I'd just fallen overboard.

"You're a very good stalker," I said to Macey when I returned. "You know my measurements and everything."

She rolled her eyes, but they were full of mirth. "I take my stalking very seriously."

The boat wasn't far from the harbor now—thank God—but I sat next to her on the deck. Macey wrapped the blanket over my shoulders and pulled me into her.

"What happened?" she asked.

"My ankle is weak as shit," I said, rolling it out. Still a little numb. Still a lot painful. "The boat hit a small wave and I totally lost my balance."

"I won't say I told you so."

"You just did."

Now, rescued and safe, I couldn't help but laugh at the absurdity of the whole situation. Not that the evening had completely unraveled me, but it had shaken me more than I cared to admit. I needed that reassurance that I was actually here, on solid ground, not still drifting in the middle of some shark-infested sea.

I stretched my limbs out, my muscles still tight from the cold and tension, and then, with a dramatic sigh, I lay down on the deck—never mind the questionable cleanliness of it. Macey's lap was the most inviting thing in my immediate vicinity, so I settled my head there, closing my eyes for a second.

Oh, shit, my phone. After a quick assessment, it appeared to be in working order. At least there was that.

Macey ran her fingers through my hair, tugging at the edges. If I thought I found paradise earlier, I was wrong. This was it. A sigh of contentment left my mouth, and Macey's hand paused for a brief second like she was going to say something. Instead, she silently continued the motion until we docked in the harbor.

Back in the suite, I showered and changed into proper clothing of my own. This wasn't the most pleasant event to document, but after I had mentally recovered from the fall, I had to recount the events in a video. During which Macey jokingly suggested I recreate it for the viewers.

Instinct drove me to look for her now, and I found her lounging on the bed, blue light from her phone reflecting on her face. She looked up when she saw me enter.

"Hey." She placed the phone on the notebook next to her. "How are you?"

"I'm fine, stop worrying."

My body was okay, all things considered. My ego may have some long-lasting damage, though.

Slowly, she looked me up and down, pausing her gaze by my feet. "The ankle?"

The bed bounced a little when I sat on the edge. I didn't want to get too close, or insinuate anything, so I stayed by the corner. "Hurts a little. Still weak."

"Weaker than normal, you mean?"

I laughed. "You're very good at comforting me and humbling me at the same time."

Macey patted the spot next to her on the bed, and my heart kicked up its pace. I scooted closer to her. "Let me see," she said, holding a hand out for my ankle.

Her fingers felt cool against my ankle. My body must be so confused by all the temperatures it encountered in the last hour, from cold seawater to a boiling hot shower.

But this touch was different. Soothing.

Who was I turning into? Some kind of lovestruck fool who tried to kiss a girl he shouldn't be pursuing?

All I knew was as long as everything went according to plan, I'd collect a check from Opal Serenity large enough to cover three months offline, during which Daphne and I would set off for California and wherever else our hearts took us. I just needed to survive the social media jungle for a few more months until summer.

I'd been doing this for a long time. I could get through it alone. That knowledge wasn't enough to stop my stupid heart from insisting it wanted her there, though.

After a minute, Macey lowered my ankle back to the duvet. "Dr. Macey says you'll be all right, but you have to rest it for real this time."

First of all, Dr. Macey had no medical credentials.

Second, despite that fact, she was right.

Thank God I was someone who could laugh at his misfortune.

"Does Dr. Macey have some medicine to share with her injured patient?"

She rolled over and rifled through a small bag on the nightstand, pulling out a pill bottle. "I have Tylenol." She held the bottle just out of my reach when she rolled back, this time even closer to me. "And..."

Then she leaned forward to press her lips against my ankle. "A kiss to make it better."

In past moments like these, with Macey being close and flirtatious, I'd shut down. I'd been with plenty of women, sure, but none who I felt really saw me for me. Or, rather, that they even cared to see who I was under the fame.

But now, I felt more at ease.

"All my past doctors have been slacking," I joked. "I guess I'll have to keep coming back to you."

She grinned. "Sure, but don't ask me where I studied."

I took the Tylenol from her, popped two in my mouth, and dry swallowed.

A comfortable silence descended upon us. We weren't even touching, but I felt the touch of her presence everywhere.

"Who's going to take care of you when Dr. Macey is gone?" She pulled a face. "I'm going to stop referring to myself in third person now."

"I take care of me."

I felt more than saw her turn her head toward me. "What about your other friends?"

Friends.

"Don't have many of those," I said bluntly and turned my head to face her. "I prefer not to keep people too close."

Her gaze was steady and unblinking, as inescapable as if she had pinned me to the bed. "Why?"

I gave my typical speech. The one I'd reminded myself of over and over these last few years.

"Because they never stay," I said. "People are like Instagram followers. Most will either leave or decide to dislike you at some point, so there's not much of a point cultivating new relationships."

She hummed, but it was a dark sound. "That's a tragic way to view people."

"Most people only care about being seen with me instead of actually being with me," I said, then added, "Better to let them leave before you get too close and get hurt."

If the words felt tackier in my mouth than usual, well. It was probably because I nearly drowned earlier.

My opinion irritated her. I could tell by the way her bottom lip curled. A mask had appeared on her face, one that was distanced and disagreeable. I could have sworn she inched away from me.

"I agree," she said, and all the air in my lungs disappeared. *Huh?* She then added, "To an extent. People do leave, but to me, that means we should love them harder while they're still here."

She adjusted the pillow on the bed. "And to continue with your analogy, if you have one million followers, chances are some have been loyal from your first post. Those are the kinds of people you'd want as your friends. Not the ones who only show up once you're famous."

The words hit me in my chest, stinging a little.

"You can have the bed tonight." Macey swung her legs over the edge. "Good night."

"Good night."

But instead of letting her go, I grabbed her wrist. She glanced down at my hand, then at my lips. Suddenly, we both leaned in, and before I could form a coherent thought, we were kissing.

Not for show or for cameras. For real.

It felt...right. Much better than our kiss earlier by the pool. Of course, that had been good, too, but this was inherently better because it was ours.

Her lips were soft and her skin even softer. I didn't know what was in the Aruba bathwater, but it did its magic. One of her hands lifted to my cheek, and I leaned into it. I let my own hand stray around her waist.

Macey felt right in my arms. Maybe this started as something fake, but the spark between us was real. I doubted a poet could find the right words to describe it.

I traced my mouth down her jaw and then her throat, pausing there for a moment. She made a soft noise, barely audible, but it rolled through me. Her ribcage flared under my hand with every breath. All I wanted was to get closer and find out if the skin under her shirt was equally soft.

Just as my hand started to move under the bottom of her shirt, Macey jerked back, and I froze.

Between deep breaths, Macey lifted one finger to her lips. "That shouldn't have happened."

The exact words I said to her after our kiss by the pool. Did she realize how different the situations were, or did she truly not want to kiss me?

"But—"

She cut me off. "I'm going to bed. On the couch. Good night."

I fell back onto the bed, feeling something that had lingered under the surface for a while, but I only now had the word to describe: alone.

13

MACEY/NOAH

Macey

I had never been more happy that I requested four different coffees in our breakfast orders. Granted, I never had an opportunity to request breakfast via room service, let alone not to get weird looks when I asked for a latte, cappuccino, drip coffee, and a mocha.

Today? I'd take every caffeine boost I could get.

I hardly slept last night, too busy replaying the moment Noah and I kissed. For real.

God, what was wrong with me? What *wasn't* wrong would be the better question. I couldn't deny that my feelings for Noah had grown complicated, to say the least. I was attracted to him. Would probably jump into bed with him if there were no repercussions.

But oh, would there be repercussions.

Noah had referred to our pool kiss as a mistake. Then later, on the boat, he claimed our first kiss shouldn't have been for show like that. In hindsight, a kiss for show was a terrible idea—I should know by now that photographs lived forever on the

Internet—but it was necessary to convince people we were dating.

Because we were not dating.

We were just two people forced to pretend to date due to a series of extremely unlikely circumstances. *Compared to what, Macey, couples who fake date for fun?*

This wasn't a rom-com movie with a romantic montage at the halfway point. This wasn't a romance book, where the reader would discover *he loved her all along!* This was reality. Writing and influencing weren't for the faint of hearts. Things weren't going to get magical now that I suddenly had a crush.

At the end of this weekend, things would go back to normal. We'd stop posting about each other on social media long enough for people to assume that we separated, and then Noah and I could go back to ignoring each other in public. Excellent plan—10/10 stars.

Then why did I feel sick thinking about it?

I was halfway through my second coffee, already dressed for the day, when Noah bustled out of the bedroom. Of course he didn't look sleep-deprived like me. Probably dreamed of cats chasing rainbows or something.

He was dressed casually, in a lightweight linen button-down with the sleeves lazily rolled to his elbows, the fabric just barely clinging to the shape of his arms. A pair of well-worn khaki shorts hung low on his hips, and he'd swapped his usual sneakers for simple leather sandals. The kind of effortless, *I just threw this on* look that made it painfully obvious he belonged at a resort like this.

Unfair. I might have a cute white dress on, but I looked like I'd barely survived the night. The bun at the top of my head agreed with me. Meanwhile, he looked like a postcard.

Noah reached for one of the mugs, his fingers curling around the ceramic like it was the only thing grounding him. "Good morning."

"Hi." My voice came out stiff, forced. *Just act normal.* I reached for my own coffee, determined not to let awkwardness win. "How did you sleep?"

"Good." He took a sip and set the mug down on the table. "You?"

"Fine," I lied.

Noah nodded, and an uncomfortable silence settled between us, thick and suffocating. The weight of last night pressed into my chest, the memory of his lips on mine lingering like a phantom touch. Were we really just going to stand here, pretending it never happened?

He pulled out the itinerary for the day, flipping through it with unnecessary focus. I eyed the paper, willing it to say *anything* that might distract me. Honestly, they could send me to chase down gorillas for all I cared, if it meant I didn't have to survive another couple's massage.

The only big thing I'd have to survive today was the cooking class. Great. As if my culinary skills weren't already humiliating enough, now I had to endure them in front of him.

I tapped my fingers against the counter, the tension between us stretching like a rubber band, ready to snap. When it became clear Noah wasn't going to be the one to break the silence, I did.

"I can't just pretend to ignore what happened last night." I folded my arms across my chest, bracing myself. "What were you thinking?"

His fingers tightened around the edges of the itinerary. "What was I thinking?" His tone was sharp, incredulous. "You were there, too."

"I'll admit the kiss by the pool was my fault, but you were the one who kissed me last night."

His jaw dropped as he let out a silent laugh, shaking his

head. "No way. If anything, we both leaned in. We were both just going with the mood."

I scoffed. "The *mood*? If there was a mood, you completely misread it."

He quirked an eyebrow, unimpressed. "That's funny because your reaction sure didn't say that."

Heat rushed to my face. I stiffened, suddenly hyper-aware of how my body had melted into his, how I had kissed him back, how I had *wanted* to in the moment. But that didn't matter. Because it was just a moment.

"Well," I said coldly, "maybe all your time spent pushing people away has made it difficult for you to understand real people's signals."

The moment the words left my mouth, I knew I'd hit a nerve.

His expression shut down, amusement vanishing in an instant. His grip on the itinerary crumpled the paper slightly, but his voice, when he spoke, was eerily calm.

"That's rich," he said, eyes burning into mine. "Coming from you."

My stomach twisted, but I lifted my chin. "What's that supposed to mean?"

Noah let out a sharp, humorless laugh. "You know exactly what it means. Don't act like you have me all figured out. Because we both know you kissed me back."

My heart pounded. "That doesn't mean it *meant* anything."

His jaw clenched. For a second, I thought he might say something else, something that would push this over the edge. Instead, he exhaled, shaking his head like I wasn't even worth the fight anymore.

"You know what?" He grabbed his coffee and stepped back. "Forget it."

I opened my mouth to respond, but before I could, he turned

on his heel and strode toward the door, his movements stiff with barely contained frustration.

"Noah—"

But he was already gone, the door swinging shut behind him.

And just like that, I was left alone in the kitchen, my pulse racing, the ghost of last night's kiss lingering on my lips.

After spending a few minutes collecting myself—read: chugging the rest of the coffee and banging my head against the wall —I headed downstairs myself. Sure, getting into something romantic with Noah was a bad idea, but I had taken it too far. It wasn't fair of me to use information he told me in confidence against him like that.

When I didn't immediately spot Noah, panic set in. *What if he ran off the property? What if he's livestreaming our breakup somewhere?*

I checked the watch around my wrist. It was almost time for the garden tour, so he was likely...by the gardens.

This resort was way too huge. I pushed through a set of doors, only to be greeted by an empty hallway. *Wrong exit. Again.* By the time I finally stepped outside, the heat was already sinking into my skin, and I spotted him in the distance.

Thank God he was tall—he stood over all the other press team members nearby like a damn lighthouse.

"Noah, thank God I found you," I said, huffing as I rushed up to him. "Listen, I—"

"Thank you all for joining us for our tour this morning of the gardens!" a bright, cheerful voice cut in.

Fucking Jennifer.

"We are going to get started now, so if I could have your undivided attention, please."

Noah didn't even look at me.

I clenched my jaw as the group moved forward, following

Jennifer through the perfectly manicured pathways of the resort's sprawling gardens. I tried to focus—really, I did. There were so many plants I didn't recognize, some with big, waxy leaves, others with tiny, delicate petals that looked straight out of a fairy tale. Jennifer rattled off names I'd never heard before, something about sustainable gardening practices, something else about native flora...

I couldn't care less.

Because the entire time, I was only aware of *him*.

Noah walked just a few feet ahead of me, hands shoved into his pockets, his broad shoulders tense. He was ignoring me, fully committed to acting like I didn't exist.

Every time I stepped a little closer, every time I opened my mouth to say anything, he shifted just slightly, positioning himself so he was always just out of reach.

By the time we made it to the orchid house, I was ready to grab him by the arm and force him to talk to me. But just as I reached for him, he turned, finally meeting my eyes.

For a split second, hope flickered in my chest.

And then—

"My *favorite* couple! How did you enjoy the tour?"

I nearly jumped. So focused on Noah, I hadn't even noticed that the tour had ended, the group already dispersing into smaller clusters, chatting about flowers and sustainable gardening.

I inhaled deeply, trying to find my inner Zen. *You are calm. You are composed. You are not going to strangle Jennifer.*

"It was lovely," I said, forcing a smile. "Thank you for the tour, Jennifer."

"Wonderful!" She beamed, clearly thrilled to have done her part in making us more connected to nature. "I just wanted to point you two in the direction of the cooking class. It's a straight shot down this path. You can't miss it."

"Thank you," Noah said, flashing her one of those polite smiles that came so easily to him, the kind that felt effortless but held no real warmth.

"I'll see you both later!" Jennifer waved as she headed off, leaving us alone again.

We walked down the path in silence, the gravel crunching beneath our feet. I glanced at him once, twice, trying to gauge if his posture had softened at all.

It hadn't.

Outside the hut where the cooking class was held, I reached out, grabbing his forearm. "Noah."

He stopped but didn't look at me.

I swallowed hard, forcing the words out before I lost my nerve. "I'm sorry for what I said. I went too far."

A muscle in his jaw twitched. For a moment, I thought he wasn't going to respond. Then, slowly, he turned toward me. "It's fine." Noah exhaled through his nose. "Let's just get through this class."

He turned and walked inside.

———

Noah

The moment I stepped inside the hut, the thick scent of spices hit me—garlic, ginger, something citrusy that I couldn't place. The space was rustic but polished, with wide windows that let in golden light, wooden beams arching over the ceiling, and woven pendant lamps casting a soft glow over the long cooking stations.

Each station had a cutting board, bowls of fresh ingredients, and neatly folded aprons with the resort's logo embroidered on the chest. A row of gleaming pans hung on the far wall, and in the center of the room stood a broad-shouldered man with a chef's jacket and an easy smile.

Others filtered in, chatting excitedly as they claimed spots. A photographer hovered near the entrance, snapping pictures of the setup, the happy couples, the overall ambiance.

I barely resisted the urge to roll my eyes. Great. Just what I needed—photo evidence of me playing house with Macey after our argument this morning.

She stepped in behind me, hesitating for a fraction of a second before following me to an open station near the middle. I could feel her eyes on me, like she was waiting for some sign that things were normal again.

What was normal between us anyways? Over the course of the last two days, we'd played multiple rounds of push-pull, and at this point, I wasn't sure where we stood.

I pulled on the apron without a word, tying the strings tightly at my back. The sooner we got through this, the better.

The instructor clapped his hands together, his voice warm and welcoming. "Good morning, everyone! I'm Chef Luca, and today, I'll be guiding you through a hands-on experience of traditional island cuisine. We're going to have fun, get a little messy, and by the end of this, you'll have a dish that will impress anyone." His gaze swept over the room, stopping on me and Macey. "Even your special someone."

I stiffened. Macey let out a short, nervous laugh, shifting beside me.

Chef Luca grinned. "Now I assume you all came hungry?"

There was a collective murmur of agreement, some of the other pairs exchanging excited glances.

"Great!" He gestured toward the tables. "Grab the prepared ingredient baskets, and we'll get started."

Macey adjusted her apron, glancing at me, opening her mouth like she wanted to say something.

I beat her to it.

"There's a photographer in here, so let's keep up the pretending." My voice came out clipped.

Her lips pressed together, but she nodded. "Fine. I know you're still upset with me but just know I really do respect you."

Chef Luca clapped his hands together. "All right! We're starting with a simple appetizer—fried plantains with a spicy mango dipping sauce. Should be easy enough, right?"

Macey and I exchanged a glance.

I wasn't sure what her cooking skills were like, but I had a sinking suspicion they weren't much better than mine.

"The plantains need to be sliced thin," Luca continued, demonstrating with a swift, effortless motion. "Then we'll fry them until golden. Meanwhile, we'll prepare the mango sauce. Now let's get to it!"

I grabbed a plantain and the knife, lining it up on the cutting board. Macey did the same, looking far too focused for a task this basic.

"Ever cut one of these before?" I asked.

She lifted her chin. "It's a banana's cousin. How hard can it be?"

Macey pressed down with the knife and squished the plantain instead of slicing it.

I snorted. "Impressive technique."

She shot me a glare. "Let's see you do it, then."

"Okay." I took my turn, slicing through mine, albeit unevenly. Some pieces were paper-thin, others way too thick.

Macey started on the mango, attempting to scoop the flesh into a bowl. Instead, a chunk of it slipped from her fingers, bounced off the counter, and plopped onto the floor with an unceremonious *thud*.

She bent down and picked it up with an exasperated sigh. "Five-second rule?"

I arched a brow. "Go ahead. You eat it."

She huffed and threw it into the trash.

A few minutes later, we had all the ingredients in a bowl, attempting to mix the mango sauce. Macey reached for a spoon and gave it a determined stir—

And somehow, defying all logic, a thick glob of sauce catapulted out of the bowl, landing on her white dress. Conveniently, the one bit of dress her apron didn't cover.

Her jaw dropped as she stared down at the bright orange stain spreading across the fabric. A snort escaped me.

"Don't laugh!" she said, dabbing at the area with a paper towel. An orange mark was left behind. "Britney is going to kill me."

I couldn't stop the laughter now. When it appeared the stain wasn't going away anytime soon, she crumpled the paper towel and threw it at my head. "Noah!"

"I can't be blamed for this," I said, taking the bowl out of her reach.

The glare slid off her face as she chuckled too.

Despite our shortcomings, our appetizer came out pretty tasty. It may not look aesthetic by today's standards, but it tasted great.

Chef Luca clapped his hands again, drawing our attention back to him. "Now that you've mastered the appetizer," he said, his eyes twinkling, "it's time for the main course. A traditional island seafood dish: coconut-crusted mahi-mahi with a citrus salsa."

Macey and I exchanged a look. She still had a mango stain on her dress, and I was pretty sure one of my plantains had been charcoal by the time I got it out of the pan.

"Not another sauce," she muttered.

"Try not to spill this one on yourself," I said, grabbing a fillet of mahi-mahi and inspecting it like I actually knew what I was doing.

Macey mimicked me, holding hers up between her fingers. "Looks...fishy."

"Excellent observation."

"Shut up."

Luca continued explaining the steps, demonstrating how to coat the fish in a coconut and panko mixture before pan-frying it to crispy perfection. Seemed simple enough.

I dunked my fish into the beaten eggs and transferred it to the coconut mixture, making sure to coat it thoroughly. Macey, meanwhile, hesitated.

"You just gonna stare at it?" I asked.

She wrinkled her nose. "It's slimy."

I rolled my eyes. "It's supposed to be."

"I don't trust it."

"It's a fish, Macey, not a criminal."

She sighed dramatically, then finally dropped her fillet into the egg wash. But when she pulled it out, she forgot to let the excess drip off. By the time she tossed it into the coconut mixture, the crumbs turned into a sticky, glue-like mess.

"I can't believe that between the two of us, you're the better cook," she said as she tried to repair the fish.

"Well"—I dropped my fish into the hot pan—"the bar is pretty low in this instance, but I do have some cooking experience. I used to do a lot of the cooking for me and Daphne."

"Really?"

I nodded. "After Mom died, I tried to recreate her signature lasagna and nearly set the house on fire. I figured I should learn the basics, at least. We probably rotated between the same seven meals, but at least I mastered those."

Macey chewed her bottom lip and started to fry her fish. "That's sweet. What was your favorite thing to cook?"

"Grilled cheese, definitely. I—" *I'll make it for you sometime*, was what I wanted to say. Instead, what came out was, "I'm a fan of cheese."

"Me too," she said. "My roommate, Kira, is a better cook than me. She bakes a lot, so every weekend I get to indulge in all the chocolate I want."

"Sounds like a dream." Using the tongs, I flipped the fish. "Who's Britney, then?"

Macey squinted and looked at me. "Huh?"

"Earlier, you said *Britney's going to kill me.*"

"Oh, right. Britney is one of my best friends, too. She's a barista in The Burrow Café, which is in the same building as my office, but she's also in law school. And then there's Ariadne. She's a computer genius and one of the most selfless people you'll ever meet."

A tiny pang of jealousy hit me. Not about any of those girls specifically but because I didn't have a group like that. It wasn't until recently that I realized I lacked a steady, stable crew of people to rely on. It'd just been me, Daphne, and occasionally Nathan for so long.

"They sound like great friends."

We finished preparing the rest of the meal, and to my surprise, it turned out half decent. Flavor, texture, all there. Luca gave us all a few minutes to sit and eat.

I took a break after inhaling my fish, leaning back in my chair with a satisfied sigh. What started off as a tense cooking experience had somehow morphed into a good time. Macey had a way of doing that—making things better, even when they didn't seem like they could be.

"I forgive you, you know."

The fork paused halfway to her lips. "You do?"

"What you said...it's true. I've separated myself so much from other people that I do forget how they feel." I ran my hand over the back of my neck. "I didn't realize not responding to your messages last year would be so hurtful. Sometimes I get overwhelmed by DMs and stop responding. Not that it's an excuse. Is that why you hated me for so long?"

Macey twirled her fork against her plate, her gaze dropping for a moment. "It's one reason. You exemplified the things I hate about influencer culture: free press for little work, ignoring writers and bloggers who work hard, and just generally belittling others." She sighed. "But now I realize I was wrong about some of that."

"I'm sorry for my past actions. I never intended to hurt or offend you."

She studied me for a second before setting her fork down. "You don't have to apologize."

I exhaled, mustering a little courage. "Maybe I can buy you dinner tonight to make up for it."

"Noah, we're at an all-inclusive resort."

"Right." I dragged a hand down my face, feeling like an idiot. "Maybe a walk on the beach instead."

Her lips quirked. "That would be nice."

14

MACEY

I curled my toes into the damp sand with each step, my sandals swinging from my fingertips. It was hard to believe we were already closing in on the end of our last full day in Aruba. This was a grounding moment, though, just the sound of the waves, the soft give of the earth beneath me, and Noah.

Strokes of gold and pink painted the sky, the last traces of daylight melting into the horizon. The waves lapped at the shore, their foamy edges catching the sunset's glow before retreating back into the endless blue.

"I can't remember the last time I slowed down like this," I said, turning my face to the sky.

Noah's voice was light, teasing. "Work keeps you that busy, huh?"

"I think the problem is that when I'm not working, I'm too busy feeling anxious about the next time I have to work, so I don't get to enjoy my free time."

"Sounds stressful," he said. "Is that really what you want to be doing?"

A question I had asked myself a million times over again. "Not forever," I answered.

Noah shoved his hands into his pockets. "I was thinking: maybe you should start a small travel blog, then leave the magazine once you build a following. You're certainly talented enough for it."

That wasn't the worst idea. I'd have to be careful about not letting Victoria see it, considering it could be considered a conflict of interest. Which wouldn't be that difficult. New blogs popped up every day, but only a few grew a successful following.

Up ahead, a sandcastle sat near the tide, its towers misshapen and slumped as the ocean crept closer. I veered toward it and crouched down to trace a finger along one of the crumbling walls.

"What about you?" I asked.

Noah sank onto the sand, stretching his legs out in front of him. "I don't think I'd have much success starting a blog of my own."

I rolled my eyes. "I meant what are you planning to do next?"

"Oh." He dragged a hand through his hair, his fingers ruffling through the waves like he was stalling for time. "I'm planning to take a break from social media. Daphne and I want to do a big cross country summer road trip, and I've been saving to have enough cash to afford the social break."

Noah Hansley, with his one million followers and endless brand deals, wanted to quit social media? I thought he was joking, but he stared at me with a serious expression.

"A road trip? Now I'm the jealous one." I dropped down beside him, the sand cool beneath my palms. "And after that?"

"I have no idea." His voice was quieter now, almost lost beneath the sound of the waves. He stared straight ahead, where the ocean stretched into forever.

This uncertainty in him caught me off guard. Noah always seemed so sure of himself, so at ease with his place in the world. But here, stripped of filters and curated captions, he wasn't the guy I'd built up in my head. He wasn't untouchable. He didn't even seem all that happy.

And the strangest part? I wanted to change that. I wanted to be the reason he felt a little more certain, a little more steady. Maybe even a little more *himself.*

I nudged his knee with mine. "Well, maybe that's the best part."

He turned to me, brow furrowed. "What is?"

"Not knowing." I drew lazy circles in the sand with my finger. "You get to figure it out. No deadlines, no pressure—just seeing where life takes you."

Noah huffed out a laugh, but there wasn't much humor in it. "That's one way to spin 'aimless drifter.'"

I frowned. "You're not aimless. You're just...recalibrating."

He let out a breath, tipping his head back to look at the sky. The sunset had deepened, the pinks and oranges giving way to dusky blues. The first few stars had started to flicker in the distance. "I've spent so long chasing after the next thing—next brand deal, next trip, next post—and now that I'm recognizing I hate it, I don't really know how to change my patterns."

I studied him, the way the flickering light from the water cast soft shadows across his face. The way his fingers sifted absently through the sand, like he needed something to hold on to.

"Well," I said after a beat, "I happen to be very good at helping other people figure their lives out."

His lips quirked, and this time, it felt real. "Oh yeah?"

"Yeah. It's a great distraction from how I also don't know what I'm doing."

"That's not true," he said. "You've got ideas, plans. You just haven't taken the leap yet."

I shrugged. "That's one way to look at it."

His gaze met mine, something flickering behind his eyes. "We can help each other, then."

I leaned my head against his shoulder, feeling the warmth of his skin through his shirt, the steady rise and fall of his breath. The air between us felt charged, like the moment before a storm —expectant, waiting.

The tide rushed in, lapping at my toes, but I didn't move. Neither did he.

I wanted to kiss him again. The thought had been creeping in all night, sneaking up on me like the tide inching closer to shore. But now that I was here, pressed against him, I was too afraid to move. Too afraid that if I did, I'd ruin whatever fragile, uncertain thing was forming between us.

Because this wasn't just some fleeting, vacation-fling kind of attraction. It wasn't just curiosity.

It was something I actually wanted.

And that terrified me more than anything.

The plane ride home was considerably more comfortable than the last. I didn't need much to get comfortable, but Noah, the diva that he was, settled in much better this time.

We had a row of three seats to ourselves, and we settled our things, plus a variety of airport snacks, onto the seat between us.

The rest of the press trip had gone smoothly. Dinner, photos, and long, drawn-out goodbye speeches. This morning, we enjoyed one last breakfast as I lamented over not having a permanent butler to deliver me breakfast each morning.

My phone began to light up with notifications. Generally, I ignored them or kept my phone on silent, but I had already decided to pass the flight time by rotting my brain on social media sites.

"What is happening?" I muttered to myself as I unlocked the phone.

When I opened Instagram, it nearly combusted on itself. Truthfully, I was losing track of my follower count because it increased every time I opened the app. Since I wasn't an influencer, I didn't check my profile too often, but it was getting tempting to check frequently.

Now my follower count stood at 100,000. Crazy to think that just one week ago it was a fraction of this. The first surge was due to the viral video, but what led to it now?

"Noah," I said and received a raised brow in response. "Did you just get a bunch of followers, too?"

"Not sure," he said absentmindedly. "Too busy trying to understand why all my comments and DMs are asking why I'm not single any—oh."

"Oh?"

He held up his phone in front of my face. My first thought was that he needed a new screen because his was cracked in the corner, but that was quickly overshadowed by the photo on the screen.

Us. Kissing. By the pool.

I was the one who instigated the kiss, but I didn't expect Opal Serenity to post it to their feed so fast. Not when there were hundreds of other photos taken during the weekend that they could have posted instead.

The caption read *The resort pool provides the perfect ambiance for couples to relax together.* Posted ten minutes ago.

My eye twitched. I slowly banged my head against the seat in front of me. "I wasn't ready for this to happen yet."

The middle-aged man in the seat turned around to glare at me. "Excuse me—"

"Sir, I'm in the middle of a crisis," I pleaded. "Please let me have this."

He looked at me like I was crazy—maybe I was—but he turned back around.

And oh, poor Noah. He must be freaking out. Anonymous girls on Instagram were terrifying. If I had to choose between fighting an army of wrestlers or an army of anonymous Internet girls, I'd choose the wrestlers.

His whole brand centered on being the center of the female gaze. If everyone thought he was taken, that would ruin his image. Normal girlfriends probably weren't okay with their boyfriend posting shirtless selfies for all the world to see.

I could fix this.

"Noah, I am so sorry," I said once I had damaged my forehead enough from the banging.

His brow furrowed. "Why are you sorry?"

"I have a plan. When we get back to Chicago, you can announce our breakup. Tell the world you ended things with me. Then you can go back to being the single bad boy of Instagram, and maybe I'll get some pity points out of it."

"First of all, no one will believe I broke up with you." He shook his head, like the idea was unfathomable. "Second, why do we need to do this?"

"Everyone in the world thinks we're dating." Was it possible that ocean water had sunk through his ears and into his brain? Did he need medical attention? "Now that we've left the resort, we can put an end to it. Or just make them think we dated briefly."

Noah shoved his phone into his pocket. Honestly, it was a miracle that thing was still working after he fell into the ocean with it. "Or," he said slowly, "we can let them go on thinking we're dating."

Scratch my earlier thought. I must be the one who had ocean water in the brain. "What?"

"If we continue to fake date, I can post about you, too. You'll get tons of new followers and drive traffic to your blog."

"What blog?"

"*Your* blog." He put his hand on my shoulder. "It's now or never. If I've learned anything about you this weekend, it's that you're letting other people decide what direction your life goes in. I think you should go after what you really want. I'll help you."

Oh, shit. Was this happening? Was I finally going to take the leap and start my own blog?

"What do you want in return?"

He dropped his hand. "I want your help, too. I have no idea what I want to do after the road trip. Unlike you, I have no direction in my life, and it's time for me to change that."

I exhaled slowly and rubbed a hand at the base of my neck. Would the public believe it? What reason would someone like Noah have to date me and me him? As the resident conspiracy theorist, Ariadne would say that many famous couples were faking it. If larger celebrities could do it, then why couldn't we?

Maybe *could* versus *couldn't* wasn't the real problem. The problem was if we *should* do it. It would help Noah, and it would really, really help me get a new blog started.

God, I couldn't believe I was considering this.

"Okay." I met Noah's eyes. "If we did agree to fake date, how would we go about it?"

"The setup is already there," he said. I thought of the photo Opal Serenity posted of us and all the questions I'd have to field once we landed. "All we need to do is continue the cute online presence and go out once a week together so people think we're on a date."

Simple enough, but I wondered how this would impact Noah and me. We'd been getting along well, and I didn't want to ruin that. I liked to think that I could conquer my unreciprocated crush on him and that we could be friends. Go on runs together. Cook matching savory and sweet breakfast foods together. Occasionally make out.

Wait, friends didn't do that.

Fake dating could change things for the worse, but it could also be a bonding opportunity. Sure, it would be the most bizarre bonding ever, but those were where the memories were, right?

I was crazy for considering this. Certifiably insane.

"It could work…" I debated. "We'd need a few ground rules, though."

"Like?"

"One, we shouldn't see other people. Your followers are probably more skilled than the FBI and they'd find out immediately."

Green eyes narrowed. "I don't cheat, Macey."

I couldn't help but flinch. Hadn't my ex once said the same thing? Noah had proved to me that he was different—and that not all influencers were the same—but it was difficult to believe that unwaveringly.

"It's not technically cheating since we're not together."

Noah only glared back at me.

"Second, we should have an end date, so we can plan out how much content we need and how many dates we need to go on. Do you have one in mind?"

He thought it through, tilting his head. "How about May 15? Right before my road trip."

That was two months from now. Plenty of time to convince the world that we were in love and then fell out right when the honeymoon period ended.

"That works." I held out a hand, which he took. "So we've agreed on our fake dating plan?"

Noah nodded once. "Until May 15, I'll make sure everyone believes you're my girlfriend."

He shook my hand, and we flew back into Chicago as a fake couple.

15

NOAH

Within a week, everyone in Chicago and beyond knew that Macey and I were dating. We agreed to share the truth with only our closest confidantes—Nathan and Daphne for me, three friends for Macey. She referred to them as "The Burrow Bitches," so truthfully, I was a little terrified of them.

Nathan had laughed through the phone when I told him and wished me good luck. Daphne told me I was a loser in that ever-sweet tone of hers.

Ladies and gents, my family.

Typically, it was customary for a man to plan the first date. I had no idea how important customs were when it came to fake dating, but apparently, that didn't matter as Macey showed up at my apartment this morning, claiming she was taking me on a date.

A *surprise* date.

Our journey to Grant Park was full of my frequent requests for information on what we were doing, to which Macey refused to answer. After a few attempts, I gave up.

A familiar environment greeted us when we arrived. Banners and decorations at the start line, support stations filled with bottles of water and snacks, a DJ in the grass and a table of medals. We were at a 5k. Did she think my ankle had healed in the last week?

It was feeling better, but I definitely wasn't in the condition to run right now. Not to mention the only reason it felt better was because I hadn't been running.

"I really appreciate this, Macey, but I can't participate," I admitted with a brush of my hands on my knees.

Macey grabbed my hand and dragged me toward the fountain. "We're not running this 5k."

"If we're not running, then why are we here?"

Now that I took a clearer glance around the park, a few things appeared different. Namely, the runners themselves. Most people wearing a number didn't look like a typical runner. They all had adaptive equipment like racing wheelchairs, hand cycles, and prosthetic running blades.

Pop music played over the loudspeakers as an energetic woman with a microphone welcomed participants and supporters. One man, wearing the number 1 and who was missing his left arm, walked up the stage as everyone cheered.

"This is the annual Ability Run 5k." Macey squeezed my hand. "And, honey, you and I are volunteering."

How narrow-minded of me was it that I didn't even know this annual event existed? Or perhaps I did—it was possible every thought of mine vanished with the weight of Macey's hand in mine.

She froze suddenly, dropping it. "I hope that's okay. I usually volunteer here every year, and I thought it would be something fun for us to do. I didn't think that maybe it would be hard being at a 5k without the ability to run."

"What?" I almost laughed. "Of course it's okay. I don't think I could have planned anything better."

Macey beamed. "Great. You and I are volunteering at the registration and information station. Just follow my lead."

Minutes later, we found ourselves behind a large white table, wearing matching blue T-shirts that said "Volunteer." My volunteer experience was limited, but I found that a smile and a polite hello came easily.

The jobs weren't difficult—we signed people up for the race and gave them a number and a T-shirt. This 5k was different than any I'd run before, and not just because of the runner's adaptive equipment. Camaraderie felt like the theme of the race, whereas every race I'd run before had an air of competition to it. Inspirational stories were shared on stage here as well as the purpose of the fundraising. All proceeds went to local charities.

Everyone here was unified and motivated. They helped each other, with volunteers ready to support any runner who required assistance.

To my surprise, many of them seemed to know Macey, greeting her with smiles and hugs that lingered just a little too long for my liking. One old gentleman with a patch over his right eye clasped her hand, holding on just long enough for me to wonder if I should step in. Cute, or just bold? Either way, I wasn't a fan.

"Macey Monroe!" he exclaimed in a raspy voice. "I thought we weren't ever going to see you again."

He glared at me, like it was somehow my fault he hadn't seen Macey in a while.

Macey laughed. "I'm sorry, Bob, work has been crazy. You know I wouldn't miss the 5k for anything, though."

"I know, I know." Bob continued to stare at me, his narrow eyes deepening the wrinkles there. "And who is this lucky fellow working with you?"

"This is Noah." Macey paused. "He's my boyfriend."

As if to prove a point, I threw an arm over her shoulders. *That'll show him.*

She glanced at me out of the corner of her eye but didn't say anything else.

"Boyfriend?" Bob laughed. "Lucky fellow, indeed. You better not keep her from us, young man."

"I wouldn't dream of it," I said truthfully.

Macey handed him a stack of information along with a number that read 133. "Bob, he's a volunteer, too."

Yeah. And I'd be at the next 5k too, Bob.

Was I...jealous of an innocent old man? God help me.

"We'll be seeing you around then, Noah." Bob pinned his number to his T-shirt and left with a wink.

The race began shortly after with a burst of enthusiasm as participants crossed the start line. The route was designed to run through Grant Park's greenery, past flower gardens and along paved paths that offered glimpses of Lake Michigan.

The course itself was inclusive, with clear markings and smooth surfaces to accommodate all types of mobility aids. Spectators lined the way, waving signs with positive messages and cheering loud enough to make my head spin.

"What now?" I asked now that registration had closed.

"Now," said Macey, "we get ice cream and cheer them on at the finish line."

Amid a sea of healthy food trucks serving kale wraps and quinoa bowls, there it was—a lone ice cream truck, like a sugar-coated rebel. I hadn't seen one since I was a kid, and honestly, part of me still suspected they were just elaborate fronts for money laundering.

I couldn't believe how much fun I was having. Until now, volunteering had been in a completely different circle than dating in my head. Though I guess anything could be a date if you were with the right person.

Fake date, the voice in my head reprimanded me.

The teenager inside the truck handed me my order, rocky road in a waffle cone. Macey received her cup of mint chocolate chip gleefully.

"Don't judge," she said, grabbing a plastic spoon.

"You can't ask that of me," I said. "People who order toothpaste ice cream deserve to be made fun of."

"It's called taste," she muttered. "Let's go sit in the grass for a few minutes."

Under the shade of a tree, we leaned back and enjoyed dessert. Macey took a few minutes to capture the perfect selfie of us, but by the time she did, my ice cream was half gone.

We had agreed to alternate who posted pictures of us each week. Technically, neither of us had posted one of us yet. We had only liked and reshared the photo from Opal Serenity. I was sure she'd make a big splash with the picture, and I'd rather she get the flurry of love than me.

"So if you weren't a full-time influencer, what would you be doing?" Macey asked, her plastic spoon resting against her bottom lip, her eyes steady on mine.

I had to think about it. "Maybe I would have gone back to college and finished my degree."

She dipped the spoon back into her cup, finishing the last bit of ice cream with a slow lick that made my pulse jump.

My ice cream was long gone, but my hands still felt sticky—a discomfort that conveniently mirrored the knot tightening in my chest. I fished around in my pocket for a tissue, more to stall than anything else.

"What's the readmittance process for Cornell like?"

Embarrassed, I admitted, "I have no idea. It's way too far to consider reapplying."

She didn't judge my ignorance. "What were you studying?"

Flashes of my time at Cornell came to me in emotions. The

pride I felt holding the acceptance letter. Freshman year, the nerves before meeting my random roommate. The challenges I faced in classes. The pure joy, and exhaustion, of hours spent in the architecture studio.

"Architecture."

"That explains the LEGOs."

"I like that there's so much to it," I said. "You've got the engineering side, but then you also have creativity, like design and drawing."

"What did you want to do as an architect?" Macey smiled when I abandoned the grass to join her against the tree. "Before you had to move home, that is."

"I wanted to work on residential homes. As a kid, everything in our house was always falling apart. We were fine, but it made me want to learn to design houses that are functional, safe, and look good."

The issues in our house were never anything that couldn't be dealt with. Mom did a good job at patch fixing what went wrong, but there were engineering failures present from the start.

More so than ever, I wished I could go back and fix them. If there was a way that I could improve the functionality of homes for kids in need, I'd do it.

"I think that's wonderful," said Macey. "Why not pursue that when the social career is done?"

"I never got my degree," I reminded her. "I doubt Cornell would take me back. And I don't have much of a desire to move back to New York."

It was true, but it wasn't the whole truth. Something deeper kept me tethered, a weight I couldn't shake. I hated lingering too long on that chapter of my life—college, funeral, and endless frozen casseroles—because it all felt like a giant, unfixable failure.

Logically, I knew I'd built something for myself. The

paycheck was proof enough. But fulfillment? That had always been just out of reach.

Opportunities to go back and finish my degree had come and gone, but I'd always found excuses to avoid them. It had felt like that door was closed for good.

"Would you be open to doing something similar yet different?" She pressed. "Maybe a local university?"

I hesitated, caught off guard. Most people didn't ask about my life beyond the surface—the content, the trips, the numbers. They assumed they already knew me, or at least the version of me they saw online. It was rare for someone to want to dig deeper.

And maybe that was why it made me feel a little shy, a little unsteady, to have Macey looking at me like she actually *wanted* to hear my answer. Like she wasn't just humoring me.

Talking to her felt easy in a way I wasn't used to. There was no need to spin a story or play up a persona. And despite everything she'd thought about me before, she wasn't dismissing me as just some influencer anymore.

"Maybe," I said.

Just then, there were cheers in the distance. Craning my neck, I noticed confetti and balloons were being popped, too.

"People are heading to the finish line." Macey shot up. "C'mon, let's go greet them."

As we walked toward the blue-and-white striped banner, I asked the question that had been plaguing me for the last hour. "Why did you really bring me here?"

Eyes trained on the finish line, she answered, "You can't run right now, so I thought I'd bring the run to you."

A smile graced my lips of its own accord.

It was exciting to see everyone finish the race, even Bob and the long hug he gave Macey. From under his arms, she winked at me. Together, we handed out snacks and bottles of water. Even though I hadn't run a single second today, I felt like I was on an adrenaline high.

I attempted to get Macey to let me walk her home under the guise of the audience that could see us, but she declined. Multiple times. I didn't let it faze me. Nothing could ruin the good mood I was in.

It had been a while since I was in such a pleasant headspace. I walked home alone with an extra pep in my step. Honestly, was I in a teen rom-com movie, or what?

Too bad the extra pep didn't make it all the way to my apartment. In the elevator, I opened my phone to see how many followers Macey gained after posting the photo, already planning a congratulations text message for later.

But instead of love and happy words, all I saw were horrible comments.

He'll drop you soon enough

She's not even that pretty

When do you think she'll get a boob job?

What the fuck was wrong with people? It was like the anonymity of the Internet shrouded any sense of decency that people had.

I couldn't spend any longer reading through the disgusting comments. I was torn between calling Macey to warn her about checking the comments and not wanting to bring them to her attention.

I just hoped that when she inevitably saw them, I'd be there to remind her they weren't true.

16

MACEY

The Burrow Bitches

Kira: How is this your life?

Macey: Honestly, I'm asking myself the same question

Britney: fake dating sounds hot

Ariadne: It sounds like a terrible idea. I can't wait.

The next few dates went as smooth as the first. I would use the word perfect if I didn't think that might jinx the next one.

Every time I returned home, I had to remind myself that this was all fake. Not only that, but we were on a real deadline. The expiration date of our relationship lingered in the back of my mind, souring our sweetest moments.

I had willingly agreed to the deal, though, so I had no one to blame.

My feelings for Noah confused me. It was like one day I was content accepting that our relationship would never be more than fake dating turned friendship, but the next night I was dreaming about him. I wished emotions came with a manual.

Deep down, I recognized the signs that I already liked him as more than a friend. The way he listened to my problems and meanderings, the way his smiles planted butterflies in my stomach, and the unshakeable faith he had in me. He proved over and over again that he wasn't who I once believed he was.

Our newfound ability to open up to each other only increased our mutual respect. That was something I craved in a relationship: respect for each other's craft and respect for their decisions. While Noah might encourage me to make a different decision at times—from the toppings on my tacos to my 9-5 job —he always respected my final choice.

My heart fluttered knowing he liked my independence and my dreams.

Damn, why was it acting like that? The bar for men was so low nowadays.

The mascara smudged my bottom lashes when I swiped too hard. Kira and I were getting ready for a few drinks at Rose Buds to celebrate Britney's internship offer. She'd be working this summer at George Mathers LLC, a well-known local law firm.

Summer was coming quicker than I thought possible, and Britney's new job had me wondering what I'd be up to. Noah shared all of my articles on his social channels, and I hated to admit it, but that got lots of new eyes on them. My numbers were up so high even Victoria couldn't chastise me.

But...a part of me still questioned *what if*? What if the blog I just started became successful? What if people were interested in me, outside of being a *Roamer's Digest* writer and a fake girlfriend?

What if I was honest with Noah and told him how I was

starting to feel? I took an anvil and immediately squashed that what if.

"Is Noah coming tonight?" Kira asked innocently. She sat next to me in front of the full-sized mirror we leaned against a wall in our apartment.

"No," I said. "Why would he?"

Despite the world seeing us as boyfriend and girlfriend, our close circles had never crossed.

Kira applied a mauve lip color and blotted off the excess. "Because Xavier is coming tonight. I thought it'd be a good time for everyone to meet."

I nearly dropped the hair curler in my hands. "Who is Xavier?"

"I'm pretty sure I mentioned him..." Kira avoided my eyes, staring at herself in the mirror. "We've gone on a few dates."

The words shocked me the moment they came across my ears. Kira had dated a few guys in the last few years, but it never turned into anything serious. I had always hoped she'd find someone great, but I suspected she still compared every guy to Landon, the boy who had broken her heart years ago.

"I think you might've mentioned him once or twice—in passing, super casual. You know, the kind of casual that doesn't scream 'we're dating!'"

Raking through my brain, I wondered how I missed this. Kira wasn't always forthcoming when it came to stuff like this, but maybe I'd been too self-absorbed lately and missed the signs. I vowed to pay more attention.

Kira shifted in her seat, her violet skirt shifting up her thigh. She wore an all-colorful look while I went with a classic black dress. "It's new."

The implication was there: new like Noah.

"Noah and I have gone on dates, but they aren't real," I

defended, searching for the hairspray scattered somewhere on the ground.

"Uh-huh," Kira said as she threw me the bottle.

"What is that supposed to mean?"

"Nothing. That's just the sound of me acknowledging that you think they're fake. Can I get an invitation?"

"To our dates?"

"No, to the land of delusion you recently moved to."

I rolled my eyes and finished setting my hair. When was the last time I went out with soft curls instead of the usual braid I folded my hair into? "If you saw us together, you'd believe me."

"Invite him then."

Kira was challenging me: invite Noah out tonight and prove to her that we were only fake dating. But how did you show your best friend that you were only fake dating a boy you actually liked while also showing the world that you were really in a relationship?

My head swam.

"Fine." I could never turn down a challenge. Besides, it wasn't our usual date night, so he was likely busy. "I'll call him right now."

I dialed Noah's number and Kira tried to hide her grin.

After a few rings, he answered.

"Macey? Is everything okay?"

I could almost picture the confused look on Noah's face.

"Yeah, everything's fine." I looked over at Kira once before taking the plunge. "Do you want to go to Rose Buds with me and a few friends tonight?"

A brief silence. "I was supposed to see my cousin Nathan tonight, but...maybe I can bring him?"

Damn it.

This wasn't supposed to be a mix and mingle type of night. It was supposed to be a girls' night to focus on Britney. But here we were.

"Of course," I confirmed.

Kira's all-knowing smile was fully strapped on her face now.

"What time?" Noah sounded like he was walking through his apartment, banging on things here and there.

"We'll be there in about an hour."

"Great. I'll see you then, Scribbles."

The phone clicked off.

Kira's eyes widened as she turned to me. "Scribbles?"

I sighed. "Don't ask."

It was a quick Uber ride to Rose Buds. Outside, Ariadne and Britney waited for us, deep in conversation.

"I hope we can find a table," said Ariadne. She brushed a stray curl behind her ear with one hand, pushing the door open with the other. "There's a lot more people than normal here tonight."

Rose Buds was packed, which was unusual but not totally uncalled for. I couldn't blame people for going out on a Saturday night. A familiar jazz album played as we took a lap around the area. Beams of colorful light from the ceiling cut through the dimness of the bar, lighting up our outfits as we walked. Someone in the corner handed out free samples of an energy drink.

We were still scanning the bar for a free table when I spotted a familiar face. And a not-so-familiar face. Noah leaned against a table, drink in hand, as he chatted with the man who must be his cousin.

"I recognize Noah, but who is the other guy?" Britney asked as we walked toward them. "He's hot."

"He's Noah's cousin," I said offhandedly, attempting to dodge an intoxicated man trying to chicken dance his way through the floor.

Nathan lifted his glass to his lips as he listened intently to Noah speak. The glass looked like straight whiskey.

To Britney's observation, he was attractive, all sharp lines and dark features. Soft-looking, near-black hair swept behind his ears, and he had green eyes that were a few shades darker than Noah's. His clothes looked custom-made and expensive.

My eyes didn't linger on him for long, catching as they always did on Noah instead. If Nathan was a lion in lion's clothing, then Noah was a sheep in lion's clothing. By now, I recognized that Noah only wore brand name clothing when we were out in public. At home, he lounged in clothes that could have been bought on the sale rack at a thrift store.

Tonight, he dressed like a model for a New York magazine, and he looked the part too. Wavy hair, relaxed posture, and eyes that begged for a free drink. His freckles glowed under the flashing lights.

"Scribbles." Noah's easy smile filled me with warmth. "I got you a lemonade. Bear's finest."

I took a small sip of the tart liquid. "Thank you."

Britney coughed quietly, pulling me out of my pathetic feelings.

"Oh, right. This is Britney, Kira, and Ariadne. My three best friends. Everyone, this is Noah."

Noah greeted them all with a wave. "Nice to meet everyone. This is my cousin, Nathan."

In between the greetings and general get-to-know-you questions, I drifted back into my own head. I wasn't sure how to act around Noah tonight. We were out in public, so we had to at least keep strangers thinking we were together, but friends and family who knew the details of our arrangement surrounded us.

Then Noah's hand grazed my lower back, and my mind went blank. Who would have thought that was a good cure for my anxious thoughts?

Britney flipped her long, red ponytail over one shoulder and asked Nathan, "What are you drinking?"

He gave her a polite smile, but his eyes lifted over her head to glance at Ariadne, who was too busy complaining about her day to Kira to notice. "Macallan. What did you guys—"

"Sorry I'm late." A man with a dark hair and darker brown eyes pressed a kiss to Kira's cheek. He was paler than me—which was saying something—with thick eyebrows that took up a good chunk of his forehead.

Was I off my observation game, or did that kiss make Kira a little uncomfortable?

Britney turned her cheek toward me and whispered in my ear, "What the hell?"

"You're not late." Despite her near flinch a moment ago, Kira carried on like everything was great. "Guys, this is Xavier, my boyfriend."

Silence like an awkward pause settled in.

The air felt much different than when I introduced Noah earlier.

Okay, Macey, take one for the team. I was likely the only person here who knew about Xavier, which wasn't great considering I'd only known about him for an hour.

"It's so nice to meet you." I shook his hand. "I've heard great things."

It wasn't technically a lie if I had heard those things on the car ride here.

Britney and Ariadne froze, their wide-eyed stares defying all biological need for blinking. I half expected one of them to keel over from oxygen deprivation. Luckily, Noah stepped in, smoothing things over with a handshake for Xavier. Britney, after what felt like an eternity, retrieved her jaw from the floor and turned away from Nathan, zeroing in on Kira's new boyfriend like a detective on a high-profile case.

In between her aggressive questions, Noah brushed a hand against mine. "Should we hold hands?" His pinky intertwined with mine. "Just in case anyone is watching."

"Good thinking." I flipped my palm up on the table. "We probably should. Just in case."

Thank God Kira was too busy answering questions about her relationship to address whatever was happening in mine.

I felt sorry for anyone who would have to face Britney in court. She interrogated Xavier like he'd just robbed a bank, not dated our friend. Still, her questions came from a good place. Kira didn't exactly glow when Xavier was around—nothing like the way she used to light up with Landon. Before that idiot wrecked everything, of course.

Out of the corner of my eye, a familiar figure sat down at a table and I jumped.

Holy shit.

Victoria was here. Why was she going out to a bar on a Saturday night and why did it have to be the same one I frequented?

Anxiety spiked in my chest, but I tried to tame it. I was doing so well from a work perspective. My numbers were up. Page views, clicks, comments—everything up, up, up.

But I guess it didn't matter how well you did at your job. A negative boss could still endlessly make your stomach curdle just at the thought of actually doing the work you're good at.

"You okay?" Noah squeezed my hand. "Looks like you just saw a ghost."

I forced a laugh to break through the bubbles in my stomach. "Victoria is here."

Noah's gaze followed mine. Victoria was seated at a small

table with a man who looked to be in his fifties. She looked good —really good—in a black dress that, frankly, reminded me of a longer version of the one I was wearing.

"Do you want to leave?"

"No."

He turned back to me, a confused look on his face. "Isn't it weird that she's here? I mean, what are the odds she shows up the one night you and I do?"

I wasn't sure how Noah factored into Victoria's sudden appearance, but whatever. "I'm sure it's just a coincidence."

"You should go talk to her," Noah suggested, leaning in a little too eagerly. "Maybe this is your chance to level the playing field. You know, so you can stand up for yourself."

I couldn't help but laugh. He had to be joking. "No way. What if she finds out I'm starting a blog?"

I'd really be in trouble then.

"She won't." He stood, proving he was very much serious. "I'll go talk to her then."

"Excuse me?" I grabbed his bicep and yanked him back down. "What is wrong with you?"

"You're tense just being in the same room as her. This is something you need to deal with."

"I don't need to do anything, Noah," I snapped, my hand dropping to my glass. "There's no reason to confront Victoria tonight." I took a slow sip, letting the silence linger. "And please don't ever fight my battles for me."

Britney tried to pour some levity into the situation. "Don't think you're off the hook from my questioning, Hansley." She pointed a manicured finger at his chest. "It's your turn to prove to me you're good enough for our Macey."

"Can't prove what isn't true," said Noah, simmering down. Victoria forgotten. "But I'm trying."

Britney sighed. "Good answer. I'm still questioning you, though. What is Macey's favorite color?"

"Light blue."

"What's her favorite food?"

"Mint chocolate chip ice cream." He pulled a disgusted look.

"And her biggest fear?"

Noah paused in contemplation. He looked down at me and said, "Confrontation."

Well, ouch.

Ariadne pushed away Britney's finger, which was still pointed at Noah. "Okay, okay. We're here to celebrate your law internship offer, not turn into lawyers tonight. I'm going to get a drink."

Nathan watched her go for a second and, before she reached the bar, downed the rest of his whiskey. "I'm getting a refill."

I sipped my lemonade and pretended not to see Britney's disappointed face. It wouldn't last, though—she could get nearly any other guy in here if she tried.

She sighed dramatically. "How is it we're celebrating me tonight, yet I'm the only one without male attention?"

"Don't worry." Kira placed her chin in her hands. "I'm getting some weird vibes from that guy." She glanced at Noah. "No offense."

Noah shook his head. "None taken."

"Britney, I have no doubt that you'll find someone to go home with tonight," I said.

"Maybe." She did a sweep of the room with her eyes. "Oh, that's someone from my corporate law class. Be right back."

By the bar, Ariadne and Nathan were engaged in conversation, voices too low for me to make out. Ariadne scowled; Nathan looked pleased.

A smile crept on Kira's face as she leaned over the table toward me. "Three dollars that Nathan buys Ariadne a drink."

I studied Ariadne, whose crossed arms grazed the bar and expression was firmly set on the bartender. Leaning as far away from Nathan as possible. She was one of the most stubborn people I knew. If she hadn't shown any interest in him by now, she wasn't budging. "You're on."

"Is there a gambling problem I should know about?" Noah interrupted.

"The stakes are low enough not to be concerned," I said.

He finished his beer. "Why don't we see who's the winner of your bet while I get another drink?"

"Sure." I grabbed my lemonade and followed Noah. "Only because I like to win."

"We'll see!" Kira's voice followed.

Noah tried to order a specific drink—some variation of a whiskey sour—but Bear only shook his head and said he knew a drink Noah would like more. Seconds later, a small glass was pushed in front of Noah.

Instead of heading back to the table, Noah sat down on a barstool, nudging for me to do the same. Oh. Okay. Alone at last. Just the two of us. Out in public, with our friends watching not so subtly from a distance. I could handle this like a normal person.

Just say something normal, Macey.

"Did you know that male whales tuck their genitals inside of them when they're not mating?"

"Same," said Noah.

Was I drunk? Was it possible to get drunk off of the drinks your friends consumed? Maybe when Noah blinked next, I could leap behind the bar and hide.

"What?"

"I'm kidding, Macey." Noah's smile, the one normally reserved for private occasions between us, appeared.

"Oh, of cou—"

"It's too big to tuck anywhere anyways."

Oh.

Great. Now I was thinking about Noah touching his genitalia. About me touching his genitalia. I hated the word genitalia. Cock. Penis. Dick. We should make the word genitalia illegal in sexy mind scenarios. It really dimmed the mood.

"Are you blushing?"

"No!" I turned my head away. "It's just been a long week."

Noah's eyes softened. "Is it the comments again?"

Over the past few weeks, I had been inundated with comments from random people on Instagram. Mostly fans of Noah's, but a few other stragglers too. Many people were positive and encouraging of our relationship, but some got...intense. Not in a good way.

My DMs were flooded with ignorant comments and immature insults about my appearance and intelligence. I'd come to the conclusion that ignorance, paired with access to anonymity on social media, was lethal.

More importantly, I didn't understand the *why* behind the hate. If you wanted to hate me for my chipped fingernail polish or my inability to parallel park, sure, but supposedly hooking up with a guy was not a viable reason.

So yeah. The whole scenario sucked. Definitely wasn't on my Bingo card when we agreed to fake date.

"Yes," I said. "But it doesn't matter. I don't care what people think."

Noah's finger traced the rim of his glass, moving down to catch the condensation before it hit the top of the bar. "It's not always about not caring what other people think. It's about caring what the right people think. You don't have to make any changes based on the right people's opinions, but they can put things into perspective."

"What do you think?"

His finger froze on the glass, and he pushed it an inch away. "I think if people on the Internet got the chance to know the real you, they'd never leave a mean comment again. People don't want to acknowledge their jealousy in a healthy manner, so they take it out on the object of it through insults, then convince themselves that person is the problem. But you're not the problem. You're what they aspire to be, and they hate it."

There was a familiar sting in the back of my eyes. "Because they think I'm dating you."

"No," he said. "Because you're a successful, independent woman. One who's effortlessly beautiful. If only they knew that fake dating is a perk for me, not you."

A laugh escaped me, a little wet and bubbly. "I wish everyone on the Internet was as nice as you're being to me right now."

"I can be nice to you as often as it takes to make you forget they're not."

My breath hitched, and for a moment, the rest of the world blurred into the background. I leaned my head against his shoulder, feeling the warmth of him against my cheek as he murmured, "But I have to insult you once more, though."

"Huh?"

He laughed and pointed behind me, to where Nathan was handing Ariadne a drink. "You are horrible at taking bets."

A smile crept onto my face, and I hid it in his shoulder, my laughter muffled against him. "Yeah," I said softly, the words more for him than anyone else. "I really am."

17

NOAH

Once, when we were kids, Mom took Daphne and me to a local coffee shop for her birthday. All she wanted to celebrate was us, a hot latte, and a slice of cake. The coffee shop we went to was a little rough around the edges, but they always had a fire brewing in the corner.

Daphne and I sat on a rug on the floor, splitting a cup of hot chocolate. Mom reread her favorite romance book as her kids played endless games of tic-tac-toe. After an hour, a barista brought a slice of red velvet cake with a lit candle as everyone in the coffee shop sang Happy Birthday.

"Coffee and cake can solve anything," the barista, an old woman with gray hair, said.

I had taken those words to heart.

Mom had a bad day? Coffee and cake.

Daphne experienced her first heartbreak? Coffee and cake.

That simple piece of advice changed the way I approached my problems for years.

Now, as I stood outside my neighborhood coffee shop, scrolling through Instagram, I wished solving my current problems were that simple.

There were a lot of frequent commenters on Macey's Instagram. One account in particular, *Fishly541*, left rude comments daily. Even though I was normally very good at ignoring the rude comments on my own photos, for some reason, I struggled to do the same with Macey's photos.

Your not even that good a writer.

I rolled my eyes. If you're going to hate online, at least use proper grammar.

Wait. It wasn't until I reread the comment that a memory from Aruba connected the dots. Macey, by the pool, complaining about her boss. *She used the wrong version of your versus you are again.*

There was no way Victoria was leaving rude comments on Macey's Instagram...right?

I shook off the thought, pushing the door into the coffee shop instead.

The coffee shop smelled like fresh espresso and something sweet—maybe cinnamon, maybe vanilla. It had that effortless charm of an indie coffee shop, exposed brick, hanging plants, and shelves lined with coffee beans in glass jars.

My gaze swept the room, landing on Macey instantly. She was tucked into a corner booth, already deep into her laptop, a half-finished iced coffee beside her. Loose strands of hair had slipped from her braid, framing her face as she chewed her lip in concentration.

I made my way over, dropping into the seat across from her. "Tell me you're not already stressing over this."

Macey glanced up, startled, then rolled her eyes. "I have to stress. This is my future." She gestured to the screen as if it held the keys to her destiny. "My blog, my brand, my livelihood."

I reached for her drink, taking a sip without asking. "And that's why I'm here—to make sure you don't spiral into a black hole of overthinking."

"Rude," she muttered, swatting at my hand, but she was smiling now.

I leaned back, stretching my arms along the back of the booth. "All right, let's get to work. Show me what you've got so far."

She shifted her laptop in my direction. "It's called *Macey's Miles*. I'll be focused on travel blogging for now, but maybe I'll expand my silos as I grow."

On the screen, her homepage was clean and modern. It had a crisp white background, bold but elegant font, and a logo that suited her perfectly: stylish yet approachable. A soft blue-and-gold color scheme tied everything together, giving it a polished, professional feel.

"It looks good," I said, scrolling through the pages. The navigation was smooth, the branding consistent. The only thing missing? Content.

"There's not much here yet," I pointed out.

Macey sighed, rubbing her temple. "I know. That's the part that terrifies me. A blank website feels way more intimidating than a blank notebook."

I smirked. "That's because a notebook doesn't have the entire Internet waiting to judge you."

She groaned. "Not helpful."

I turned the laptop back toward her. "Then let's fix it. I'll help you make a content plan. Blog posts, Instagram, engagement strategies. We have to tie them together." I took out my own phone. "Actually, I use an app to plan mine. I wonder if I can add you as a user so you can try it out."

I looked up from my phone to see her staring at me with a soft smile. "What?"

"Nothing." She shook her head. "Thanks for offering to help."

"It's part of our deal," I said.

"Right." Macey tucked her chin, focused again on her computer. "Our deal."

I cringed, knowing I'd said the wrong thing, but unsure how to make it right.

She pushed her coffee cup to me. "If you're getting a coffee, can you get me a refill? It's only fair since you had the last sip."

"Yeah, I can do that."

I returned a few minutes later, two coffees and a slice of cake in hand. My respect for servers increased tenfold. Balancing items on your forearms was difficult.

Macey craned her neck. "What kind of cake is that?"

"Carrot." I handed her the second fork. We both took a bite.

Yeah, coffee and cake really could make anything better.

She got up and joined me on my side of the booth. "Can you show me how to use the app? I can't figure it out."

"Sure."

She handed me her phone, and I went to the homepage of the app. Macey scooted in closer, so our thighs were touching, and suddenly, it was like my brain short-circuited. All the buttons looked the same.

"I...don't remember."

"You don't remember?"

We were arm to arm now too. Macey wore a thin tank top, so I could feel every inch of her soft skin against mine. Did she know what she was doing?

Macey laughed and poked my bicep. "I thought you said you've been using this for years."

"Yeah, but sometimes when I get distracted my mind goes blank."

"Distracted?"

Ah, shit. Didn't mean to say that either. "By the cake."

"Oh, right." Macey cut another piece off with her fork. "It is really good."

Don't stare at her mouth. Don't get distracted by her tongue licking the cream cheese frosting.

Too late.

I turned away. "How about we work on your debut post instead?"

"Sure." Macey pulled her laptop closer to her, settling into this side of the booth. "I've got a few ideas."

We spent the next hour writing and rewriting her debut post. Macey made a list of posts she wanted to write during her first six weeks, and we got the start of a content plan going.

Fueled by cake, we also linked her Instagram to her blog. She could slowly transition into one online presence: *Macey's Miles.*

It'd be a long, slow process, but I had full confidence Macey knew how to conquer it.

During our planning, a few more nasty comments made their appearance. Macey brushed them off, even though it was clear they bothered her. Trolls had taken over the Internet. It was like people forgot that the influencers and celebrities they followed were actual people with real emotions, not just characters in a movie.

I tried to bring them up to Macey again, but she claimed the angry comments and the bad press would be worth it for her blog. She had stuck her chin up and said she was going to "fake date me even harder now."

I had no idea what that meant, but it scared me a little. I wasn't terrified of the thought itself, but instead by how much I wanted it.

There was an even scarier thing—the more Macey gave me, the more I craved. I felt like a puppy, all too eager to accept whatever scraps she threw my way that day. A smile when she saw me. A glare whenever I said something stupid. A touch when she thought someone was looking.

Macey was fine leaving the comments alone, but something about them left me feeling unsettled. Especially with the new suspicion that some of the commenters may be closer to Macey than she realized.

"Oh, shit." Macey frantically shut her laptop. "We're going to be late."

"Late to what?"

She grinned. "We have an appointment."

———

When Macey said appointment, my first thought was *Not another massage appointment, please.*

As it turned out, Macey had something completely different in mind.

We walked across the lawn at the University of Illinois Chicago. It felt like another world being here—old stone buildings towering above us, ancient-looking archways, the whole place humming with the quiet intensity of people who actually knew what they were doing with their lives. Students rushed past, some deep in debate, others sipping coffee from biodegradable cups, all of them looking like they belonged.

I, on the other hand, stuck out like a sore thumb.

"Are you sure we're allowed to be here?" I asked, hands shoved in my jacket pockets as I scanned the quad.

"Technically? No," Macey said breezily, tossing me a grin. "But students sit in on random lectures all the time. No one's going to stop us unless you, like, raise your hand and ask what's on the midterm."

"Wait, we're going to a lecture?"

She quirked an eyebrow. "Did you think we were going to just wander around the campus and go home?"

I shrugged. "I thought maybe you wanted to show me your old college haunts."

"Nope. I don't think I ever stepped foot into the architecture department."

"Why are we going to the architecture department?"

Macey paused to lean against an empty wall, tilting her face toward the sun. "It's part of our deal, remember? I'm supposed to help you figure out what you want to do and who you want to become after your road trip. You studied architecture before. Why not finish your degree?"

I glanced around the student body, trying to picture myself as one of them. It felt like too much time had passed, like I couldn't stuff the current version of myself into the body of an older version of me.

"It's no Cornell," she said slowly, "but it's still a good university. If you gave it a chance, I think you might like it."

"I'll consider it." It was enough to earn a small smile.

She led me into one of the older lecture halls, the kind that looked straight out of a movie—high ceilings, massive windows filtering in the pale afternoon light, rows of wooden desks worn smooth by decades of restless students. The room smelled like coffee and old paper, and something about it made my stomach twist.

Macey slid into a seat near the back and gestured for me to sit. "Look studious."

I dropped into the chair beside her. "Do I look like someone who blends in here?"

She gave me a slow once-over—the leather jacket, the worn jeans, the fact that I was a grown adult sneaking into a college class on a Thursday evening.

"Not even a little," she admitted. "But if anyone asks, just say you're auditing."

I smirked, leaning back in my chair. "You just wanted to see me in a classroom setting, didn't you?"

She scoffed. "Please. My daydreams of you don't include you stressed over a final exam."

"Daydreams of me?"

She blushed, but before she could fire back, the professor cleared her throat at the podium.

"Tonight," she began, adjusting her glasses, "we'll be discussing the evolution of the modern house."

Macey shot me a look that was half *how perfect is this?* And half *pay attention*.

I did. More than I expected to.

For the first time in a long time, I wasn't thinking about my next post, my next flight, my next anything. I was just here, sitting in an old lecture hall, listening to ideas bigger than myself.

The temptation to get back into a learning environment bit me harder than I expected. Whenever I thought about college before, a slew of excuses usually accompanied it: too much time had passed, I was too old, there was no point in me getting a degree anymore.

Now the list of excuses grew smaller and smaller.

At the end of the lecture, we left with the crowd. We walked down the breezeway where, at the end, Macey handed me a small card.

"What's this?" I asked.

"The professor's business card. She's a department head. If you're interested, I think you should set up a meeting with her to talk about enrolling here and finishing your degree."

I pocketed the card but didn't say anything. That was a decision I'd have to sleep on.

"Thank you," I said, pulling Macey into a hug.

She rested her cheek against my chest. "You're welcome."

18

NOAH

The next morning, I caught myself grinning like an idiot. Cooking eggs? Done while grinning. Making coffee? Done while grinning. Editing photos using an app Macey recommended? Done while grinning.

I was turning into such a sap. A part of me understood it was inevitable, though. In fact, I thought it showed emotional intelligence to openly admit to myself that it was happening.

Falling for Macey Monroe? Done while grinning.

We obviously had an unconventional relationship—one that was languid, shifting a little more and more toward *something* every day. I liked the pieces of us that were malleable. It meant we were constantly changing for the better.

I didn't realize how much I needed someone close until Macey had forged a space for herself. I suspected the new space close to my heart was five-foot-three and wouldn't stretch to accommodate anyone else.

She pushed me, encouraged me, took care of me—all the things I felt I could only give to others but never receive. Macey gave them to me without a second thought.

I liked that there was room for me to fit close to her, too.

Neither of us was perfect, but if I could encourage her to become the person I knew she was capable of...well, that made me feel pretty good about myself.

The fake dating scheme was doing well. Macey's articles on *Roamer's Digest* were taking off, which no doubt fueled the fire that her boss aimed in her direction. A boss should want to see their employee succeed, but from what I'd observed, all Victoria wanted for Macey was to crash and fail. Macey normalized it as the red flag rose higher in my mind.

During these last few weeks, Macey and I were invited to almost identical events. Though we both were selective in what we attended, that only meant she was gaining recognition in the community, which would be a huge asset for her blog. *Macey's Miles* was doing well for a new blog, and I had no doubt it would only continue to grow.

Roamer's Digest wasn't invited to cover the opening of Sushi Nirvana—exclusive lounges weren't exactly up their alley—but Macey loved sushi. So when the Sushi Nirvana's public relations team asked me to bring Macey, I knew we had to go.

"How many rolls do you think I can eat before I explode?" Macey asked as soon as we were seated at the table of Sushi Nirvana.

She placed her hand on the table next to mine, and it was like a tangible representation of everything I felt. It danced on the edges of her fingertips—whatever we could be, it lingered on her outstretched hand. There were mere inches between our palms, and I could reach through the space to grasp hers, but it felt different now. The urge to always touch her, to always exist in the same space as her, tore me up from the inside.

There was only one barrier to clear, unfiltered honesty, but I wasn't sure if I had the strength to break through. The fear of rejection lingered in the back of my mind like smoke on clothing.

I could hear a voice in the back of my head, maybe mine, that suggested that was the main reason why I preferred to tuck away any chance of getting close to anyone. I'd made a habit of dumping water over the sparks of a relationship before it could ignite. But the ember between Macey and me raged to flames.

And I burned.

Realizing that Macey was still waiting for an answer, I stuttered over a response, "With that attitude, they'll have to roll us out of here."

She laughed. "Who would have thought you were so good at bad puns?"

Not me.

Small chatter scattered throughout the lounge as servers brought out samples on small, round plates. I didn't know anything about sushi. Serving fish raw should be criminal, in my opinion, but Macey had provided me with a top ten ranking of her favorite rolls on the walk here, so I knew she was excited.

In between bites, Macey said, "Did I tell you about the drama between numbers five and fifty-seven at the 5k?"

"No." I attempted to lift the roll with chopsticks, but it fell off and into the soy sauce. Why did I bother? "Tell me."

"Okay, so you know how..." Her voice trailed off.

My eyes still set on the roll that mocked me, I asked, "What?"

A second passed.

"Calculator Cal is here," she said in a small voice. Curious. Disappointed.

I lifted my head to observe the man who had just entered Sushi Nirvana and was making his way to the press table. He looked around thirty, with the kind of hair that looked like it belonged in a shampoo commercial—thick, glossy, and wavy. His smile was perfectly crooked and disarmingly sincere, but it faltered when he spotted Macey.

"Who is that?" I asked. "I don't see a single calculator on him."

Macey placed her chopsticks on her plate. She suddenly looked sick. "My coworker."

An ID badge sat around his neck, like the one I wore, and as he grew closer, I noticed it said *Roamer's Digest*.

"I can't believe it," said Macey, stunned. "Victoria told me there weren't any press events this week."

"She lied to you?"

That was it.

I didn't care that there wasn't any proof that Victoria was behind one of the harassing Instagram accounts. I would confront her myself if I had to.

Calculator Cal looked for an ID on Macey, only to realize there wasn't one. Plus-ones didn't have IDs.

To his credit, instead of taking the empty seat at the end of the table, he beelined toward us, his expression tightening with every step.

"Macey?" His voice was high-pitched, panicked. "What are you doing here?"

She twisted in her seat to meet Calculator Cal's eye. "I was going to ask you the same thing. You're covering this for an article?"

"Yeah." He nodded, smoothing a hand down his tie like it might help him recover some composure. "Honestly, I was surprised Victoria suggested me instead of you, but I figured..."

"Figured what?"

"Since your articles have been doing so well, and you started a blog, you'd quit *Roamer's Digest*."

Macey reared back, her waist colliding with the table. I instinctively scooted an inch closer. "I would never do that. And how did you know I started a blog?"

He scoffed, gripping the back of the nearest chair a little too tightly. "I do competitive intelligence, remember? I keep track of every blog that could be a competitor."

Macey's fingers clenched around her napkin, twisting the fabric as her breath hitched. "You didn't tell Victoria, did you?"

"Of course not," he said, lips pressing into a thin line. "But it seems like you need to figure out your priorities."

The words landed hard, and I could see the way Macey swallowed them down, forcing herself not to react. Experience made her an expert at masking her emotions around coworkers, but I wasn't a coworker—I could see the way her shoulders curled in, the way her jaw tensed, the way the light in her eyes flickered just a little dimmer.

This wasn't just about Victoria giving the assignment to someone else. It was about Cal's jealousy, his resentment wrapped in a smug, professional tone.

Calculator Cal gave us a tight smile, waved, and stalked off to claim the only empty seat on the far side of the table.

Macey exhaled slowly, staring at the untouched drink in front of her.

I leaned in, lowering my voice. "Hey."

She blinked, looking up at me.

"Want me to 'accidentally' spill a drink on him?"

It wasn't much, but it was enough to make her laugh, even if just for a second.

Macey let out a heavy sigh and rubbed her temples with her fingertips. "I don't have a good feeling about this."

"Me neither," I said. "You can't work for them anymore."

"I *can't*?" She turned a lethal eye toward me.

Walk it back, Noah. "You can do whatever you want, of course," I hastened to clarify. "But I don't think you should. Your blog has real potential. Besides, your coworkers are jealous, your boss is trying to ruin your career, and you look miserable just thinking about it."

"Calculator Cal didn't do this out of jealousy," she said. "He was just doing what he was told."

She notably didn't correct my two other statements.

I hesitated. Should I tell Macey about my suspicions that Victoria was one of the ones leaving rude comments? The *Fishly541* account had left more comments recently, and the tone of the comments matched the tone of Victoria's articles.

But also, Macey had already been hurt by so many other anonymous messages online, I didn't want to twist the knife.

"Macey, you should know—"

Just then a server dropped another plate on the table between us. Macey's eyes brightened. "Unagi! My favorite."

One thing I learned from watching *Friends* reruns was that unagi was a state of total awareness. I shivered watching Macey shove one into her mouth. Maybe I never finished that episode.

After finishing the plate in record timing, Macey turned to me. "I thought that would make me feel better, but I was wrong."

Suddenly, it became too much. The constant reminders about what kinds of comments waited for us on Instagram. The surface-level small talk around the room. The coworker who had unknowingly taken an opportunity away from Macey.

Too. Much.

I shoved my chair back and stood, offering a hand to Macey. "Let's get out of here."

She stared back at me. "Don't you have to post like, five photos tonight?"

I didn't give a shit about any of that, but for the sake of my manager Ezra's anxiety, I pulled my phone out of my pocket and snapped a few pictures. They looked like they were taken by a five-year-old, but oh well.

"Done," I said. "Now let's leave before they bring out more raw fish."

We meandered slowly back to my apartment.

All things considered, Macey was reacting well. It was good to know she handled bad news and others' mistreatments better than I did. I just had to press on the issue one more time.

"Why are you so afraid of quitting *Roamer's Digest*?" I asked, peering down at her. "For real?"

"For real?" She shot me a small smile. "I've always done what I thought was the right move. I wanted things with stability that helped me achieve my goals. Quitting a job to focus on a blog I just started sounds terrifying." She nearly tripped over the sidewalk. "Also, what would my parents think? I'd be crushing my mom's dream."

"Right." I sighed, remembering what she had told me about her mother. That she had always dreamed of working for a magazine but never had the opportunity. Seemed like she was living vicariously through Macey. "What does your dad think?"

Macey laughed. "Matthew Monroe has always been a free spirit. He always told me to listen to my heart. He'd probably find a way to justify any decision of mine.

"They do want me to be happy. But Dad has also said that being happy requires some level of comfort. They were both teenagers when I was born, so they were always making things up as they went. I love them, and I know they love me, but I can't help but think I ruined their dreams."

"Ruined?" I slowed my pace, turning to face her. "Scribbles, you're not capable of ruining someone's dreams. You are the dream."

She let out a soft scoff, kicking a loose pebble along the sidewalk. "But they wanted to travel the world," she said, exasperated. "Mom wanted to work for a magazine. I'm not sure what Dad wanted to do, but I doubt it was to spend nights changing diapers while his friends went to bars."

I reached out, brushing the back of my hand against hers as we walked. "That just means that when they got you, they got new dreams. Better ones, too. It's not your fault." She didn't look convinced, her brows still furrowed in thought, so I added, "Next time you see them, ask them about their dreams. I think the answer might surprise you."

She didn't say anything, just stared straight ahead, her lips pressed together like she was tucking the thought away for later.

The city stretched around us, a blend of quiet and movement. We were nearly at my apartment now, just a block away. I could already see the warm glow from the lobby lights spilling onto the sidewalk, feel the familiar weight of my keys in my pocket. But for some reason, I wasn't in a rush to get inside.

"Have you put any more thought into applying to the University of Illinois Chicago?" she asked.

"I had a meeting with the professor the other day." I missed the metro and had to sprint a few blocks to be there on time, but I made it. "She thinks I have a good chance of getting in as a transfer student on rolling admission for the fall semester."

"Oh my God!" Macey came to a sudden stop, and since we were still holding hands, so did I. "Noah! That's amazing."

Her eyes were wide with excitement, her fingers tightening around mine. The rush of her reaction hit me harder than I expected, like warmth spreading through my chest. I wasn't used to people celebrating my wins like this—like they mattered.

She took a step closer, her other hand still clasped around mine, her enthusiasm radiating between us. The space between our bodies felt smaller. I swallowed, suddenly a little unsteady.

"Being back in the classroom reminded me of my passions," I admitted, my voice quieter now. "I think it's time for some new goals."

Macey's expression softened, her fingers trailing up to my face as she pressed a warm palm to my cheek. "I'm so proud of you."

Her touch was gentle but grounding, like she knew exactly

how much this meant to me without me having to say it. I leaned into her hand instinctively, caught in the moment, caught in her.

And then, like it was the most natural thing in the world, she lifted onto her toes, closing the last bit of distance between us.

Our lips met in a kiss that was soft and unhurried. The only thought left in my head was *finally*.

19

MACEY

The Burrow Bitches

> Britney: wait, you haven't slept together yet?

> Macey: Nope.

> Ariadne: It's a fake relationship, Brit.

> Britney: so? i bet he's really good at it

> Macey: I bet he is, too

> Macey: ...Not that I've thought about it

> Kira: Me thinks the lady doth protest too much

If I had a nickel for every time I found myself spontaneously entering the apartment of the guy I was fake dating, I'd have three nickels. Which wasn't going to pay for anything, but it was still a lot.

"I'm surprised," I commented as Noah flipped the grilled cheese in the pan with precise accuracy.

He pressed the spatula on top of the bread. "About?"

"That someone as fit as you puts three types of cheese in their grilled cheese."

Smile on his face, he turned down the heat on the burner. "One isn't enough. Neither is two. Also, this is one of the few dishes I can make well, so I like to add as much pizzazz as I can."

I sat at the kitchen island—because of course his apartment kitchen had one—and glanced out the tiny window. Translucent yellow curtains covered it, and the tiny opening brought in just enough wind to make them flutter.

I needed the chill the wind brought me, after feeling all the warmth from our kiss.

"Did your mom teach you?"

"No." He plated the sandwich, setting it on the island next to me. I wasn't surprised he was making himself food, considering he hardly ate at Sushi Nirvana. Two glasses of water appeared next. "Daphne did."

He took a bite and white cheese dripped out one side of the bread. "Really?"

"It's her favorite thing to eat, and she was determined that I learn how to do it before I went to college. After Mom died, it was all we ate for like, a month. That and sympathy casseroles."

Something squeezed inside my chest. My heart, probably.

I conjured a mental image: a twenty-one-year-old Noah running after his fourteen-year-old sister, trying to feed her grilled cheese sandwiches and make sure she did her homework before bed. Picking up whatever work he could to have extra cash after the bills were paid. Questioning why so many people liked his photos on social media.

Noah Hansley, who months ago spoke to me exclusively in sarcastic comments, now offered me parts of himself that I doubted he had offered anyone else. They sat heavy on me like a key in my pocket, something hidden in plain sight that I touched every few minutes to remember it was there.

"It must have been hard on you."

Sandwich halfway to his mouth, he froze. "It was. I went from having no responsibilities beyond passing finals and making my bed to all of a sudden caring for a whole human being. Daphne had always been a priority, but it felt like she then became my entire life. I was so angry at first. At my mom for dying and leaving me with all these responsibilities. At Daphne, too, for being the reason I dropped out of college."

He picked at the edge of the sandwich that was a tad burnt. "Then I realized my anger was masking my sadness. That no one made me do anything. I'd do it all again for Daphne to have a fair chance."

I handed him a napkin that had been sitting on top of a pile of mail. "Fair chance at what?"

"At life, I guess." He shrugged. "Most of what I've heard about foster care isn't great. I thought I could do better."

"And you did. You shouldered a lot. At so young, too."

"Like I said, I'd do it again." He munched boyishly on his sandwich and finished it in minutes.

Noah absentmindedly washed the mixed dishes in his sink —the plate from the grilled cheese plus the pan and spatula, a ceramic mug that read *#1 brother*, and a bowl with a chip on its edge. He grabbed a nearby black-and-white rag and proceeded to dry them. The whole scenario felt so domestic—dinner and doing dishes—and it filled me with want. Not want for one thing in particular, but for...everything.

Emotional intimacy was real, I thought as a tingly sensation fluttered through my stomach. I felt now, more than ever, that I could trust Noah. That he trusted me.

There was only one more thing I needed to know.

"Noah?"

"Hmm?" He opened the cabinet above the sink and placed the mug inside it. I'd need a stool if I ever wanted to get up there.

"Why are you fake dating me, instead of dating someone for real?" Before he could answer, I rambled on, "You want to quit social media, so couldn't you have done a few more brand deals and clocked out? Or just tell your audience that you want to take a break?"

It wasn't that Noah didn't have a valid reason for us fake dating, but after spending time with him, I gathered that he'd been wanting to quit social media for a long time. Sure, I agreed to help him figure out what to do after, but anyone could do that. He could've hired a professional life coach. Was I nothing more than an opportunity that fell into his lap that he decided to leverage?

Noah sighed before coming to stand in front of me. My back pressed against the island, and he towered over me. Uncontrollable thoughts raced through my "emotional intimacy turns me on" brain. Things like *kiss him* and *climb him like a tree.* I silenced them.

"You're probably expecting an elegant explanation about why I suggested the ruse in the first place. But the truth is, I have no idea what the fuck I'm doing. I thought honesty wouldn't be enough, and I needed a plausible excuse."

Classic case of quarter life crisis, then. Why go for a tattoo when you can quit your job and get a fake girlfriend?

"When we left the resort, I realized if we went our separate ways and things returned to the way they were, I would die inside. And I had no idea how to fix myself or my life, but I thought I'd have the best chance of it with you by my side."

Breath left my lungs with a *whoosh.* "There's nothing to fix about you, Noah. I don't think any of us know what we're doing, but what's important is who we're with."

"I like being with you." His hand came to touch my collarbone, his thumb running back and forth around the base of my neck.

I rested my hand over his. "I like being with you, too."

Sex had always been a simple thing in my mind. When you liked someone, and they liked you too, sex was the logical next step. It was like the next stage of a relationship, nestled between feelings and trust.

My past sexual experiences were all within the clear lines of a relationship, although I admired people like Britney, who didn't need those lines. It had always been too difficult for me to separate feelings and sex. They bled into each other on a level I couldn't control.

Standing here in front of Noah, breathing the same air, made me realize how layered and nuanced the whole experience could be.

Those clear lines that I mentioned, the relationship ones I liked to be in before sex? Yeah, they were looking really blurry right now.

Noah's gaze traveled down my throat, pausing at where our hands were connected, leaving shivers on my skin. He stepped closer, our feet grazing, and my other hand went to the back of his head. I was shaky but confident. I knew I wanted this.

I stretched to the tops of my toes, nose brushing against his, and kissed him.

The kiss started off slow. Hesitant. Two sets of warm lips, pressed together but not connecting. For a second, I feared I'd misjudged the entire situation. That while maybe Noah was attracted to me and respected me, perhaps he didn't think anything further was a good idea.

Maybe it wasn't.

"Is this okay?" I pulled back just enough to whisper into his mouth. "Because it's okay if you don't want me."

His eyes darkened as our foreheads rested against each other's. Noah's hands touched me slowly, more like a gentle caress. It took me out of my comfort zone—I was used to fast movements and rushing to get all items of clothing on the floor.

Noah didn't rush this. In fact, he seemed to relish taking his time. Widening his palm across my waist, letting each finger explore. His thumb slipped underneath my shirt, sending a line of goose bumps up my spine.

"You think I don't want you?" His hands tightened on my waist and brought me closer to him. Instinctively and a little roughly. Like he wanted to pull me inside himself.

The hardness on my belly punched a moan out of the back of my throat. I leaned further into him, and his Adam's apple bobbed with a swallow.

Slowly, as if he had all the time in the world, he adjusted his position to press a hot, open-mouthed kiss underneath my jaw. I wondered how such a small action could be felt all the way down to my toes. "Why do you think that?"

His hands moved down my body, lingering on my ass for half a second before he lifted me onto the counter. Beneath the hem of my shorts, the granite cooled my flaming hot skin down. I was pretty sure I was on fire. Or close to it. "Answer me, Macey."

"Because you're so confident in everything you do and everything you post," I admitted. "But you hesitate with me."

Noah's mouth dragged down my neck, teeth scraping against my skin. He paused at the strap of my shirt. "Why do you think that is?"

I whimpered, unsure when this had turned into a question-and-answer session. "I don't know."

He tugged at the strap of my shirt with his teeth and I gasped when it hit my skin.

This close, I smelled the aftershave Noah used—herbal, with

a hint of mint. When I looked down, he was staring back up at me. His green eyes, normally bright and clear, were entirely different shades now, pupils wide.

"Because you made me nervous," he said. "At first, it was because of how confident you were in yourself and your choices. Then it was because I realized that not only was I incredibly attracted to you, but I also cared about you." He pressed his forehead against mine again. "That's not a combination I often feel."

What we had went beyond surface-level attraction. Don't get me wrong. I thought I could do my laundry on those washboard abs, but that wasn't the sole reason I wanted him. It went beyond, to the soul of the man inside. Though at this moment, I was admittedly more focused on those abs.

And his lips. Soft, fluffy, kissable. Begging to be bitten.

As if he could read my thoughts, Noah was now the one kissing me. *Finally*.

Our lips opened and we completely ravaged each other's mouths. It was instinct that had me spreading my legs, giving him space to make a home in between my thighs. He settled against me like he belonged there.

Noah was relentless in his actions, his hard body pressed against mine, desperately seeking anything I'd give him. My hands flew to his chest while his palms roamed down my sides. I hoped he couldn't feel how fast my heart was racing.

There was no trace of the nerves he talked about now. Patience was gone, too. He shimmied my body forward, leaving me on the edge of the counter. Hands, both mine and his, shoved at my top, briskly pulling it over my head.

The same sense of urgency came over me as I pulled at his top. In a swift motion, he loosened the buttons that I missed, and it then joined my shirt and bra on the floor.

I feel the same, I wanted to tell him. *It's more than just attrac-*

tion. I care. So damn much. I wanted to scream it to the world, post it on social media, write it on a public billboard. Explain it to anyone who would listen.

But despite that, I couldn't find the best way to put it into words right now. I wrote words for a living, yet I couldn't find one to describe this moment. Joy. Bliss. Excitement. Every word in the English language paled compared to what I was feeling.

So I tried to show him. My hands reached for his cheeks, slowing down the kiss into something more tender, more sensual. And I hoped he understood what I was trying to get across because he responded so well. Tugging my lower lip into his mouth, giving a gentle bite right in the center. Licking the tingling sensation away.

His lips traveled up my cheek, across my forehead, and back down again. He was either trying to taste every inch of me or mark his territory. I liked the thought of both way too much.

A shiver coursed through me when he kissed me again.

Wanting the rest of his clothing gone, I tugged at his pants. As soon as they were off, I arched my back, looking for the friction I had only gotten a taste of earlier. My shorts rolled off smooth as butter, and then Noah gave me what I wanted. His hardness pressing into me, shooting small sparks through my body, even with the barrier of our underwear.

I felt him hot and thick as he rocked against me, and my eyelids fluttered shut. He moved again, and based on the way my toes curled, I was pretty sure I could come from this alone.

"More," I demanded.

I reached down to tug off his underwear, but he grabbed both of my wrists, pinning them behind my back with just one hand.

"Not until you come first," he rasped into my mouth. "Can I touch you?"

"Yes." I arched into him. "Everywhere."

Before I exploded, ideally.

He swept his mouth over me as if he really was trying to touch me *everywhere*. Drawing one nipple into his mouth, he alternated between slow tongue movements and gentle bites. Little nips that had me gasping and squirming on the counter. Once he was satisfied, he manipulated the movement on my other breast.

I was aware that his free hand was constantly moving, up and down my back, side to side over my stomach. But I didn't take a minute to process where it was going until his fingers reached the band of my underwear.

By the time he hooked his pinky under them, I was desperately ready.

"Everything about you is so pretty," he murmured, stroking his thumb back and forth over my hip bone. "Your face, your ambition, your Elsa hair, your stalking."

I opened my mouth to protest the last one, but then he pulled my underwear down.

"I bet your pussy is too."

Heat flushed from my hairline down to my toes.

When his fingers touched me, the sound that escaped my mouth was borderline inhuman, but based on the sound he made in response, he liked it.

Noah carefully observed my face as his fingertips sank so easily between my folds, parting and gliding until they settled over my clit. Rubbing in slow, small circles until my mind went empty. I never really understood how someone could forget their names during sex, but I got it now.

"I was right," Noah said in awe. He wasn't talking to me, though, more to himself.

One finger entered me, and I squirmed a little against Noah, but he still held tightly to my wrists. Fuck, that shouldn't be so hot. Was this a kink I had gone years without knowing I had? Maybe I should have explored more in college.

A second finger matched the motions, curling perfectly right *there*. My head lolled back, and Noah followed. His torso leaned over mine, lips kissing my cheek, my temple, my nose as his fingers hit there, there, there.

"Don't stop," I panted. Which then made me nervous because a lot of men hear the words *don't stop* and interpret it as *change it up*. Noah didn't. He kept going, deep breaths by my ear only turning me on more.

Shortly, I tumbled over the edge. I was pretty sure this was what people meant when they said they saw stars—bursts of color popped up against my eyelids.

"So pretty." Noah was as coherent as I was right now—which was to say, not at all. "You deserve pretty things. Pretty things to wear. Pretty things for me."

My hands were set free as he shoved down his underwear, cock springing free. I reached for it, but he beat me to it, closing a fist around it and tugging once. We could add that to the list of things that had no need to be that hot. He was just the right size for me. A little pink, with thick veins. Perfect.

I wanted to stroke the little line of hair below his navel, but he stepped out of reach. He reached into the pocket of his discarded pants and I heard a familiar ripping of foil. My heart continued to pound inside my chest as he kissed me once more, aligning himself with me.

"Okay?" he whispered.

"I thought we moved past the hesitating—"

He nudged the head against my opening and we both gasped the moment he entered. A few seconds of uncomfortable stretching gave way to the perfect feeling of having him inside me.

I looked up at him. His eyes were closed, half-moons against his soft cheeks, constellations of freckles shining around them. "Noah?"

"Hmm?"

"I'm glad I have you in my corner."

One hand caressed my cheek. "You'll always find me there."

And then he pulled back and thrust again. And again. The motion made my entire body pulse with need as I constantly moved my hips, trying to invite him closer. My thighs trembled, and I was thankful to be sitting.

He moved inside me until I could feel his cock twitch inside me, like a rhythm. My head fell forward, saved by Noah's shoulder. I sucked a bruise on his shoulder, kissing it better afterward.

My ankles crossed behind his back and my heels dug in. If only I could melt fully into him. His thrusts moved from slow and steady to fast and hard, his hands on my back keeping me stable. Pleasure zipped up my spine.

Composure transitioned to clumsiness on both of our parts as we fully lost it. We both let out a giggle, followed by a moan when he slipped out and had to nudge his cock back inside. All I could focus on was how smoothly he slid in and out. How good it felt.

"Sweetheart, you have to tell me"—he paused for a grunt when I clenched around him—"what you need."

I fisted my fingers in his hair and pulled my head off his shoulder. "Kiss me."

He did, open-mouthed and wet, but I didn't care. Our tongues met at multiple angles as he went deeper inside me. He trailed his mouth up my cheek, toward my ear so that I could hear the breathy moans he emitted.

It was that sound—the confirmation of pleasure from both of us—that had me coming once more.

Noah shuddered in my arms, and he muttered more

nonsense. Words about how silly it was to be nervous over this, how he couldn't believe how much time we wasted apart, how soft I was.

And then when he let go, too, I smiled, thinking how we couldn't possibly waste any more time.

20

NOAH/MACEY

Noah

The morning sun filtered through the blinds and reflected off my kitchen counter. I had woken up early after hardly sleeping all night. Not like me, considering I usually slept like a rock. But it was difficult to escape reality when I wanted to stay awake just a little bit longer.

Macey, on the other hand, passed right out. She was still asleep in the bedroom.

Determined to surprise her, I decided to try my hand at making breakfast. Thankfully, I had groceries delivered yesterday and a full fridge. The issue was that I couldn't cook many breakfast dishes well. Not unless I had a chef like Luca in front of me giving specific instructions.

I was pretty sure I had an old cookbook in here somewhere. That would have to be a substitute.

Filtering through the contents of the pantry while being as quiet as I could, I searched for the book. It had to be on one of these shelves. So far, I had found old receipts, dusty Tupperware, and a half-empty bag of flour. My hands gripped the edge of the book at the back of the shelf and I pulled it out.

One dust off later and I had in my hands *50+ Simple Comfort Recipes for Beginners.* Perfect.

Leaning against the counter, I flipped through the pages in search of something easy. And something that wouldn't take a million years, because I was starving. After a minute, I had a plan.

A frittata for both of us.

French toast for Macey. Plus a bite for me.

Soon enough the kitchen smelled of cinnamon, and eggshells cluttered the counter. I glanced frequently at the cookbook as I stirred vegetables into the skillet. Not professional-looking by any means, but it was better than grilled cheese for breakfast.

The bedroom door opened with a soft creak, and moments later, a soft hand pressed against my back. Macey stood next to me, her hair down and tousled from sleep, a smile on her face. She wore one of my old T-shirts, and the sight of it made me want to drag her back to the bedroom.

Breakfast first.

"Good morning, Scribbles." I inserted the skillet into the oven. "Breakfast will be ready soon."

She gasped when she saw the bread and cinnamon sugar on the counter. "Are you making French toast?"

"Yes."

"You're willingly touching carbs. Who are you and what have you done to Noah Hansley?"

I grinned. "I'm evolving."

Her eyes raked down my body—okay, I "forgot" to put on a shirt—and went back to the stove, where I was starting to cook the French toast. "I like it. Is there anything I can do?"

Using one hand, I pointed to the coffeepot on the edge of the counter. "Want to get coffee going?"

Macey coughed into her elbow then nodded. "Easy."

"How did you sleep?" That was the kind of question boyfriends asked, right?

She measured out the ground coffee and added it to the filter. "Good. I don't usually knock out like that."

Our eyes met. She blushed and looked back down.

I didn't know why nerves were starting to overcome me now, especially when last night I was so confident, brazen. It was easy, acting with my body, doing anything to find Macey's pleasure. Sure, I might have spent the night replaying the moment when she put her hand around my cock and squeezed perfectly like she had been studying it for years, but well. She was always the bold one between us anyways.

"Macey, last night—"

"Noah." My name on her lips didn't sound right. It was more of a croak or a gasp.

Macey pressed both palms against the counter, leaning forward. Something shifted in her expression as her breathing became shallow.

"Macey?" I moved the frying pan off the burner and put a hand on her shoulder. "What's wrong?"

"Something...in the air." She tried to take in a deep breath, but her shoulders shook with difficulty. "Like smoke or fire or..."

Dust.

Like I had just dusted off an insanely old cookbook, plus whatever else lingered in the back of the pantry. *Fuck.*

"Where's your inhaler?" I pressed one hand to her cheek. Her breathing grew more labored. "Sweetheart, where is it?"

She flopped a hand in the direction of the bedroom and croaked out, "Purse."

Without thinking, I darted across the kitchen, knocking over one of the barstools. My hands trembled as I rifled through her purse, finally pulling out the inhaler.

Macey sat on the floor, back against the island. Exhausted.

Sweat dripped down her brow, like the action of breathing tired out her body.

"Here," I urged, handing her the inhaler.

I squatted in front of her. My own breath caught in my throat as I watched her struggle to use it. For a few agonizing minutes, I could do nothing but listen to my heart pound in my chest and hold her free hand.

She took a few puffs in between deep breaths. It terrified me, how much something like asthma could impact not just your quality of life but your life in general. I made a vow in this moment to be more cognizant of our environments and Macey's response. Maybe I could keep an inhaler stored in my apartment, too.

Logically, I knew this wasn't my fault, but I couldn't stop the feeling that I could have stopped it somehow. Order in fancy breakfast. Take her out.

How long had it been? A few minutes. Felt like hours.

Slowly, Macey's breathing began to steady, the color returning to her cheeks. I let out a breath of my own.

She leaned her head forward onto my shoulder, and I rubbed her back.

"Are you okay?"

I felt more than saw her nod.

"Yeah. Just want to rest a little while."

"Of course." Her hair was silky soft under my touch. "Let's get you back to bed."

I helped her to her feet and back to the bedroom. Even though her breathing was stable, I could tell it had taken a toll on her. Physically, yes. But emotionally too. Like it was something she didn't want me to see. I didn't like that. I wanted to be there for her, asthma attack or not.

As I pulled the covers over her body, Macey curled in on

herself and held tightly to my pillow. I sat on the edge of the bed, gently stroking her hair as she drifted back to sleep.

Remnants of fear still lingered in the back of my mind. This was normal for her but terrifying for me. I hated that it was part of life for her. But that was the thing about chronic illnesses—no matter how much you hate them, they won't go away. All a loved one like me could do was educate myself on the best way to help and be supportive when they needed it.

I planned to stay here, watching like a guard, until she woke up again.

I texted Daphne while I waited.

> Noah: How do I help someone who's had an asthma attack?

> Daphne: ask google, not me

> Daphne: wait, what happened??

> Noah: Long story. Macey had one.

> Noah: She's okay now, just sleeping.

> Daphne: let her sleep. Then give her food.

> Noah: You think that'll help?

> Daphne: sleep and food are the tickets to any woman's heart

> Daphne: ...unless you have a spare pair of lungs

A deep stench thwarted my plans to stay here until Macey woke up. It couldn't be dust. There wasn't *that* much in the pantry.

Already on my feet, my body recognized the source before my brain caught up. It was burning. The fucking frittata was burning.

I ran back to the kitchen and threw open the oven. Thank God something like this wouldn't catch fire or else my entire apartment would be up in flames right now. I pulled the skillet out of the oven, mentally scolding myself. The entire thing was black, almost ashy on the ends.

First the dust. Then the burnt frittata.

Macey probably thought I was trying to kill her.

Macey

I knew Noah wasn't trying to kill me. It wasn't his fault my lungs didn't work fully. Don't get me wrong. They worked hard. It was just that their best wasn't always good enough.

I sat on the edge of Noah's couch, hands still trembling as I held the glass of water he brought me. The remnants of the wheezing echoed in my chest, a ghost of the attack that had taken me by surprise. My nap only lasted twenty minutes, enough to ease my frantic heartbeat. I took a sip of water, letting the coolness soothe my throat, but my mind was far from calm.

Why now? Why here? Besides the obvious—dust and who knows what else in the air. Last night was perfect in every sense, but now I had to go and ruin the moment.

It was bizarre, feeling the sting of both frustration and a strange sense of pride. Maybe I should just be proud, though. My lungs had fought back. They'd kept me here, in Noah's apartment, instead of the nearest walk-in clinic.

I hadn't felt that way in a while. The tightness, the desperate clawing for air, the panic that gripped me until I had my inhaler in hand.

This wasn't something to be embarrassed over. It wasn't like I chose for this to happen at the worst time possible, and Noah, well, he didn't seem to mind. He'd been nothing but concerned. He stroked my hair during my earliest parts of slumber, whispering something like, "You're okay, sweetheart," on repeat. Chanting it like it was a reminder for him as much as it was for me.

Still, I couldn't help the flush creeping up my neck at the thought of him seeing me like that. Vulnerable.

Noah busied himself in the kitchen, giving me space but close enough to be there if I needed him. Would he worry every time I coughed or took a deep breath? The last thing I needed was for him to be concerned if I went on a mind-clearing run.

A small part of me was relieved. Relieved that he hadn't run away, that he was still here, making coffee as if this morning hadn't shaken me to the core.

One more sip of water, and I let myself breathe a little easier.

The room was quiet except for low-fi music playing from Noah's phone in the kitchen. He wasn't a fan of silence, I'd noticed. The dishes clinked in the kitchen, and I found myself oddly comforted by the normalcy of it all.

Noah leaned against the entryway of the living room, catching my eye. "How are you feeling?"

His voice was gentle, concerned but not overbearing. He didn't hover.

"Better," I said. "Thanks."

He nodded, giving me a small smile before returning to his task. I watched him for a moment, the ease in his movements, the way he seemed unfazed by what had just happened. It was almost like this was another part of the morning routine—nothing more than an unexpected detour.

Moments later, he returned with two mugs of steaming

coffee and two full plates of French toast. Covered in syrup and strawberry preserves. *He remembered my favorite topping.*

I took the mug in my hands, embracing the warmth it provided.

"I heard black coffee can be good after an asthma attack," he said as he sat next to me on the couch.

"You heard?"

"Well, I read it online." He cut into his toast. "It can relax airways and reduce inflammation in your lungs."

I paused before I could even cut into my breakfast. "You researched asthma?"

"Of course." He acted like it was no big deal. And maybe it wasn't. Asthma wasn't a super rare condition by any means, but most people didn't learn about management beyond an inhaler.

I blurted out, "I'm sorry."

His brows furrowed in confusion. "For what?"

"For...that." I gestured vaguely. "For having a full-blown asthma attack literally hours after sleeping together for the first time."

Noah shook his head. "You don't have to apologize. It's not your fault."

"I know, but..." I trailed off, trying to find the right words. "I feel like I ruined the moment."

"You didn't ruin anything. Last night was amazing and so is this morning. Your asthma attack didn't change anything for me, except that now I want to be here for you even more."

A sense of relief washed over me, mingled with a deep affection.

I looked down at my plate, the French toast suddenly seeming more appetizing. I shoved a piece into my mouth. Slightly burnt on the edges, but it tasted good all the same. "I'm just not used to people being around when it happens."

"Get used to it, Scribbles," Noah said, voice teasing. "Do you have a spare inhaler?"

"I have one somewhere in my room."

"Maybe we should keep one here, or I could carry one with me. Just in case." My face must have echoed the surprise I felt because he rushed to continue. "I know you're usually prepared, but if something happens and you don't have it, I'd like to be able to help."

A lump formed in my throat. No one had ever offered to do something like that for me before.

Part of me wanted to protest, but I shoved that part of me down in favor of moving us forward. Any instinct I had to deny his request wasn't about needing help. It was about letting someone in again.

"Okay." I smiled. "I'd like that. But…"

"But?"

"I hate black coffee." I held my mug out toward him. "Do you have any sugar?"

His laugh echoed across the apartment, but he brought me a few sugar packets without complaint.

It tasted much better now. "Did you even post the Stories from Sushi Nirvana?"

Noah cursed under his breath and reached for his phone. "I knew I forgot something. Sushi sneak peek, yada yada."

The sugar in the coffee and the breakfast were working their magic. I knew Noah had attempted to cook us something healthy before he ruined the dish. In my opinion, it was a sign from the universe to stick with delicious, non-healthy breakfasts.

"You are a terrible influencer," I said. "How do you get away with so much?"

He shrugged, eyes trained on his phone. "I pay my manager a lot of money."

"Does he know about the fake dating?"

Noah's torso stiffened, but he continued swiping through his photos. He posted a selfie he took of us when we first walked in. "No, he doesn't."

Seemed like a bad strategy to lie to your social media manager about a key element in your life. I mean, I was letting my coworkers and boss think I was dating Noah, but my column wasn't my personal brand. Not like how Noah's social media was all about him.

I wanted to ask Noah what this meant for us. Were we just going to continue doing the same old deal of posting a photo of us together once a week for two more weeks, then shake hands, and say *see you later*?

If we didn't have the presence of more than a million people looming over our heads and rushing to comment their thoughts on our relationship, maybe it'd be a little easier. But it was one thing to present yourself to an online audience and another to someone you cared about in reality.

"He'd probably yell and throw something at me if he did know," said Noah. He finished posting the photos and dropped his phone onto the coffee table.

"Throw something? Are you in an abusive relationship with your manager, Noah?"

"Ha. No. He usually picks something soft to throw at me, don't worry."

"Like a sock?"

"That, or something easily found in his kitchen, like a bell pepper."

"Speaking of, thanks for making breakfast." I set my empty plate onto the coffee table. "I actually can't stay too late. I told Kira I'd help her bring some art supplies home."

"You're sure you're feeling better?" Noah asked as I gathered my purse and slipped on my shoes.

"Oh, yeah, just like new."

"Don't forget what I said about the inhaler." Noah pulled me into a goodbye hug. I could have sworn I felt his lips on my hair. "Let me take care of you, please."

"Only if you let me do the same."

He snorted into my hair. "You've been doing it for weeks."

Unconsciously, maybe. We took care of each other. I leaned into Noah's chest and breathed easier than I had all morning.

21

NOAH

Time was a human construct, but I had never felt the constrictions around me as much as I did now. May 15 loomed in the near distance. Two weeks, to be precise. And I was in the exact same place as I was when Macey and I struck the deal—confused and lost.

The one thing that had changed? Now I had something to lose.

Someone to lose.

We were on our second to last fake date this evening at a pop-up photography exhibit. I had spotted it the other day on the way home from the gym. Sometimes, our pre-planned outings were brief: a quick coffee break in a popular coffee shop, a walk through the park, or lunch at the newest café.

Today, I wanted to take Macey somewhere I knew she'd like.

And yes, I was well-aware this was real-boyfriend behavior, but I didn't need to expand on the psychology behind the decision. We had already started crossing the line anyway. Tonight would be the night I said something about the real feelings that had been boiling inside me. For better or worse, she deserved to know the truth. Even if I was terrified about how she'd respond.

Was it fair for me to even ask Macey to take a chance on someone so unstable, who had no idea what he was doing in life? What she needed was dependability and stability. I wasn't sure if I was in a place where my life included those things, no matter how much I wanted them.

Still, I wanted that chance. Wanted the opportunity to turn myself into a better version of myself, one that was worthy of her. I just wasn't sure how.

Soft, ambient music played as we filtered through the exhibit. The space was an eclectic mix of industrial and chic, with exposed brick walls and concrete floors juxtaposed against elegant drapery and plush seating areas. Spotlights illuminated the photographs, making them stand out vividly against the muted backdrop of the gallery walls.

"Thanks for bringing me here," Macey said as she stared straight ahead at a jungle landscape photo.

"You're welcome," I said, feeling pleased. Then I explained my reasons for selecting this date. "I thought it would be a good place to get photos for your blog."

"Thanks." She sounded pleasantly surprised. "I've pretty much stopped trying to get Victoria to consider my photos for articles, which, by the way, are still performing amazing. My blog viewership has slowly been increasing, too."

"I know," I commented. "I check every so often."

"Stalker," she teased. "I appreciate it, though. I've felt a little off ever since seeing Calculator Cal at the restaurant opening. He never said anything about me being there to Victoria, so she doesn't know I know, but the office still feels hostile. My career is really important to me, and I can't help but feel like I'm being pushed out."

A hot coil of frustration curled in my stomach. It wasn't fair what was happening to Macey, and now I knew I needed to do something about it. Macey's career was important to her, and I wanted to help her succeed.

"Macey, there's something I should tell you about your boss," I started, then hesitated. Was this really the right time to tell her about my theory?

I looked at her face—wisps of hair from her braid falling onto her forehead, glitter on her eyelids that only accentuated the joy in her deep brown eyes—and I couldn't bear upsetting her tonight. I'd tell her another day.

There was still time.

"What?" she asked, my blank expression probably confusing her.

"Your boss sucks." I forced a nonchalant laugh.

She laughed along with me. "Yeah. She's not always so bad, but she's much harder on me than everyone else. I've tried so many times to patch the holes in our relationship, but I've never succeeded. I think she's made me stronger, though, even if she didn't mean to."

"It's not on you to fix someone else's insecurities."

"You think that's the reason? She's insecure?"

I nodded. "You're confident and good at what you do. Most people would want to partner with someone like that, but a few will do what they can to drag you down with them."

"Maybe you're right," she said. "But there's got to be something more to it. I don't know."

She started to move toward the next photograph in line, but something caught her eye. "We have to see this." She giggled as she dragged me across the gallery floor. We landed in front of a large portrait.

It was a whale.

Ever since the Whale Fest event, she was oddly obsessed with whales.

"Did you know," Macey started, "that whales use physical touch to maintain social bonds?"

I stood behind her, close enough that strands of her hair brushed my chin. "Oh?"

"They swim close together, rub against each other, and even hold fins like how people hold hands."

I enveloped her body within mine, placing a hand on her hip. When I rubbed a thumb over the space in between the end of her shirt and the top of her skirt, a gold and glittery thing that hit mid-thigh, a shiver skated down her body.

Masculine pride filtered through me. *I did that.*

It was borderline pathetic how fast Macey consumed me. The entire cast of *Die Hard* could enter through the front door, and I'd never notice. I wouldn't take the opportunity to meet the stars of my favorite movie if it meant not touching Macey for a minute.

"What else did your whale book teach you?"

"Um." Her breath caught when I moved both hands to her waist, holding gently. "In some species, males and females form long-term partnerships. Which is a big deal, when you think about how many animals are only with each other for one goal, like breeding."

"Is that what you want?"

"Breeding?" She sounded horrified.

"No, Scribbles." I placed my chin on top of her head, taking a minute to observe the photo in front of us. A wild whale in the ocean, free and happy. "Long-term partnership."

"It is," she said, then leaned back into my chest. "What about you?"

I swallowed and took a deep inhale as I wrapped my arms fully around her. "I never thought I was capable of that."

"And now?"

"Now I think I am."

We stayed like that for a minute, unmoving, content to be close to each other. Staring at a simple photograph. Fortunately, most of the guests didn't have an interest in whale photography, so it was just us in this corner of the gallery.

At least it was, until I heard footsteps approach.

"They're taking photos of you," Macey said under her breath.

Out of the corner of my eye, I saw a pair of girls, probably around Daphne's age. One held up a phone unabashedly as the other hastily threw hers back into her bag.

"Not me," I corrected. "Us."

One girl, the brave one who still held up her phone, shouted, "Kiss!"

Her friend turned away in embarrassment.

Did people think we were trained animals who did things on command?

"No, thanks. His lips are chapped," Macey joked to them.

A joke at my expense, but it was better than the alternative: a forced kiss for other people's viewing pleasure. I pinched her side, and she let out a giggle.

"So?" The girl looked like she was going to protest further until her friend dragged her toward the next exhibition room.

Once they were gone, I asked in mock offense, "I have chapped lips?"

Macey shrugged, turning around in my arms. She touched one finger to my bottom lip. "You can borrow my lip balm."

Did she notice the way my breath grew heavier after her touch? This close, it'd be impossible not to. It was hard not to look at her, but at the same time, it was more difficult to look. Every time she tilted her head, I had to press down the desire to reach out and kiss there, right at the point of her pulse. I flicked my tongue against my lips and turned away.

"You're going to regret saying that."

"Why?"

I glanced around once, then twice, noting a lack of guests in the immediate area. When I stepped back, I tugged Macey back with me until we were both fast walking toward the edge of the gallery. Near the corner, to the reading room.

It was unlocked, and we slipped in unnoticed.

"Noah?" Macey asked into the darkness as I found the light switch and turned it on.

I didn't answer, instead stepping in front of her and tugging at the elastic band at the end of her braid. I placed it in my pocket, working slowly to undo each fold of the braid. Her hair felt soft and silky in between my fingers, and it looked almost white against my palm.

When I reached the base of the braid by her scalp, I tugged. Macey followed the movement easily, tilting her head up and to the side for me. Right where I was craving earlier. I planted a kiss on the underside of her jaw.

"What are we doing?" Macey's voice was a hushed breath that turned into a moan when I moved my lips down her neck, pausing at the spot that I gathered she liked most.

It happened so fast—and I was already so lightheaded, intoxicated from contact—that we found ourselves falling against the couch in the corner of the room. Macey hit the cushions, me leaning over her, the high velvet back of the couch engulfing us. My knee pressed into the cushions between her legs.

"You said you didn't want to kiss my lips because they're chapped." Not a great joke considering I did use Chapstick regularly. "So I'm working around that."

"But I like kissing you," she said in a low voice, like a prayer.

My mouth found its place by the shell of her ear. "I think you'll like this, too."

Pinned as she was under the weight of my body, Macey's eyes widened. "We're in public."

"We don't have to do anything you don't want to do." I emphasized my point with one quick peck against her cheek.

"No, I want to. It's just..."

"We'll have to be quiet."

My mind began that slow, familiar melt into mush. One hand fisted in the glittery fabric of her skirt, even though she already pulled us close together with a knee hooked around my waist. I reached down to hook that leg over my shoulder and pressed an open-mouthed kiss on the skin of her ankle.

A short exhale left Macey's mouth. *Ticklish, then.*

Slowly, I moved up her legs, suddenly very grateful to whatever intelligent person invented skirts. When I got to her knee, I moved to the floor, sitting on my own knees. Macey was a mess of anticipation and excitement. She stared down at me, heat in her pupils, as I traced my tongue against the fold of her knee.

I made quick work of the silk underwear beneath her skirt, then carefully tossed it onto the couch so it wouldn't be lost later.

Her hands tangled in my hair as I gave a first long, languorous lick. Macey fell back against the cushions with a soft moan, cushioned by her palm against her lips.

"Quiet," I reminded her before drawing her clit into my mouth and sucking, reveling in the way she panted.

The thought that anyone could come in at any moment and see the most beautiful girl in the city, skirt pushed up to her hips, with the luckiest bastard kneeling before her—well. It was dangerous and disastrous, and the only kind of bad idea that I enjoyed participating in. From the way Macey responded, she did too.

"I—" But she didn't finish her sentence as I upped the intensity, licking and sucking until she was dripping all over me.

I pulled back for a second, rubbing a finger where my mouth had been previously. I admired the sight before me, how Macey's spine left the cushions, eyes harshly shut. I spread her thighs wider and sucked a bruise on the tender skin there.

Her whimpers escalated into muffled squeals as I alternated between fingering her and worshiping her with my mouth. Fast, even strokes across the entirety of her. Swirling a fingertip over her swollen bud until she rolled her hips, trying to get more.

"Noah." My name broke out as soon as she moved her hand off her mouth. Instead, she fisted my hair again, muscles taut.

"You taste better than I imagined." I buried my nose and inhaled. I wanted to stay here forever. I wanted the chance to stay here forever.

Macey pushed herself up by her elbows. "You...imagined?"

I slid two fingers in and lifted my head. "Often."

She gazed down at me, her eyes half-hidden with desperation and desire. Maybe something else, too. Trust. Care. Certainty.

My cock was hard against my pants, but my heart had never felt so soft. Fuck. It was like she had beaten down every last layer between my heart and the world.

"I always did," I admitted, pushing my fingers deeper. She was so tight around my knuckles, and I felt the stretch. "Always knew you were beautiful. Never thought we'd have a chance."

A shudder rolled through her, at my words or my actions, I couldn't tell. So I continued with both.

"I love the way you always smell like coconut sunscreen, and the braid down your back, and that you always see the best in people." I lowered my head. "Like me."

I timed the next swirl of my tongue with a flick of my finger, hooking against that spot. Macey shoved a hand over her mouth once again as her muscles went taut, clenching around me as she came.

Desire burned in my veins. Even though I'd love to lock us in here for the rest of the night, that wasn't an option. Still, I leisurely took my time as Macey came down from the high, relishing in the quiet whimpers that gave way to silence. I gently placed her leg back on the couch.

She leaned up to push our foreheads together, and a thrill of delight exploded in me. "It's easy to see the best in you, Noah."

22

MACEY/NOAH

Macey

The Burrow Bitches

> Ariadne: What's the status? Are you guys officially dating now?

> Macey: Um

> Britney: friends with benefits?

> Macey: Well

> Kira: Still "fake dating"?

> Macey: Hm

> Ariadne: Still fake dating and unable to express your true emotions. Got it.

"I have a problem."

I buried my face further, my arms pressing against my words.

The bright industrial light of The Burrow Café did nothing to ease the headache creeping into my temples.

I didn't sleep last night. Hardly slept the whole weekend. Every time I laid my head on the pillow, all I could think about was Noah and everything we did behind closed doors. Then I thought, *I should call him.* It was only after my phone was unlocked and in my hand that I realized it was 3:00 a.m.

And that Noah wasn't even my boyfriend. Technically.

Hence, the problem.

"Which one?" Britney called from the other side of the counter. Her hair was pulled into a tight bun as she frothed milk in a container.

I lifted my head and imagined I looked as pathetic as I felt. No amount of concealer could hide these baggy eyes. "First of all, rude. Second, you know which one."

Britney hummed as she poured the milk onto the cappuccino. I eyed it carefully, curious what latte art she'd create this time. "Yeah, I do."

I sighed. A few months ago, things were turning around for me. My column was successful, I was single and sufficient, and I had hit a new 5k record time.

Now Victoria continued to treat me unfairly despite my success, I was in a fake relationship with a guy I liked for real, and blogging took up most of my free time. Oh, and the cost of inhalers went up again.

"Life sucks." I dropped my chin into my hands, well aware I was being dramatic. But I deserved a few minutes to vent.

"Correct."

Britney passed the cappuccino to me. A heart stared back.

My hands wrapped around the cup as I let it warm me up. "You're supposed to tell me everything is going to be okay."

"If you wanted that, you would've gone to Kira or Ariadne,"

she said. "Now that you're well aware you've dug yourself into a hole, what are you going to do about it?"

Britney was right—that was why I subconsciously sought her out. Everyone needed a kick in the ass from a friend every now and then.

"I'm going to be honest about my feelings," I grumbled.

"Hell yes, you are." She encouraged me with a large smile. "But first you're going to drink the amazing coffee your friend made you."

I took a sip and glanced at the time. Fifteen minutes before I had to be back upstairs and in the office. I didn't usually come to the café during my lunch break, but I had struggled to concentrate all morning.

"Besides," said Britney, "I've seen the way Noah looks at you. There's no way he doesn't reciprocate your feelings."

"I didn't say—"

"You didn't need to." Her emerald eyes softened. "Try not to worry about it too much. Your pinky has more chemistry with Noah's big toe than Kira and her new boyfriend do."

I choked on my coffee. Suddenly grateful I was wearing a black blouse, I dabbed at the spill with a napkin. "Don't say that. You know it's hard for her."

Xavier seemed nice. Sure, he didn't have much of a personality besides that, but Kira was content with her choices. And we needed to support that.

"I know, and I get it. That doesn't mean she needs to settle."

Also a fair point.

Ugh. Why were relationships so complicated?

"Fucking bastard," Britney suddenly seethed, standing straight and placing her palms on the counter.

"Xavier isn't a bastard," I defended.

"I wasn't talking about him," she said.

Immediately my body identified the bastard she referred to.

My stomach curled to the point where if it hadn't been Britney who served the latte, I would have demanded a refund. Something hot and sticky and full of anger paraded its way into my chest. It was like sharing a space with the guy who cheated on me had my organs on the brink of dysfunction.

Part of working as a columnist in the same industry as my influencer ex-boyfriend meant I'd have to see him on occasion, but I shouldn't have to see him like this. When I was already at a rough and raw moment, stressed about things that didn't involve him.

It took only a second to realize without a shadow of a doubt that the man who'd just walked into The Burrow Café was Kyle Arnold. Famous, pretentious local influencer. Also my ex-boyfriend.

What the hell? This was strictly my territory.

"Do you want me to beat him up?" Britney asked as Kyle headed for the counter. She was serious.

"It's fine," I said, distracted. My heart pounded *fight, fight, fight.* "I got this."

As usual, Kyle was dressed in his finest athleisure. He was a little tanner than the last time I saw him, like he'd spent the entire week sunbathing instead of trying to be in the background of every other influencer's picture.

Kyle hadn't changed at all. Not physically, at least. Although he was a few years older than me, he was very boyish in appearance. Light brown hair with small curls, like he had attempted to style them but failed. Tall and lanky, yet his movements were very poised.

I usually avoided contact with him. The last time we talked was at a world showcase event at the Bean last year, during which he teased me, claiming, "You're probably going to write something ridiculous about this event, like a beyond the plate segment."

And then I wrote it to spite him.

Ironically, the conversation before that included him begging me to take him back after I saw him in bed with another woman. I had laughed in his face, and days later overheard him telling people that I was a "lucky nobody" he had been with, along with a multitude of other insults.

Now I realized those insults came from his true fears: that I was a talented woman who climbed her way from the bottom and had the potential to surpass him.

We weren't even in a competition, but he saw everyone as a competitor.

That's what happened when you viewed life in terms of a competition: you had to wave to everyone you saw on the way up when you came crashing down. And for the people he crushed, like me, all I offered him in response was a middle finger.

There was nothing I wanted from him. Any opportunity for a meaningful apology was long gone.

Britney was busy with another customer when Kyle sat on the stool next to mine. Unsurprised to see me.

"What do you want?" I cut right to it.

He frowned, the mole on his chin moving with the movement. "Why do you assume I want something?"

"Because you're in The Burrow, my territory. So you must want something from me."

Kyle had the special ability to maintain an arrogant demeanor at all times. Even now, he leaned his elbows on the counter, the picture of poise.

"All I want is a cappuccino," he said dryly. "But since you are here, let me offer my congratulations."

Every hair on my arms stood up straight. "On what?"

"Hitting half a million followers," he said.

Could I believe him? Obviously not. The man didn't like any form of espresso, yet claimed he wanted a cappuccino. I rushed to check my phone. Yep. There it was—500,000 followers. *Holy shit.*

It was a great milestone to reach, but I didn't feel any flood of joy at the realization. All it brought me was questions of where to go from here. As if I needed more of those.

"I underestimated you, Macey," Kyle said casually. His eyes refused to meet mine, too concerned with observing the box of pastries near the register.

"What is that supposed to mean?"

"Your strategy game is perfect. Upgrading from me to Noah to get that much more influence. Great work, truly."

I slammed my phone on the counter so hard I was surprised it didn't shatter. I didn't bother asking how he knew Noah—everyone in this business in Chicago knew Noah in one way or another.

"That's not what happened. You cheated on me, Kyle. And I have never used you or Noah for followers. You know I don't care about that stuff."

I wanted to punch him in the face. I wanted to throw a tomato at him. I wanted to write a public exposé about him. Five thousand words, single spaced, Times New Roman because he hated that font.

He laughed. "Then why did you jump so quickly to look at your follower count?"

"That's not...it isn't..."

Was Kyle right? Had I become just like him, caring what others thought and always looking for the next level? *No. You know yourself, Macey.* If I was only concerned with follower count, fake dating the man about to drop off the face of the earth would be a terrible idea.

But I couldn't say that to Kyle.

"It doesn't matter." I dismissed it. "You can say whatever you want, but the truth is you're an egotistical loser overly concerned with your public appearance. You hurt me once, and you're incapable of hurting me again. So I strongly suggest you leave me alone."

I grabbed my coffee and stood up. "And you know what? Dating Noah is an upgrade from you. Because at least he would never lie to me."

"But would he keep secrets?" Kyle stood as well, our eyes catching like two boxers about to battle.

I was about to answer with a confident no, but something made me stifle it down.

"Get the fuck out of here." Britney rushed through the gate to our side of the counter, pushing on Kyle's shoulders. "I'll poison any coffee you order here or in a mile radius. I've got connections."

I stood frozen in my spot as Britney, who was at least half a foot shorter than Kyle, pushed him out. Heaving in a deep sigh, I fled the café, heading toward the elevator.

Only to forget I was in heels and running was a really bad idea.

I tripped next to the elevator. Though I caught myself before I landed on the ground, the contents of my purse tumbled in a few directions. Squatting down, I hastily reached for them all and shoved them back in an order that would make my headache worse later.

Why would Kyle go out of his way to come here and tell me this? Was it an attempt at a brag? A subtle insult?

Maybe he's jealous.

No, that would be ridiculous. He was the one who ruined everything in the first place.

The last item back in my purse was a set of notecards. Weird. I hadn't used notecards since my seventh-grade science fair, where I focused on the question: *Does music impact the growth of plants?* Scientists may say no, but my daisies that listened to classic rock grew five times more than the others.

The handwriting on the notecards wasn't even mine.

I flipped through them as I entered the elevator.

To Macey,

I can't be there every time you read a bad comment, so I hope this helps. Grab a card every time you need to be reminded how amazing you are.

Noah

Curious, I pulled out a card from the middle of the pack.

The people who leave mean comments are the ones without any self-confidence. I love how bold and confident you are.

I tucked the rest of the notecards into my purse but folded this one into my pocket.

Noah

It had been a long time since I was inside an office that wasn't a doctor's appointment or Nathan's fancy corner office.

I didn't like it.

Why was every office temperature set to below zero? Was it some intimidation tactic: *I don't need a parka because I'm tougher than you?* I shivered as I took a seat in front of the glass desk. On the other side, a velvet rolling chair whirled around to face me.

Victoria.

Macey's boss. And the user behind the *Fishly541* account.

"Noah Hansley," she said. "I recognize you. Any reason why you bombarded past my assistant and into my office?"

Victoria looked different from her photo on the *Roamer's Digest* website. As editor-in-chief, nearly everyone rolled up to her in some capacity. Chin-length brown hair hugged her jaw, and bright red lipstick blinded me. She looked like every leading villain in a movie about magazines.

Macey described her as intimidating, but all I saw was an average human who hid behind anonymous accounts like a coward.

"I think you know," I said.

Her eyebrows furrowed. "I think I don't."

"It's about how your actions are impacting Macey," I explained. "She's your top employee and a damn good one at that."

She impatiently tapped her pen against the table. "If you're referring to withholding event invitations from her, it's nothing personal. I have to give other writers opportunities no matter how much they're trending online."

"That's not what I'm referring to. Though that's a problem, too. If event staff want Macey there, it's not right to sub her out with another employee. There has to be another way to handle that."

And a way that didn't involve hurting Macey.

She pursed her lips, and I imagined her defenses rising. "Your subtle insults aside, tell me what you're referring to."

"Fishly541."

"Excuse me?"

"The anonymous Instagram you've been using to post all those negative comments about Macey."

The pen in her hands froze mid-air. Victoria moved in slow motion, like she was walking through molasses. She folded her arms and leaned back in her chair. "There are negative comments about Macey?"

This was getting frustrating. She was a great actress. "I know you've been undermining Macey for months. Frankly, it's embarrassing that you've stooped to the level of anonymously posting horrible things about your employee."

Victoria blinked, then let out a snort. "What kind of fanfiction are you writing?"

I didn't follow.

She dropped the pen onto a stack of files and sighed. "I would never do that. I don't know why you would even think that."

"But the writing and tone of the comments are the same as your articles. You've written specific things that only people who know Macey would know."

"I don't know what comments you're even talking about." She threw her arms wide, exasperated.

I pulled up Macey's Instagram on my phone and handed it to her. Victoria took it apprehensively and spent a few minutes scrolling through the comments. She scoffed and handed it back to me.

"I don't know what kind of macho man shit you're doing barging in here like this, but this sounds like something you should talk about with Macey, not me."

Victoria wasn't behind the account? I looked for common traces of lying—damp palms, fidgets, lack of eye contact—but all I saw was sincerity. That, plus the desire to punch me.

Okay, I understood the intimidation now.

"You really have nothing to do with this?"

She only glared. "Get the fuck out of my office."

I let out a short breath, and then I got the fuck out of her office.

It was almost 5:00 p.m. at this point, so I had two options. One, try to sneak out of here unnoticed. Two, purposely seek out Macey.

Those options were taken from me when I realized that Macey's desk was a few steps down from Victoria's office.

"Noah?" Macey poked her head outside her gray cubicle. "What are you doing here?"

Excellent question.

"Looking for you." I tried for suave. "Thought I could walk you home."

"Really?"

Please don't push this further.

I nodded.

"That's sweet of you. Give me a minute to pack up."

I admired her desk as she shut down her laptop and pushed her notebooks to the side. Pushpins held up a calendar with inspirational quotes as well as Polaroid pictures of her and her friends. There was one older couple in the photos—based on the similar smiles, they were her grandparents. A collection of succulents in pots gave color to the space, and she added a small amount of water in them before she was ready to go.

In the elevator, Macey asked, "What did you do today?"

I hated lying to her. Really, I did, but I didn't want to stress her out over this right now. Especially considering the embarrassment I felt over being wrong about Victoria.

"Talked with Nathan, went on a long walk around the neighborhood, donated to whale conservation," I joked.

She laughed. "That sounds like a better day than mine."

Bright sun greeted us as we exited out the revolving door. It wasn't until we were outside that I realized I had no idea where to go next. I had never been to her apartment before. Macey turned right and I followed.

"Not a good day?"

"It had its ups and downs," she said. "I found the notecards you left in my purse."

I wondered when she would find those. It was a hasty idea, done after seeing how defeated she looked at some of the comments. She smiled, and I realized there was nothing I wouldn't do to see it again.

"I hope that wasn't the low of the day."

"The opposite, actually."

Mental fist bump.

"My low was so crazy you probably won't believe it."

The smell of fresh bread from the cornerstone bakery flooded my senses, intertwining with my curiosity. I was half-tempted to pull us inside to get the details and a croissant at the same time.

"My bar for crazy things is pretty high," I said. "Tell me what it was."

She eyed me hesitantly. "Kyle came into The Burrow Café."

I racked my brain for an explanation of who that was to her and why it mattered, but I came up with nothing. "Kyle who?"

"My ex-boyfriend."

Oh, lovely. Time to have the ex talk right before I intended to ask Macey for a real relationship. I didn't particularly relish hearing about her past boyfriends.

I almost tripped over a crack in the sidewalk. "Why was your ex-boyfriend at The Burrow Café?"

"I don't know." Macey shrugged. "He was being weird, and Britney kicked him out."

"Weird?" I pressed. "Weird how?"

Macey swung her arms back and forth as we crossed the street. In the distance, someone cursed out a car that ran a red light.

"Congratulating me for reaching half a million followers while insinuating I used you and him to get those followers," she answered. "And he had the audacity to imply you're a liar."

Despite the sun warming our skin, I felt very, very cold.

"Don't worry," she continued, reaching to squeeze my bicep. "I know you're not."

Any thoughts of croissants left my head as nausea rolled in my stomach. Parts of the complex situation floated through my head like jigsaw pieces, and I tried to put them together. So far, I was hitting mismatched pairings.

"Thanks." I had a bad feeling about this situation. "You've never really talked about him before."

Some of the light left Macey's eyes. "His name is Kyle Arnold. Maybe you know him. He cheated on me, then begged for me to come back. When I said no, he told everyone I was a nobody. Hurt my reputation almost as much as he hurt me. Then he had the nerve to say I was lucky to have dated him because I got some followers out of it."

My feet froze in the middle of the sidewalk. Or maybe that was my calf muscles. Either way, I was incapable of walking.

I did know Kyle, albeit not well. We ran in similar groups. I faintly remembered Kyle mentioning he went on a few dates with a writer at *Roamer's Digest*, but I had no idea of the full story. Didn't really care to know, considering he dated a lot of people.

Now I wished I had asked for more information so I could at least try to understand the audacity he had to treat her like shit. To make her feel subpar.

Kyle must have never experienced what I'd incurred these last few months: the way that air rose out of my lungs when I looked at Macey for too long, the itch between my fingers when her palms were close to mine, the sense of emptiness when we parted ways.

The Macey of today paused a few feet ahead of me. With the setting sun, she looked ethereal—like an angel of good fortune.

"You okay?" she asked.

"Yeah." I found my footing again and caught up to her. "I know him. I thought he was an okay guy, a little desperate for fame, but apparently, he's an asshole."

"Oh, he is. Let me tell you about the time he..."

Macey recounted an old story about Kyle as dread pooled a hole in my stomach. It felt like all the progress I made these last few months came to a halt.

I knew how much it killed Macey that her ex-boyfriend lied to her, and here I was, doing nearly the same thing.

23

MACEY/NOAH

Macey

Since I left the apartment so early this morning, I beat the rush and didn't have to elbow fight with anyone on the street. In fact, I made it to the office in record timing. I spent the whole entire walk to work internally reviewing my blog strategy and also the write-up for a local restaurant review I needed to finish for *Roamer's Digest*.

Things were busy but good. So good that I was able to easily put the image of Kyle's face out of my mind. There was no point in letting an encounter with my ex-boyfriend ruin my mood. Not when I finally felt like things were coming together.

The office was quiet when I dropped my bag off at my desk and powered up my computer. It was acting extra slow today. I gave it a loving pat on the side, hoping that would stir it into operating faster.

"Macey?" Victoria called from her office. "Is that you?"

"Yes!" I yelled, a quick glance proving we were the only two here.

"You're here early," she said. "Can you come into my office?"

I rebooted my computer, hoping that would fix the issue, and headed into Victoria's office. In one hand, the latte Britney made me. In the other, my notebook. I felt ready to take on the world.

Victoria gestured for me to take a seat. The sharpness in her gaze made my stomach knot. "Do you know why I called you in here?"

I frowned, a bad sense of foreboding igniting already. It slithered down my spine, cold and unwelcome. I tried to toss it aside, considering I couldn't place a single reason. "No, I don't."

She turned her monitor around, displaying my Instagram profile. Odd, considering she wasn't the type of boss to mix work with play.

"I did some digging, and there are things I can't ignore."

With a click, she opened a new tab that displayed *Macey's Miles*, my blog.

Well, fuck. A sharp pulse pounded at the base of my skull. I thought I had more time. The blog hadn't been live that long. I had intended to work at least a few more months as I expanded it, then find a way to take it full time.

How the hell did she find this? There was no way Victoria had stumbled upon it herself.

Calculator Cal. It had to be Calculator Cal. Had he shown her? The thought made my stomach churn.

Victoria's gaze stayed level, unreadable. "Did you attend the press sneak peek of Sushi Nirvana?"

"Yes," I answered, hesitant but truthful. "As Noah's plus-one."

"That might be true, but you attended a press event on your own, unaffiliated with *Roamer's Digest*, despite the fact that *Roamer's Digest* was covering it."

My pulse roared in my ears. "I'm not following." That wasn't entirely true—I *was* following. I just didn't like where this was going. For good measure, I added, "I haven't gotten paid for anything." That had to count for something, right?

Victoria rubbed her temples. "Payment doesn't always come

in the form of a check. There's a conflict of interest here. I can't have a writer on staff creating competing content."

I thought about how I explained my contract to Daphne and Noah all those months ago. *If I'm not writing about it, I usually turn down free gifts because it could turn into a conflict of interest.*

I fought for calm, but a tremble zipped through me. There was no real defense for my blog here. I knew the risk when I made it. When Noah encouraged me to start it.

"I'm sorry, but I have no option other than to terminate your employment with *Roamer's Digest.*"

My hands went numb. My fingers were so tight around my cup that they trembled. The words split me open, punching my insides until they fell out. *Terminate your employment.*

What the fuck was happening?

"You're...firing me?"

"Effective immediately," said Victoria casually as if she hadn't turned my world upside down.

"But I've given so much to *Roamer's Digest,*" I sputtered. "Thousands of hours. I gave up my nights and weekends to cover events for you. My articles have been doing so well, and you're going to throw it all away? There must be some way we can meet in the middle."

"You're young," Victoria said simply. "You'll bounce back from this."

It didn't feel like that was true.

When she said, "You can pack your things before the rest of the office comes in," I thought I was going to cry.

Instead, I swallowed the tears and stood on my own two feet.

Palm pressed to the door of Victoria's office, I remembered something Noah said. *I look at you and see a girl with incredible potential, yet she's terrified of standing up for herself.*

Not any longer.

"I'll go," I said, meeting Victoria's eyes. "But wherever I go next, I won't allow myself to be treated like a second thought again. You may have been forced to give me opportunities, but you also took many away. You never posted my photos. You edited my articles so much they barely had my voice anymore. Why, Victoria?"

I didn't need her to reply. "Is it because you knew that if you allowed my creativity to shine, that something like this would have happened? Because maybe that's true. I considered myself lucky to be working here, under you, and look where it got me. Maybe if I had listened to myself, I would have outshone you a long time ago."

I still could.

If I wasn't so present in the moment, I might have brushed off the look on Victoria's face. Where I expected anger, I only saw pride.

I swung open the door to her office, letting myself out for the last time. I threw my things into a box and waltzed out of the office with my head held high.

It didn't matter if you felt like throwing up the whole time, if you'd ever stood up for yourself in the workplace, you were a badass.

Noah

I had been enjoying a quiet morning off, just me and my LEGOs, when a pounding sound started from outside.

When I opened the door, Macey stood there, shoulders tight, arms crossed like she was holding herself together. Her eyes, usually full of fire and mischief, were shadowed with something heavier.

Something was wrong.

I stepped aside without a word, and she walked in. She didn't pace, didn't fidget. Just stood in the middle of my living room like she wasn't sure what to do next.

I shut the door, watching her. "Scribbles?"

She exhaled, slow and shaky. That was all it took for me to cross the space between us. I didn't touch her, but I was close enough that she could if she wanted.

"What happened?" I asked.

She hesitated, then lifted her chin like she was trying to will herself into holding it together. "I just got fired."

I ricocheted a step backward. "What?"

That didn't make any sense. Macey was the best employee there. While I didn't think Victoria was supporting her growth, she had also confirmed she wasn't anonymously trashing Macey online.

"Yeah," she sniffed. The crack in her voice nearly undid me. "I thought I had more time."

Before I could think, I pulled her into my chest, stroking a hand up and down her back. She was tense, every muscle drawn tight. "What do you mean?"

"Victoria pulled me into her office and told me she found my blog." Macey let out a bitter laugh that rumbled against my shirt. "Calculator Cal must have shown it to her. I mean, it's my fault for thinking I could juggle both, but it still sucks."

Shit.

The words slammed into me like a brick to the chest. Yesterday, I showed Victoria Macey's Instagram, which I had forgotten was connected to her blog. This was my fault.

I thought I was helping, standing up for Macey, putting an end to the rumors. But all I did was put a spotlight on her—on her blog. On the very thing she wasn't ready to share.

My stomach twisted. Macey thought Calculator Cal had ratted her out. She had no idea I'd set this in motion.

I swallowed hard, guilt clawing up my throat.

I rested my chin against her hair. "It's not your fault. You have every right to be upset."

She exhaled, her breath shaky against my chest. She felt so small like this, so exhausted. "I don't know what I did to Calculator Cal to make him show my blog to Victoria."

I had to tell her the truth.

There was no way around it. Not if I wanted to be the kind of person she could trust. Not if I wanted to move forward with her without this gnawing at me, eating me alive.

I had fucked up. Now I had to own it.

"Macey," I said quietly.

She pulled back just enough to look at me, her brows drawn tight.

"I don't think it was Calculator Cal who told Victoria about your blog."

Her expression flickered with confusion before hardening. "Who was it, then?"

I swallowed. "Me."

Macey's eyes widened, and she stepped out of my arms like I'd burned her. "What?"

I forced myself to keep going. "I've had this theory for a while that Victoria was behind one of the accounts bullying you online. Yesterday, I went to her office to confront her about it. I wanted to put an end to the mean comments."

Macey's whole body went rigid. Then—

"You *what*?" she exploded. "You went to my boss's office and accused her of cyberbullying me? Do you know how bad that makes me look?"

"I think the only person it looks bad on is me," I said, trying to keep my voice level.

"Well, you're not the one who lost their job today."

I took a step toward her, but she jerked back. "Macey, I didn't mean—"

"Why didn't you *tell* me about your theory?" she cut in. Her voice was rising, thick with disbelief and something else—hurt.

"I...tried. Once or twice," I admitted. "The timing was never right."

Her mouth fell open, and she let out a bitter laugh, one that sent ice-cold dread through my chest. She whispered under her breath, "Kyle was right."

I stiffened. "Kyle?" My voice came out sharp, my own frustration snapping. "Your ex-boyfriend?"

"Oh, don't try to turn this around on me," she shot back. "Kyle implied that you might be keeping secrets. I stood up for you. Defended you. And now I feel like an idiot because guess what? You were lying to me this whole time."

Kyle? What the hell did Kyle know about anything? A jealous ex grasping at straws, trying to wedge himself between us. Just another influencer trying to climb to the top. And now Macey was quoting him like he was some kind of prophet?

I clenched my jaw, forcing down the sharp words fighting to escape. This wasn't about him. This was about me screwing up.

I exhaled slowly. "I'm sorry, Macey." And I was. More than she probably realized. "I shouldn't have kept this from you."

Her arms stayed folded tight across her chest; her stance guarded.

"But look on the bright side," I tried. "Getting fired isn't the worst thing. Now you can focus all your energy on your blog."

Macey inhaled sharply, her nostrils flaring, and when she spoke, her voice was pure venom.

"Are you serious right now?"

I sighed. "I just want what's best for you."

She threw her hands up, pacing a tight circle. "Sure, as long as it's also what you want, too. God, you're being so controlling right now."

"Controlling?" I flinched like she'd slapped me. "I'm not trying to control you."

"You're acting like a controlling boyfriend. You don't need to protect me or fight my battles for me. I'm more than capable of doing that on my own."

My heart pounded, her frustration spilling into the room and leaving no space for anything else. "I know you can. I was just trying to help. We're close enough for that."

She stopped pacing long enough to fix me with a look that cut straight through me. "Your help got me fired, Noah." Her voice trembled—not with sadness, but with pure, white-hot anger. "And you're not even my boyfriend."

The words hit harder than they should have. I clenched my jaw, forcing myself to stay still, not to reach for her, even though some instinct deep in my bones demanded to.

Macey's breath came quick and uneven, but she wasn't finished. "The only reason we've been faking a relationship is because you suggested it would benefit our careers."

"I think we're at the point where we can both acknowledge we had more reasons for agreeing to fake date than that."

Her gaze locked onto mine like a shot fired point-blank. "Like what?" she bit out, her voice low and sharp. "Or is that another secret you're going to keep from me?"

I ran a hand over my face, dragging in a breath that did nothing to clear the knot in my chest. "I'm sorry for not telling you about Victoria."

I should have stopped there. But, like an idiot, I kept talking.

"But I was afraid you'd get scared."

Macey's head jerked back like I'd physically pushed her.

Shit, shit, shit.

"Scared?" She said it full of spite, hardening the consonants. "Why did you think that?"

"Because change scares you. You hate confrontation. I don't

think you would have ever confronted Victoria if she hadn't initiated it."

In a moment, the crackling anger fled the room, leaving behind tense silence. Macey breathed hard and sniffed once, like she'd just run up and down the unsafe apartment stairs five times.

"Maybe not," she said, quiet and steady, "but that wasn't your decision to make."

"Macey—"

"We're close enough to May 15." Her tone was detached now. Final. "Let's end this fake relationship now."

No.

No, no, no.

Words clogged my throat, burning, but my mind was blank. Totally useless, giving me nothing to fix this.

Macey opened the door, pausing just long enough to throw me one last look. "I'll let you have the honor of publicly announcing our breakup."

24

MACEY/NOAH

Macey

The Burrow Bitches

> Britney: Macey what's wrong babe, you haven't responded to any of the tiktoks i sent you
>
> Ariadne: Did something happen with Noah?
>
> Britney: do we need to beat him up?
>
> Kira: I'll go knock on her door
>
> Kira: ...Macey where are you?

Nothing seemed bad when you were burrowed under the covers. The darkness brought a sense of safety over me—here, I didn't have to deal with my problems.

It reminded me of when I was a kid, playing house with my parents in our one-bedroom apartment. We had lived there until I was ten, when Dad got a big promotion at work, and we upgraded to a two-bedroom. When we played, we'd use a blanket as the pseudo roof of the house, and somehow, all three of us crammed onto the floor, staring up at the blanket above. It was dark and quiet, two words that normally meant scary, but with my parents, it was calming.

Nothing existed under the covers now, so I couldn't feel the effects of everything I'd lost in the last twenty-four hours.

My job.

Noah.

My dignity.

I poked a head outside of the blankets, only to still be met with darkness. Rain fell outside in furious sheets as angry bolts of lightning cracked through the skies. If I wasn't so pathetic, I'd get up and turn on the light switch, but that sounded like too much work.

My shoulders ached from my hunched position. I stretched them out, lifting my arms above my head, and then collapsed into the fetal position.

I didn't know how long I was curled up in bed before I heard the front door open. Kira must be home.

"Macey?" she called. A moment later, she pushed open the door to my room.

When she saw my sorry state, she ran towards me and placed a hand on my forehead. "What's wrong? Are you sick? We've been texting you all day."

Let's rip the Band-Aid off.

"I got fired today," I said. "And Noah and I got into a huge fight."

"Oh my God." Kira dropped her purse onto the floor and kicked off her flats, then climbed into bed next to me. "Tell me everything."

I did. Starting with Noah going behind my back to confront Victoria, to how I was then fired the next day.

Kira listened intently, nodding at the right places, offering me silent understanding. But when I was finished, she exclaimed, "This is amazing!"

What.

The.

Hell.

She added, "Not the Noah stuff—I'm going to kill him for that—but everything with *Roamer's Digest*."

I glared at her. "Why would you say that?"

"Macey, my best friend, I say this with love," she said, squeezing my cheeks with her palms. "*Roamer's Digest* was a great place to start your career, but think about all the late nights you spent fixing articles, the weekends you spent dreading Monday, all the effort you put into appeasing Victoria. You got comfortable being walked over, and it's time for you to do the walking now. You would have stayed there forever, making excuses about why it's not the right time to chase your dreams. Sometimes the universe recognizes the bullshit we tell ourselves and gives us the kick we need to put ourselves first. That might mean getting knocked to the ground, but you pull yourself up again even stronger than before."

Hot tears pricked the back of my eyes. "I don't feel stronger."

"That's the thing. Sometimes other people recognize your strength before you do," she said. "And that leaves you no choice but to trust the potential your loved ones see in you."

There was a beat, and I tried hard to stop the rising tears, but it was impossible. I frantically wiped under my eyes.

Kira's words reminded me of Noah, who always encouraged me to take my work into my own hands. My career was important to me. I wanted to grow and be the best version of myself, but had I even been happy at *Roamer's Digest*? Or had I tolerated it for my mother's sake?

I had struggled with standing up for myself. I knew how to be my own advocate in a personal sense, but replicating that in a professional environment was much more difficult for me. But now, I wondered, what was the worst thing that could happen if you stood up for yourself? You get fired?

That happened to me anyways.

Before I knew it, the tears had taken over. They tore themselves from my body, leaving me tense and trembling, gasping for air between wracking sobs. The tears were just as much for losing my job as they were for losing Noah.

Kira and I lay there in silence for a few minutes after my tears dried. Some energy had returned to my body, but I still felt defeated.

There was a loud knock on the door before someone let themselves in. Ariadne and Britney pushed the door open.

"We brought cookies." Britney set a cream-colored box on the bed. The Velvet Whisk was the best bakery in town, and my stomach rumbled looking at it. "Chocolate chip."

For all of Britney's jokes and lackadaisical attitude, she knew how to be empathetic. It showed on her face as she sat on the corner of the bed. Ariadne climbed over me to perch on the other side.

They were worried. I hadn't checked my phone since this morning, but I was sure there were lots of unanswered messages.

Ariadne's warm gaze caused another swell of emotions to form in my throat. "Do you want to talk about it?"

I recounted the story to them.

When I was done, Britney jumped off the bed. "I'll kill Noah. I will shove this box of cookies down his throat, make him choke on the only thing good in this world, and then—"

A laugh escaped me. "No, no, we don't need to kill him."

"Or waste a perfectly good box of cookies," said Ariadne through a mouthful of chocolate.

Britney huffed dramatically but sat down again. "What do you need us to do then?"

"Nothing," I said. "Just stay with me a while longer."

Ariadne smiled and threaded a hand through mine. "That we can do."

Tomorrow will be better.

And if not, I'll keep saying it until it's true.

Noah

The rhythm of my footsteps barely drowned out the chaos in my head.

I'd barely slept the last few days. Instead of staying in bed this morning, I laced up my running shoes at dawn and took off, hoping I could outrun the thoughts clawing at my brain.

Spoiler alert: I couldn't.

My ankle was doing much better, but I welcomed the pain of the dull ache today.

The park was quiet this early, with only a few other runners and dog walkers scattered along the trail. The air was crisp, the kind that bit at my lungs in a way that almost felt good. Like maybe if I pushed myself hard enough, I could burn through the ache sitting heavy in my chest.

But every stretch of pavement, every curve in the path, felt like a new place to replay the last few months.

Macey and I had walked through this park once. It was after a press dinner that went too long, and neither of us wanted to go home yet. She had kicked off her heels and made some grand speech about how *bloggers weren't afraid to walk barefoot in the city*. I'd called her a lunatic, she'd called me a snob, and we had ended up on a bench, sharing a bag of convenience store peanut M&M's at midnight.

The same bench passed by in a blur.

I picked up my pace.

Macey wasn't wrong last night. I *had* made decisions for her. I thought I was protecting her, but I was just deciding for her, as if I knew better.

She was right about something else, too. I had suggested the fake relationship because it made sense. Because it was mutually beneficial. Because we could both get something out of it.

But somewhere along the way, it stopped being about that.

I stopped thinking about the benefits and started thinking about her.

How she made everything feel lighter. How she challenged me, pushed me, made me laugh even when I didn't want to. How she looked at me like I was someone worth trusting.

Except she didn't now.

I exhaled hard, shoving my hands onto my hips as I slowed to a stop near the water's edge. The lake was still, the surface reflecting the sky above.

The whole point of this run was to clear my head, but all it had done was solidify what I already knew.

I wasn't ready to let her go.

And I sure as hell wasn't going to let our last conversation be the way this ended.

After running as much as I could before my ankle—and, let's be honest, my lungs—needed a break, I checked my phone's notifications, only to be flooded with missed calls from my sister. For someone who claimed to have phone anxiety and got nervous calling the dentist's office, she had left me an unsettling number of messages. I scrolled through them with mounting dread, my stomach tightening with each notification.

Was something wrong? Did something happen to Daphne?

Oh.

Oh, shit.

I double-checked the date on my phone. May 15. My heart sank. I had been so consumed with my failed fake relationship with Macey that I had completely forgotten the date. Daphne's semester had ended, and she was flying into Chicago today. Right now, actually.

We were supposed to be packing up for our big summer road trip—the cross-country adventure we'd planned since last year before everything in my life went sideways.

What the hell was I going to say to Daphne? I couldn't cancel the trip. We both needed this. But it didn't feel right to leave Chicago with my life in shambles. My thoughts whirled in panic, my brain trying to grasp a solution as if I could fix everything in the short time before she arrived.

I checked her location on my phone. She was almost at my apartment. If I hurried, I could beat her there.

But first—a pit stop. I jogged down the street, my mind racing as fast as my feet. I needed a peace offering, something to soften the blow of my negligence. Donuts. Mario's Donuts. Her favorites. I grabbed a half dozen and sprinted back to my place, barely beating her to the door.

I unlocked the apartment and left the door slightly ajar, knowing Daphne would let herself in like she always did.

"Way to leave me on read!" Daphne's voice rang out the moment she stepped inside, her tone laced with teasing accusation. But her expression softened the second she saw the white box in my hand, her eyes lighting up.

"Are those Mario's Donuts?" she asked, her voice a mixture of excitement and exasperation.

"Only the best for my best," I said, grinning as I opened the lid to reveal her favorite treats.

Her hair had grown longer, I noticed. Now it fell in tight curls down to her mid-back. When had that happened? Had I really been so wrapped up in my own drama that I missed these small changes?

She dropped her suitcase by the door and plopped down on the couch beside me, then crossed her legs. "I know you're trying to butter me up with donuts before apologizing for ghosting me. And just so you know, I'm going to need a lot more sugar to forgive you for leaving me hanging all morning."

"I can arrange that," I said, handing her the first donut as a peace offering. "I really am sorry. Today was...well, let's just say it wasn't my best day."

"Oh, how the tables have turned." She took a giant bite out of the cheesecake donut and spoke through a mouthful. "You know, I've been waiting for the day you went through an existential crisis while I was the stable one."

I raised an eyebrow, taking a slower, more controlled bite of my own donut. "What makes you think I'm having an existential crisis?"

Daphne rolled her eyes in that way only she could—exaggerated, like she couldn't believe I was asking something so obvious. She picked apart another donut, intent on tasting every flavor in the box.

"Please," she said, "I can see it in your eyes."

"What, do they look bloodshot?"

"No," she said, her voice softening. "They look like mine did last year—before I had any clue what I was doing with my life. And guess who helped me figure it out?" She jabbed a finger into my chest. "Now it's my turn to help you."

I sighed, running a hand through my hair as I leaned back against the couch cushions. It felt strange, confiding in Daphne like this. Growing up, I'd always been the one fixing things—her problems became our problems. Mine were never hers.

But now, sitting here with her, it struck me that we weren't kids anymore. She wasn't the little sister who needed me to pick her up from school or help her with homework. She was an adult, smart and capable in ways that surprised me sometimes.

"Fine," I said, giving in. "This week has been rough."

I told her everything—about Macey, about my mistake with Victoria, about the way I'd let everything fall apart because I didn't know how to hold on. Daphne listened without interrupting, nodding thoughtfully as if she were mentally cataloging my problems, sorting through them like some puzzle she was determined to solve.

When I finished, she sat back, crossing her arms. "You know, when I said 'existential crisis,' I didn't think I'd be right, but damn, Noah. You really went all in."

I groaned and dropped my face into my hands. "I know. I've screwed everything up."

"Maybe you've screwed some things up," she corrected, her voice light but firm, "but not everything. You're being dramatic."

"I'm not being dramatic—"

"We can fix this."

"*We?*" I looked up, confused.

"Yes, we." Her tone was matter-of-fact, no room for debate. "We can't go on our road trip until you settle things here."

I started to protest. "Daph, you don't have to—"

"Noah, stop." Her voice turned serious, and I stopped mid-sentence. "I know you think you have to handle everything on your own, but you don't. People care about you. I care about you. You put everything on hold for me when I needed help. Why can't I do the same for you?"

I stared at her, at the conviction in her eyes.

"Because you're my little sister. It's different."

"It's not different," she insisted. "Not when you're family."

She paused, giving me a knowing look before adding, "And I'm sure Macey would be interested to hear how you truly feel about her."

My heart thudded in my chest. Macey. It was always Macey.

"I don't know—" I began, but Daphne cut me off, her voice growing impatient.

"Stop overthinking. Just answer this: What do you *want*, Noah?"

I hesitated. What *did* I want? For months, I'd been running in circles, trying to keep everything together without asking myself that simple question.

"I—" I stammered, unsure of what to say.

Daphne poked me again, relentless. "What. Do. You. Want?"

"Macey," I blurted out before I could stop myself.

She got up, grabbed a notebook from the shelf, and flipped it open, pen in hand. "Perfect. Because we are not leaving until I help you win her back."

I nodded, still reeling from how quickly she'd taken charge of the situation.

Daphne smiled, her eyes gleaming with determination. "Let's get to work."

25

MACEY

The Burrow Bitches

> Kira: Everyone chime in with their inspiration to Macey today!

> Kira: I'll go first. Macey, you're a talented writer who's gonna go far.

> Ariadne: You don't need a man to be successful! You're an independent woman

> Britney: you're a bad bitch with a fat ass

> Kira: Not quite what I had in mind, but I agree

> Macey: I love you guys

Today I discovered that I had a limit on the time I could spend pitying myself. Turned out it was three days. I spent three whole days in bed wallowing, eating nothing but Chinese takeout while binge-watching *Love Island*. Both the US and UK versions.

After a brief stint of considering applying to be a contestant on the reality show, I realized I had spiraled enough. I wasn't made to be on TV. I was made to be a writer.

And I wasn't going to let this setback ruin my career.

I jumped into gear, prioritizing my goals and how to achieve them. Personal goals, especially dating-centric goals, would have to wait. Top of my list?

Growing my blog.

Getting fired was an experience unlike any other. Days ago, I thought my worth had been demolished because of it, but it made me realize how much I was worth away from *Roamer's Digest*.

I could do this. I knew I could.

I just had to figure out…how.

There were so many ways to improve but also so many ways to fail. I found myself with a newfound respect for anyone who started their own business. Without the set boundaries of an employer, how did you know what to do?

I guessed that was the point. You did whatever you wanted.

Write what you know was one of the first pieces of advice I ever received. It'd worked well for me in everything I'd done. So now I'd start with what I knew.

My laptop lit up with enthusiasm as I began typing—if only my brain could match that energy. I'd tried working from my apartment earlier, but the couch had me convinced it was a sanctuary for movie binges, not productivity.

The original plan was to camp out at The Burrow Café, but the idea of bumping into someone I knew felt counterproductive. Instead, I opted for a charming little neighborhood café with the coziest chairs and cheesecake so good it could solve existential crises.

I had only been here a few minutes, in the corner booth, when someone I knew walked in. Not just anyone.

Noah Hansley.

And he was wearing...a tie?

He paused in the doorway, his gaze sweeping the room like he was searching for someone. Was it me? Surely not. His wavy hair was smoothed back, his stubble freshly shaved, and his outfit—sharp and undeniably expensive—made him look like he'd stepped out of a high-end ad campaign.

Why was he so dressed up? Oh no. Was he on a date?

Fortunately, my corner booth was well hidden, so I was able to watch him walk to the table where a familiar-looking woman sat. I had to hold back a grin. That wasn't any woman—it was the professor whose lecture we sat on at the University of Illinois Chicago.

Despite my residual anger toward what Noah did, the sight flooded me with joy. I hoped that meant good things for his application for the fall semester.

I turned back to my work, though the weight of seeing Noah still pressed against me. My fingers hovered over the keyboard, my mind already racing through everything on my to-do list. But something was different now—I was doing everything for *me*, not for anyone else.

Maybe, just maybe, I was building a better future. One where I could be happy and fulfilled. Or at the very least, one where I spent fewer late nights eating ice cream while revisiting old articles, searching for clarity that never seemed to come.

After a few minutes, I finally checked my email inbox. Spam, spam, new comment on the blog, spam, invitation to a resort, spam.

Wait.

I clicked on the email, my stomach twisting before I even read the subject line.

It wasn't just any invitation—it was for a couple's vacation.

My throat tightened.

Delete.

The email was gone, but the thought remained, stubborn and unshakable.

Memories of Opal Serenity crept in before I could stop them —the way the ocean breeze had tangled my hair, the lazy mornings in a bed too big for just me, the way Noah had looked at me across the breakfast table, his usual sarcasm softened into something real. Something dangerous.

I had gone into that trip thinking I knew exactly who Noah was—just another arrogant influencer with a carefully curated life and a knack for getting what he wanted.

But I had been so wrong.

He was different. So much kinder, more genuine than I had let myself believe. He remembered the little things, noticed details about me that I hadn't even realized were worth noticing.

Now everything felt wrong.

I pushed back from my desk, rubbing my hands over my face. I was still angry with him. Still hurt. Still not ready to forgive him for making decisions about my life like I wasn't capable of handling it myself.

But damn it, I missed him.

I missed his teasing, his unwavering confidence, the way he could read my moods with just a glance. I missed the way he made everything feel lighter. I missed his presence, even though he was on the other side of the café.

What was I supposed to do with these feelings?

I sighed, leaning back in my chair, staring at my empty inbox like it held the answer.

It didn't.

And right now neither did I.

"Where's Noah?" my mom asked, her tone casual as she poured me a glass of water. "We were hoping to meet him."

I blinked, trying to shove down the pang of discomfort that hit me. Dinner with my parents had crept up faster than I anticipated. Maybe it was because I'd been throwing every ounce of my energy into my blog these past few days. Repurposing old, unpublished articles that Victoria had rejected at *Roamer's Digest* and finally using my own photography, my way. I'd poured myself into it, and it felt freeing. But Noah was still a fresh wound.

I had brought up Noah to my parents a few times. They followed my blog and occasionally checked social media, so he wasn't a secret I could hide from them anyways.

"Oh." I fumbled for a moment, even though I'd rehearsed this conversation a hundred times in my head. "We broke up."

The words dropped like stones into the room. Both of my parents froze, jaws slightly open in surprise.

The clink of silverware on plates halted, and suddenly, the air felt heavier.

"I'm sorry, baby," my mom said, her voice gentle as she sat down across from me at the dinner table. Her eyes softened with concern, searching mine for more information.

"It's fine. It happens." I shrugged, trying to brush it off, but the truth was more complicated.

"But you guys were in a fake relationship, right?" my dad asked, his brows knitting together as he stabbed a piece of sausage with a little too much force. His mustache had grown and curled at the ends. Something about that, and the tired chestnut eyes, made me feel nostalgic.

I laughed. A fake relationship sounded extra silly when my dad was saying it. "Yeah. It always had an expiration date. We just decided to go our separate ways early."

I wondered if they could understand that. My parents had

been together since they were sixteen, through every challenge and complication life threw at them. Their bond was built on years of shared experiences and resilience, forged through being young parents who had to grow up fast. I admired their marriage, their ability to weather any storm that came their way.

But Noah and I were different. We didn't have that kind of foundation. Now, without him, I feared people would start asking questions, speculating about why we had broken up. People would think they knew more than they did.

Mom gave me a small, encouraging smile, her eyes kind. Her blonde hair was pinned up today, but a few stray strands had escaped, falling loosely around her face. Dad, with the ease of a partner who had done this a thousand times before, reached over and gently tucked the loose strands back into place.

It was a simple gesture, but one that spoke volumes. He had always been good at the little things—taking care of us in the small, meaningful ways that added up over time.

Despite everything that had gone wrong between us, Noah had taken care of me, too. In his own way. He carried a spare inhaler for me, just in case. He left me notes on bad days, little reminders that I wasn't alone. And he had encouraged me to leave *Roamer's Digest*, even when I wasn't ready to hear the truth. He saw things in me I hadn't seen in myself.

"Well, he's missing out," Mom said firmly, breaking the silence and snapping me back to the present.

I managed a weak smile, appreciating her attempt to comfort me, even if the words didn't quite land the way she intended.

"Anyways," Dad said, changing the subject as he poured more sauce onto his plate. "How's work?"

Here it was, the moment every child dreaded telling their parents. *Just be honest, Macey. You've got this.*

"Actually…" I hesitated, then took a deep breath. "I got fired."

For the second time that evening, both of my parents' jaws

dropped. Mom's fork clattered against her plate, her wide eyes darting toward the ceiling as if searching for divine intervention.

"It really sucked at first," I continued quickly, trying to keep the conversation from spiraling into panic mode. "But honestly? It's been a good thing."

"A good thing?" Mom sputtered, her laugh tinged with disbelief. "Macey, this was your dream job! How could losing it be a good thing?"

I shook my head, a strange sense of relief washing over me as I prepared to tell the truth I'd been holding back for so long.

"No, Mom. It wasn't my dream. I stayed because I thought it was what you wanted for me. But I was miserable. It wasn't the worst job, sure, but it wasn't what I loved. I worked so hard, and most of it just got rejected.

"I don't care about climbing the corporate ladder. I don't care about working for a magazine. I know that's hard to hear because it was your dream once, but I think I stayed as long as I did because of how much *you* loved it."

As the words spilled out, I realized just how much I had been holding back. Saying it out loud made everything clearer. I wasn't letting her down. I was choosing my own path, and it didn't have to be the same as hers.

Mom's face softened, and she set her utensils down, then reached across the table to take my hand. Her grip was warm and reassuring. "Macey, I had no idea you felt that way," she said, her voice gentle. "I loved the idea of the job because I thought *you* loved it. But if you weren't happy, then I'm glad you're moving on. Yes, working for a magazine was once my dream, but dreams change. Now my dream is seeing you happy, living your life the way you want to. And if *Roamer's Digest* wasn't giving you that, then I say good riddance."

I swallowed hard, fighting back tears that threatened to well up. "I felt like I ruined so many chances for you to do what you loved."

"Ruined?" she echoed, her voice filled with disbelief. "You didn't ruin anything, baby. You and your father are what I love. The things that matter to me aren't my career, but the life we've built together. Work doesn't fill my heart—being with my family does. Sharing meals with you. Hearing about your day. Eating your dad's overcooked pasta."

"Hey!" Dad protested with a playful grin.

Mom shot him a teasing look before turning back to me, her smile warm and full of love. "You're my dream, Macey. And your days are too short and too precious to spend doing what you think someone else wants for you. It takes courage to stand up for yourself, and I'm proud of you for finding that courage."

"And besides," Dad added with a wink, "everyone gets fired at least once in their life. It's practically a rite of passage."

I snorted, the tension breaking as laughter bubbled up. If I ever got fired again, it would be from my own venture. The thought felt empowering, not scary.

"Thank you," I said, feeling lighter than I had in a long time. "Getting fired has forced me to think about my next steps, and I've been working on my blog twenty-four seven."

Mom raised her brows, curiosity dancing in her eyes as she released my hand and resumed eating her pasta. "And how is the blog going?"

I twirled a forkful of pasta and held it up in a mock toast. "*Macey's Miles* is going very well, thank you. It'll be a little bit of time before I'm making a full salary from it, but I've got savings in the meantime."

"That's great news," said Dad. "Good things take time."

After finishing the pasta on my plate, I spent a few minutes giving them a behind-the-scenes look at my blog. All my plans, goals, photos. It really was a relief to have not just their approval but their excitement.

Dad had just excused himself for a few minutes when Mom took my hand. "Professionally, everything seems to be working out, and I'm so proud of you. But you still look upset. Unsatisfied. What is it?"

I sighed, wishing I could bury myself in the remaining carbs instead. "It's everything with Noah. I know we weren't a real couple, but the hurt from losing him was real."

"Why did you guys break up?" Mom twisted her mouth, searching for the right words. "Or, uh, end your agreement?"

I sighed, tracing a finger along the rim of my cup. "He did some things he shouldn't have without asking me. He had good intentions, but it blew up in our faces. We got into a huge fight about it."

Mom leaned back in her chair, giving me a knowing look. "That sounds like typical relationship drama to me. I don't think you'd be this upset over someone you only had fake feelings for in a fake relationship."

I hesitated, the admission sticking in my throat. "Yeah, I guess some of it got real."

Her expression softened. "Noah seems like a great guy. I'm sorry he upset you, but if he had good intentions, I'm sure he's regretting it."

I exhaled slowly, picking at the hem of my sleeve. "Yeah. Probably."

Mom smiled, a glint of something playful in her eyes. "Maybe he's missing you as much as you're missing him right now."

My cheeks burned. "*Mom!*"

She laughed, the sound warm and teasing. "Just calling it like I see it, baby." She stood and headed toward the kitchen.

"Now, I baked some extra cookies. You'll have to take a few home with you."

On the train home, cookies in hand, all I could think about was Noah. I missed him. That was the simplest, most undeniable truth.

I turned my phone over in my hands, debating. If I texted him, would it be the start of fixing things? Or just another mistake?

Was there a chance for us to take a shot at something for real this time? No lies, where nothing was fake. I contemplated if we could handle raw honesty and feelings, without the pressure of filtering our best moments for the online world to judge.

It was scary.

But then again, so was the thought of living without him.

26

NOAH

Daphne and Nathan waited for me as I met with my manager Ezra. He had been dreading my announcement that I was taking a break from social media, but today he helped me workshop how to best deliver the message.

"Make it about the journey," he had told me. *"People don't follow you because you're this 'cool guy.' They follow you because, whether you know it or not, they see themselves in you. You're flawed. You don't have it all figured out. Neither do they. Be honest and show them that. Tell them you're still searching for yourself and invite them along for the ride. That's your story."*

So that's what I did. And then I immediately turned my phone off. The public's reaction would be a problem for future me. Not like I didn't have any other preexisting problems: I had a lot to figure out ever since an acceptance email from the University of Illinois Chicago hit my inbox.

Daphne and Nathan had taken over a bench and were halfway through the hot dogs I'd bought them earlier, each exaggerated bite clearly designed to mock my generosity.

"How'd it go?" Daphne asked, wiping a streak of mustard

from the corner of her mouth as I crossed the street toward them.

"Good," I said, shoving my hands into my pockets and trying not to sound too relieved. "I'm officially on a break for the road trip."

"Perfect!" Her eyes lit up with the kind of excitement usually reserved for free samples or last-minute concert tickets. "But it's not road trip time yet."

"Why not?" Nathan asked. "I thought you guys had been planning this forever."

"Noah has to win back Macey first," Daphne stated matter-of-factly.

Nathan arched a brow but finished his hot dog without comment. For someone who enjoyed the finer things in life, he could put away two chili cheese dogs like they were filet mignons. Clearly, Daphne had already debriefed him on my relationship drama. It was practically their love language as my sister and cousin—conspiring behind my back in the name of "fun" or, more often, "chaos."

"Go on, Noah," Daphne prodded with a knowing grin. "Tell us how you're gonna do it."

I rolled my eyes. "I'm going to the opening of the Astor Royale, a new luxury hotel, tonight. Macey will coincidentally be there, too."

"Coincidence?" Daphne pressed, tilting her head. "Or is that what Instagram stalking told you?"

I gave her a flat look. "I prefer the term strategic information gathering."

Nathan snorted. "Doesn't it feel a little backward to go to a press event after you just announced a social media break?"

"I never said I was breaking from *all* social interactions," I countered. "Just the ones that don't involve winning my ex—" I stopped myself, inhaling sharply. "Winning Macey back."

Daphne's eyes gleamed. "Oh, the drama is going to be so good tonight."

I exhaled, already regretting ever telling them anything.

A press event was the last thing I needed. My mind was already spinning with all the things I still needed to organize before Daphne and I left for the road trip. I really didn't need to stand in a crowd of over-dressed strangers plastering on fake smiles for cameras. Or, at least, that's what I thought until I noticed Macey post about the event.

This could be my last chance to see her. My last chance to make things right.

I didn't expect her to forgive me. That wasn't the point. What I wanted—no, needed, was for her to understand why things went the way they did. I wanted her to know how much I cared about her, even if it was too late. The pain of imagining her walking out of my life for good was almost unbearable.

"Shit," I whispered to myself. "I have no idea what I'm going to say."

"You have to tell her the truth," said Daphne as if it were the simplest thing out there.

And maybe it was. I used to think relationships were inherently selfish—people always wanting something from someone else. Give and take, but mostly take. But I didn't fall in love with Macey because I wanted something from her. I fell in love with her because, without even trying, she gave me everything—affection, kindness, empathy.

Maybe that was the best kind of relationship. The kind where you brought nothing to the table except yourself and somehow walked away with more than you ever thought possible.

I never had many close relationships. Never cared enough to hold on to people before they slipped away. But then there was *her.* And for the first time, I wanted to hold on with everything I had.

I just hadn't realized that holding on too tight could push someone away. Instead of letting Macey decide what was best for herself, I had tried to take over completely. I had turned us into something uneven, something controlled. But we worked best as partners—both on and off social media. Equals. I needed her to know that.

"I will," I said. "I can't leave for three months without telling her how I really feel."

Daphne grinned and clapped me on the back, nearly knocking the air out of me. "That's the spirit! Now go grovel like your life depends on it."

Nathan, who'd been playing the role of Silent Spectator up to this point, finally let out a sigh. He leaned toward Daphne, muttering under his breath, "You didn't need me for this."

She shot him a look, pursing her lips. "You can learn a thing or two from Noah. You never date! At least he's been in a relationship these last few months."

"A fake relationship," Nathan deadpanned.

"Better than no relationship," Daphne countered, flicking a fry at him. "Besides, it was never fake to Noah."

I cocked my head. "I never said that."

She sighed dramatically as if this was exhausting for *her.* "That's sibling telepathy, big bro. I won't question what works for me."

"For you?" I scoffed. "How is this for you?"

"I've always wanted a sister," she said solemnly as if I had denied her some lifelong dream.

I rolled my eyes, stealing the last bite of her hot dog as I stood. "Let's get out of here. I need to get ready for a very important event to attend tonight and Nathan probably needs to polish his shoe collection again."

Nathan flipped me off as Daphne dissolved into laughs.

But none of that mattered.

Tonight, I'd see Macey. And maybe I'd find the words to tell her everything I hadn't been able to say before.

27

MACEY

The Burrow Bitches

> Macey: Guess who's attending her first press event as Macey's Miles?

Britney: hmm i don't know, could it be chicago's newest it girl, macey?

Kira: You're going to kill it!

Ariadne: I can't wait until you're rich and famous

I had never been so nervous to do something I'd done a million times before.

Tonight was the media event for the opening of a new hotel in Chicago, The Astor Royale, and this was my very first press invite as part of *Macey's Miles*. Recent changes in my life were all sparked by covering a resort opening in Aruba, so needless to say, there was a niche here for the taking.

The nerve-wracking part was covering the event as part of

my new blog. What if someone asked too many questions about why I left *Roamer's Digest*? What if they thought I couldn't do it on my own? What if someone *laughed*?

Ugh. I was convinced that no matter how successful you were, there would always be moments of insecurity.

I hoped that if I walked into The Astor Royale with confidence, they might not even notice I was an experienced professional turned newbie blogger. To help blend in, I wore an all-black dress, silky and smooth. I took out my braid and let the soft waves flow down around my face and down my back. A little bit of dark makeup and red lipstick rounded out the look of someone who belonged.

The moon hung low in the sky just over the new hotel. Its grand facade gleamed under the streetlights, and the sound of laughter and clinking glasses echoed faintly from the lobby.

As I approached the front entrance, I saw the impeccably dressed doormen greeting guests, their sharp eyes scanning the crowd. One large man held a clipboard and pen, checking names of people as they entered. I froze.

What if there was a mistake? What if my name wasn't on the list? What if I had to do the humiliating walk of shame home, a nobody who dared to believe she could make it in this world?

My feet itched to turn back. A quiet, self-preserving part of me whispered that this wasn't my scene—that I was out of my depth, playing pretend in a space that didn't belong to me. I imagined retreating to my apartment, curling up with a pint of ice cream, numbing the sting of failure with reruns of trashy reality shows.

But then I saw him.

Kyle.

The oak tree beside me provided just enough shadow to keep me hidden, but I still felt like a total coward, lurking there as I tracked his every move.

Kyle strolled past the bouncer without so much as a pause, slipping into the hotel like he owned the place.

Was I really going to stand in the shadows and let *him*—of all people—make me feel small?

Absolutely not.

Straightening my posture, I took a deep breath and marched toward the entrance, willing my face into one of calm confidence.

The doorman with the clipboard gave me a polite but expectant look. "Name?"

"Macey Monroe," I said, steady and sure.

He ran a finger down the list, then handed me a badge. "You're all set. Enjoy your evening, Ms. Monroe."

That was it?

I exhaled, the tension uncoiling from my shoulders as I stepped through the grand double doors. Inside, the air hummed with soft jazz and the clinking of champagne glasses. Guests in designer outfits moved through the lobby, their conversations a blur of laughter and murmured business deals.

I had been bracing for rejection, for some kind of confirmation that I didn't belong here. But it hadn't come.

Because I did belong.

With a small, triumphant smile, I adjusted the strap of my bag, squared my shoulders, and stepped fully into the golden glow of the hotel.

I took a slow breath, letting my eyes sweep over the space. Floor-to-ceiling windows framed the skyline, the city lights twinkling like scattered diamonds. A sprawling floral arrangement sat in the center of the lobby, a statement piece in soft blush and ivory, no doubt strategically placed for photo ops. Servers in crisp white jackets glided through the crowd, balancing trays of bubbling champagne and delicate hors d'oeuvres.

I moved carefully, weaving through clusters of well-dressed guests. Every step felt like a tiny act of rebellion, a silent declaration that I belonged here just as much as the PR executives, journalists, and influencers who seemed to navigate the room with effortless ease.

It felt like I was living in my future.

And then I crashed into a man's side.

Oh, no. My body immediately recognized the forearm. A little pathetic that I could recognize someone from their forearm alone, but well. This was where I was in life.

"Macey?" Noah's voice was laced with confusion as his gaze locked onto me.

I instinctively took a step back, the soft *ding* of the elevator doors shutting behind me like a dramatic exclamation point to my predicament. "What are you doing here?"

He blinked, his expression a mix of curiosity and amusement. "I was hoping to see you here, actually."

"Really?" I hesitated, already feeling the heat rise to my face.

Noah shoved his hands into the pockets of his suit pants, his shoulders shifting like he wasn't entirely sure how to stand. "Yeah. I've really enjoyed your last few blog posts, and I saw you share something about tonight, so I put two and two together."

Hearing that sent a rush of emotions crashing into me— excitement, trepidation, the ache of missing him.

And then there was the simple fact that he looked *good*.

The kind of good that made my stomach tighten unfairly, like my body had decided to betray me entirely.

His black suit was perfectly tailored, skimming his frame in all the right ways. The top button of his crisp white dress shirt was undone, just enough to hint at the casual confidence he carried so well. And his hair was slightly tousled, giving him the image of someone walking the line between polished and reckless.

Not fair.

"If you're interested," he said, "I can point out some important people to talk to." He exhaled. "But no pressure."

I smiled, despite my heart kicking up. "I am interested."

Okay. Okay. This would be fine. Just a guy helping his ex-fake-girlfriend crush a press event in a hotel lobby. Nothing to see here, folks.

Noah settled himself against the wall next to me, a polite distance away so no part of us touched. Disappointment flickered inside me before I could chase it away.

"So that guy"—he pointed to a bald man dressed in Armani—"is the CEO of the hotel chain. Big talker, you'll get good quotes from him. And she"—he signaled toward the bar where a woman in a blood red dress was stirring a cocktail, "is the PR lead, Lina. She's got a lot of stories about the hotel."

"Thank you," I said. We both continued to stand there for a few minutes, watching the crowd in front of us like a wave, ebbing and flowing. "I appreciate the help."

The more I thought about Noah, the more I realized how he'd always been there. Maybe not initially there *for me* but present regardless. I realized he'd continue to be there, even if he dropped off the face of social media forever. It was like an invisible, unbreakable string ran between us, stretching vast distances and tightening in the moments that mattered most.

"Of course," he said. "I just wanted you to know that even though I'm always here to help, I don't want you to feel like I'm controlling you or forcing you to do something. You were right. I went overboard before, and I'm sorry I handled the situation so badly. All I want to give you now is honesty and direction."

My breath hitched.

"Noah, I—"

"Oh, Lina's free." He gave my shoulders a gentle nudge. "Go talk to her."

"But—"

"Macey, you came here for a reason. Don't let me get in the way of your dreams."

You're not, I wanted to scream. *Whatever dream I have, you're in it.*

The buzz of the lights overhead did nothing to combat the growing feeling of unreality that I carried with me toward the bar. I turned my head over my shoulder once and was met with an encouraging wink from Noah. I stared for a minute, gathering up all the details, like the exact shade of green of his button-down shirt and the casual way he leaned against the wall.

"Hi," I introduced myself to the grinning PR lead. "I'm Macey."

Lina, with cascading dark brown hair and the kindest gray eyes, shook my hand. "I know who you are," she said. "And what you're doing here tonight."

Nausea swam in my stomach.

"You and Noah are showing off as the power couple of the town." Lina laughed. "And I can only hope you write something amazing about tonight."

Immediately, my spiraling seized, only to be replaced by a different wave of panic. *She doesn't know that Noah and I aren't together anymore. Not that we were ever together. Ugh. I don't even know anymore.*

How should I play this?

Noah, with his bright green eyes and relentless smile, stared at us. I made eye contact with him yet again and he mouthed, "You got this."

"Yeah, we're pretty powerful," I said, then smoothly added, "And speaking of writing, did you know I've started my own blog?"

"Oh my gosh!" Lina's hand flew to her mouth. "Tell me everything."

So I did. Lina told me everything about the hotel too—history, plans for the future, fun facts. When our conversation came to a lull, I handed her a business card.

"Good for you, Macey," she said. "I hope we can collaborate again."

I thanked her and left, resisting the urge to fist-bump toward the sky.

Noah waited expectedly by the wall, having not moved an inch during the time I was gone. "How did it go?"

"Amazing." I didn't mention the power couple comment. "Thanks for the encouragement."

"It was all you, Scribbles."

"I didn't know you'd be here tonight," I said, hoping he could hear the sincerity in my voice.

"I know," Noah replied, a grin tugging at the corner of his lips as if he were in on some private joke. "I guess that makes me the stalker, then."

I tilted my head back against the wall we were both leaning on, mirroring his easy posture. "I guess we both are."

The comfortable silence between us was brief before I said, "I saw your post about taking a break for the summer. You were so open with everyone. I like that you're going to see what happens when you get back, instead of making empty promises."

"Yeah," he said, his voice lighter than I remembered it. "I finally summoned the courage to be honest with my audience." His gaze softened as it settled on me. "Thanks to you."

Was it getting warm in here, or was that just me?

"What's happening with school?" I asked, desperate for a topic change to distract me from the way my pulse had started racing.

He tucked his hands into his pockets, the sheepishness returning. "I'll be attending the University of Illinois Chicago this fall."

My jaw dropped, and before I could stop myself, I pushed off the wall like it had burned me. "No way!" Forget decorum—this was definitely hug territory.

Wrapping my arms around his middle, his surprised laugh vibrated against me. "I'm so proud of you," I said, squeezing just a little tighter.

Arms wrapped around me in turn. Noah's hugs were all-encompassing. Like I could bury myself here and stay safe forever. "Thank you. For what it's worth, I'm proud of you, too."

"It's worth everything."

After a minute, we both awkwardly stepped back.

Where did this leave us?

Ex-colleagues who ran into each other every once in a while?

Ex-friends who played nice when forced to?

Ex-lovers who were awkward all the time?

Everything was ex, ex, ex. It didn't have to be.

"I accept your apology," I said. "I know you've only had good intentions when attempting to help me."

He grinned. "Yes, but I'll plan to get your explicit approval on help in the future."

"Sounds like a deal."

When Noah, with his arms still encircling my waist, asked, "Do you want to go out for real sometime?", I thought I melted. Just a little. Maybe we could get on the same page again. A page of open communication and honesty.

"Yes," I answered.

There was a lot still to figure out, but we could at least start with one real date.

28

NOAH

"How is this romantic?" Daphne asked, trailing me into my bedroom where I rummaged through the overflowing laundry basket in the corner.

"Because we're both runners," I shot back, trying not to gag. Why did all my socks smell like they'd been fermenting in a swamp?

Daphne snorted. "And that's romantic *how*? You're both just going to end up disgusting messes."

I guess laundry had been placed on the back burner recently. Years of losing one sock to the washing machine really lowered my total count of socks owned.

"I like Macey as a disgusting mess as much—if not more— than I do when she's dressed up," I said, finally fishing out a pair of socks. Clean? Debatable. Not actively offensive to my nose? Good enough.

As I slipped them on, Daphne leaned against the doorframe, clearly unimpressed. "Have you considered if she feels the same?"

"She saw me fall off the side of a boat," I replied, straightening up. "Pretty sure sweat won't be a dealbreaker."

Daphne froze mid-sip of her water. Her metal bottle slipped from her grasp, clanged against the floor, and rolled until it hit the wall. "Wait—*what*?"

Oh, right. Had I never mentioned that?

The look on her face was pure gold, and I braced myself for the endless stream of mockery this revelation would undoubtedly inspire. Daphne didn't disappoint. "You *fell off a boat*?!"

I shrugged, casually tying my laces like I hadn't just unleashed an eternal inside joke upon myself. "You heard me."

Instead of picking up the water bottle, she collapsed to the ground and stayed there. "I never understood your fake relationship, and every day I realize I understand the two of you even less."

"You don't need to understand." I grinned, taking a quick look in the mirror. Hair? Ready to get wind swept. Outfit? All black, no leather jacket. "Besides, you're too young to date."

"What?" Daphne rushed to her feet, banging her knee on the nightstand in the process. The banging sound didn't faze me, though. I was going on a real date with Macey, and nothing was going to ruin my mood. "I've already dated like—"

I shoved my hands over my ears. "Don't tell me." A panicked thought just occurred to me. "Oh, fuck. We never talked about..."

This time Daphne was the one to shove her hands over her ears. "Oh my God. Are you going to say sex? Stop it. Stop it right now."

Did I mess this up as a caregiver? I never once brought up safe sex or...intimacy in any sense of the word. What if Daphne had gotten pregnant? Did schools still teach kids how to roll a condom onto a banana?

I cleared my throat, probably looking as awkward as I felt. "It's important to stay safe—"

"I know!" She waved her hands up in a 'stop there' gesture. "I grew up with social media and went to public school. You think I don't know how to use a condom?"

The flush on her cheeks mirrored the one I felt on mine. "Okay, I just wanted to make sure. I should have brought it up earlier."

Her eyes softened. "First of all, I'm glad you didn't. Saved us both the embarrassment. Second, not having this talk with me doesn't make you a bad caregiver. You know you're the best, right?" Her nose twisted. "Even when you're a disgusting mess who doesn't have clean socks."

I swung an arm around her. "Thank you."

"Okay, get out of here before you have to tell Macey you were late because you tried to give your little sister the sex talk four years too late."

Halfway to the door, I nearly tripped. "Four years?"

"Go!"

Chuckling on the elevator ride down, I attempted to scrub this conversation from my memory forever.

Macey and I agreed to meet at the park halfway between us, the same place we'd run into each other months ago. This time, I'd be running with a recovered ankle and with a pretty girl by my side. What else could I ask for?

She was already there by the time I jogged to the entrance. I couldn't fathom how Daphne jumped ahead to the "disgusting messes" phase because right now all I saw was beauty blinding me. Not to mention, those leggings did wonders for her ass. All I wanted to do was peel them off her and take her to—

Focus, Noah.

That could wait.

I couldn't risk screwing up the first real date between me and Macey.

"I've got to say," Macey said as I neared, "this feels a little like you copied the first fake date I planned."

She was kidding, I knew, but there was something hidden underneath the surface. An unsaid question. *This isn't another fake date, is it?*

"There are a few key differences," I said. "One of which being that I can actually run."

Her eyes lit up as she assessed my ankle. The brush of her fingers against the skin there still sent goose bumps across my body. It's nice to know that some things won't change.

"It's healed?"

"Thanks to consistent wrapping and rest. Who knew?" I joked.

Macey laughed as she scuffed her toe against the pavement. "Certainly not you. What would you do without me?"

Although the question was teasing, I took it seriously.

"Nothing," I answered honestly. "I would have done nothing. I had no idea when we flew to Aruba how lucky I was to have your unfiltered honesty."

I was by no means a romantic relationship expert. I was probably the furthest thing from it. Honesty was at the heart of relationships for me. I couldn't bear to listen to someone who only wanted to talk with me because of a follower count or because of the clout they hoped to gain.

"Wow." The upfront honesty took her by surprise, but I was pretty sure it pleased her too. "I don't think I can take too much credit. You would have gotten there without my words."

"Maybe." It was possible. "But it would have taken me a lot longer."

When Macey turned her head, a stray hair stuck to her cheek. She tucked it behind her ear. "Speaking of taking long. Are you ready to lose?"

"Lose?"

"I'm planning to beat your time, Hansley." She grinned.

Then she took off running.

Shit.

"Wait!" I yelled a few paces behind her. "You have to take the path with the spiky bushes!"

Macey listened and turned in the right direction. There was that, at least.

My ankle had healed, sure, but without my stamina, I felt like an amateur again. My legs burned, my lungs screamed, and I couldn't help but wonder: *Why did I ever think this was fun?*

Then it hit—the familiar adrenaline rush. My chest expanded, and I remembered exactly why I loved running: it made me feel invincible, like I could take on the world.

I picked up my pace, closing the gap between us. Fortunately, I hadn't planned for us to become the "disgusting messes" Daphne had predicted. In fact, we were just a few steps away from—

Macey skidded to a halt, her braid whipping around her neck as she turned. "What is this?"

I grinned, my chest still heaving.

Beneath the shade of a sprawling oak tree, a picnic blanket lay spread out, its red-and-white checkered pattern bold against the vibrant green grass. A wicker basket sat open, revealing its contents: golden croissants, wedges of cheese, plump grapes, and slices of crisp apple. An ice bucket nearby cradled two bottles of sparkling water, their condensation catching the sunlight like tiny jewels.

"You didn't really think our first date was going to be running a 5K, did you?" I asked, gesturing for her to sit beside me against the tree.

Her expression softened as she approached. Her fingers trailed over a single red rose in a small glass vase. She sat down, glancing up at me with a smile that made my pulse quicken in a completely different way.

"I don't really care what we do," she said softly, her voice carrying a weight that stopped time for a moment. "As long as we do it together."

"I know," I said. "But I wanted to do something special. Something we haven't done before. Like a symbol of something new."

"I love it." She reached for a sparkling water and cracked it open with one hand.

And then...silence.

I spent so much time thinking about setting up this date and getting everything ready that I never considered what to talk about. Not that I ever needed to think about stuff like that before.

This was awkward. Was Macey feeling as awkward as I was right now?

Think, Noah, think. What should we talk about?

University? No, I didn't want to make it seem like I was bragging.

Her blog? Maybe. I wanted to know more about it.

Our expectations? I didn't even know how to bring that up without sounding like a weirdo.

"I'm glad some things don't change," Macey suddenly said, setting the can down onto the blanket.

"Huh?" I frowned, unsure if I understood. Was she talking about us? I thought we were on the same page that we didn't want things to stay the same. Things were different now, which I appreciated.

"In front of your fans, you're this super cool dude," she continued, her voice light and teasing, "but in front of me, you're still a nervous wreck."

My jaw dropped. "I'm not a nervous wreck! I told you. I got over the minuscule nerves I had around you."

She stretched out her legs, crossing one ankle over the other, a small smirk tugging at the corner of her lips. "So that wasn't you mentally debating topics of conversation before speaking?"

How the hell did she do that?

"No."

Her gaze didn't waver, her eyes locking onto mine with that familiar knowing look. I could feel the weight of it, like she was waiting for me to crack.

And, of course, I did. It only took about as long as it took me to break into the box of croissants.

"Fine," I muttered, finally giving in, "maybe I was a little nervous. Only because I don't want to screw this up."

I dropped a croissant onto a napkin and handed it to her. As I waited for her response, I shoved half of my croissant into my mouth. How did I go so long without eating croissants? Maybe I focused too much on egg whites and protein in the morning. Were these buttery pastries the key to true happiness?

"You're not going to screw it up." Macey ripped off a small piece of the croissant and chewed it gently.

"I'm not sure about that."

"Why do you think so?"

Needing more time to answer, I finished off the rest of the croissant and dreamed about having babies with it.

I picked at the edge of the wicker basket. "I've never had to worry about keeping someone close to me before. I mean, I have Daphne and Nathan, but they're family, so they're trapped with me. Everyone else usually had a motive for wanting to spend time with me. So I learned it was best to keep everyone at a distance."

"You said you think about people like Instagram followers. They'll either leave or come to dislike you." She folded the napkin in her lap. "Do you still think that?"

That had been my philosophy for so long, but it sounded

wrong now. "I'm not sure. I mean, look at some of the shit people have said about you online."

Macey shook her head. "I'm not talking about those anonymous online jerks. We'll never figure out who they are, and they don't matter. I'm talking about the people around you, for real."

I thought about it. Really, truly thought it over in a way I hadn't before. Was it fair of me to think about people in that way? People like Macey, Daphne, and Nathan had proved that some people do stick around. That they're capable of seeing through all the bullshit you put out there and still love you anyways.

"Yes," I said and watched her eyes fill with disappointment.

Before she could turn away, I put my forefinger under her chin and lifted her eyes to meet mine. "But I'll add a third option. Some people will stick by you, too, even when you say something stupid or post a horrible sushi photo."

She cracked a smile.

"I like you, Macey, almost as much as I love you. I'm frantically trying to figure out how to get you not to leave."

"There's nothing for you to figure out." She scooted closer to me so that our thighs were touching. "I don't think you could get rid of me now. Because I like you and I love you."

Did my heart just fucking soar at those words?

Yes. And I was not ashamed.

I wrapped an arm around her shoulders and pulled her closer into my chest, feeling the warmth of her body against mine. "I love you, Scribbles."

She rested her head against my chest, her voice soft and teasing. "I love you, too. But I hope you don't mean I can't leave you in a physical sense."

"Of course not," I murmured, my fingers gently stroking her arm. "I'm never going to stop you from going places. I want to be the person in your corner, cheering you on, confident in the knowledge that you'll come back."

"We'll always come back to each other." She shifted slightly, pulling back just enough to rest her head against the tree trunk. Her eyes softened as she looked at me. "So where does that leave us now?"

"In a real relationship, of course," I said, feeling a smile spread across my face as I brushed a stray strand of hair behind her ear.

"Right." Her smile mirrored mine as she leaned into my touch. "I can't believe it took us so long to get here. What do we do now?"

I cocked my head. "What do you mean?"

"Logistically, we don't have to keep up with fake dates now. Do we say anything publicly?"

"Nah," I said, my hand moving down to rest on her leg, giving it a light squeeze. "Let people think what they're going to think."

Her eyes searched mine for a moment before she asked, "Are you happy?"

I blinked, taken aback. "This is literally the happiest moment of my life. Why would you ask that?"

"Not just about this, but in general." She bit her lip, her brows knitting together. "You're taking a social media break, you're going back to school to change careers, you're in a new relationship. That's a lot of change." Her voice softened, tinged with hesitation. "Are you happy with how everything turned out?"

I paused, considering her question. "Truth is, I'm still not sure what I'm doing." I pulled her closer, our foreheads nearly touching. "I think it'll take me a while to get there and feel completely happy and confident in my decisions. But this? Me and you?" I pressed my lips gently against her forehead, lingering there for a moment. "It will always be the one thing I'm confident in and happy about. What about you?"

Macey smiled, her hand resting on my chest. "Me?"

"It's not like you haven't had a lot of changes, too. Are you happy?" I asked, my fingers lacing with hers.

"Yeah." She nodded, her grip tightening around my hand. "I'm actually a lot happier than I thought I was going to be. Getting fired sucked, but it made me realize how ready I am for the next stage of my career." She leaned forward, her face inches from mine, her smile widening. "Starting my blog made me feel like I was in control over something I loved. Not to mention, I get to do it all with a hot boyfriend at my side."

Boyfriend.

The word sent a thrill through me, new and unfamiliar but in the best possible way. I tilted my head, my heartbeat quicking as I leaned in to brush a soft kiss on her lips. "Speaking of doing it all..." I couldn't hide the grin that spread across my face. "What are you doing this summer?"

29

MACEY

The Burrow Bitches

> Kira: What am I going to do without you??

> Macey: I'll only be gone 3 months!

> Ariadne: A lot can happen in 3 months.

> Britney: a lot ;)

> Ariadne: What does that even mean?

> Macey: Guys, don't do anything crazy without me this summer.

I'd never packed so fast in my life. Once I said yes to road-tripping with Noah and Daphne this summer, time seemed to move quicker.

Noah would never admit to what Daphne revealed in thirty seconds: that he had been putting off the start of their trip so that we could reconcile. My heart had warmed for a minute before guilt cooled it off. They had been dreaming of this trip for a year, and it was my fault they were losing time.

So we agreed to leave today. It wasn't like I had a job to show up to tomorrow or anything.

I had begun to finally feel confident in myself and in my decisions. Sure, it often felt like I had no idea what I was doing, but now I understood that feeling was normal. It didn't matter if you were in your twenties, thirties, forties, or beyond—it was okay to take your life day by day. I would much rather live life not sure what was going to happen tomorrow than face a planned day that would make me miserable.

It didn't hurt that *Macey's Miles* fit perfectly for a road trip series. It'd be my first series in my blog, but I was excited to feature *us* instead of just *me*.

Another thing I realized recently? It was okay if we all felt a little lost. I could be inspired by the friends and family who had it all together just as much as the ones who didn't.

As I shoved a pile of clothes into my suitcase, the door to my room creaked open. Kira leaned against the doorframe, her arms crossed, wearing a half-smile. "Is it crazy to leave on a three-month road trip with a guy you just started dating?"

I paused, holding up my long-sleeved Chicago Bears shirt. "Well, technically speaking"—I tied the shirt around my waist—"we've been fake dating for months."

Kira chuckled, but her smile faltered, revealing a hint of sadness. "I'm just trying to find an excuse to get you to stay."

Her words made my heart ache. I crossed the room in two quick steps and pulled her into a tight hug. "I'll be back before you even know I'm gone," I promised, my voice muffled against her shoulder. "Plus, I left extra money to cover my share of the rent, so no worries."

Kira squeezed me a little tighter before letting go, her eyes a bit glassy as she took a seat on the edge of my bed. "I don't care about the rent." She gave a small laugh, brushing her hair behind her ear. "Who else am I going to complain about work to every night? Or share a pint of ice cream with?"

I smiled as I returned to my suitcase to tuck the last of my clothes in. "You can FaceTime me whenever, and I'll make Noah pull over for ice cream."

"Deal." Kira grinned, but I could still see the sadness there. The clock on my nightstand caught my eye. Noah would be here in a few minutes.

After zipping up the suitcase, I tugged it off the bed, and Kira helped me drag it into the living room. She stood there for a moment, hands on her hips, eyes glistening.

"I'm proud of you, you know." Her voice cracked a little, and I had to blink back the tears forming in my own eyes. "I'm glad you're following your heart."

Damn it. I didn't expect to cry today. "Me too."

She sniffled and then cleared her throat. "Where's your first stop?"

"We're going to spend the night at my parents' place. Then we're heading to Detroit."

Kira's eyebrows shot up. "Aw, a family gathering. I can't wait to hear how they react when you introduce Noah as your real boyfriend."

I chuckled, shaking my head. "There's a lot to explain to them."

Noah was heading back to school in the fall, but he planned to study all summer to refresh his knowledge. I had offered to help, even if my role would mostly involve reading flashcards and teasing him with sexy rewards along the way.

Just then, a car beeped outside. "Your ride is here."

I sighed, the weight of the moment settling in. We hugged one last time by the door, and I held on a little longer than I meant to. "Don't do anything crazy without me," I teased, pulling back.

"All I do is go to work and read books," Kira said, smirking as she opened the door for me. "Trust me, you won't miss anything."

That made me feel like I was going to miss a lot.

But while leaving meant missing out on some things, it also provided the chance to have new experiences of my own.

I laughed, but as I stepped out into the hallway, a wave of emotion hit me. The adventure ahead excited me, but leaving Kira, my partner-in-crime, even for just a few months, left a bittersweet taste in my mouth. With a final wave, I headed outside, suitcase rolling behind me. Noah stood by the car, waiting with a smile that immediately brightened my mood.

I dragged my luggage down the stairs to where an SUV was parked. The beeps got more intense. *Hopefully the neighbors aren't home.*

The back seat window rolled down and Daphne popped her head out. "Get in loser! We're road-tripping."

"Okay, Regina George." I high-fived her through the window as I walked toward the trunk to pop my luggage inside.

Noah met me there, greeting me with a kiss on the forehead.

I could get used to this.

"Are you sure you're okay with leaving for so long?" he asked while opening the trunk.

In the broad sunlight of the day, Noah's skin looked as tan as ever, glowing beneath the sun's warmth. The veins in his fore-arms pulsed as he effortlessly lifted my luggage into the trunk, each movement as smooth and natural as I remembered. Even after seeing every inch of him—countless times—I still thought those forearms were the sexiest thing I'd seen.

"Spending three months with my boyfriend and his cool

sister while gathering content for my blog?" A playful grin tugged at my lips. "Yeah, I'm sure."

Noah wrapped an arm around my waist and drew me into his chest with a possessive yet tender grip. "I'll never get tired of hearing you say that."

"What, my blog?" I mumbled into his chest, still half-laughing.

"While I'm immensely proud of your blog," he whispered, his breath warm against my skin, "no, that's not it."

"Your cool sister?" I teased.

"Macey." His voice dropped, just a little, and the sound of my name in his mouth made my stomach flutter.

"Oh," I exaggerated the syllable, dragging it out in mock surprise. "My boyfriend."

He hummed softly in response, the vibration of it sending shivers down my spine. "Say it again."

"My hot boyfriend, Noah."

His response was instant, a sharp intake of breath followed by a low, guttural, "Fuck." He pulled back just enough for our foreheads to press together, the gentle pressure sending a wave of warmth through me. "Do you think Daphne would mind if we went back to your room for half an hour?"

Before I could answer, the car beeped, loud and sudden, startling me out of the moment. I laughed, my shoulders shaking as I shook my head. "Yeah, I think she'd mind."

As we climbed into the car, Noah taking the wheel and me sliding into the passenger seat, Daphne poked her head between us, her eyes wide and exaggeratedly disapproving. "If I have to see that every day, we'll need to get some doggy bags for all my vomiting."

Noah pressed a button to start the car as I watched, fascinated. "Once a drama queen, always a drama queen."

"*I'm* the drama queen?" Daphne leaned back in the middle

seat and crossed her arms. "Who nearly cried when I told him to leave the LEGOs at home?"

"I did not nearly cry," Noah scoffed. "I was just thinking of ways to keep us entertained."

"Oh, I'm sure you and your new girlfriend will find plenty of ways." She smirked.

I forgot what sibling arguments looked like. "Let's hold on the fights until day three at least," I said, then turned to Daphne. "Maybe we can find a hot partner for you this summer."

"*Please*," she said just as Noah yelled, "Not happening!"

Noah turned up the radio as we fell into comfortable silence. I opened up Instagram. While the growth in my followers count had slowed compared to the last few weeks, it was still increasing.

I gave Noah's profile @*noahhans* a quick glance. His most recent post about taking a few months off was still up, and it had been met with positive reception. The comments poured out their understanding and encouragement for taking breaks from social media.

When he returned to his account in the fall, things would be different. I knew he was a little bit worried about what people would think—it was inevitable for us all—but he knew he had the support of the people who mattered the most to him.

I held up my phone for a selfie. "Everyone, smile!"

This would be the first photo to mark the rest of the summer, and in a way, the start of our futures. And I couldn't imagine starting the journey next to anyone else.

30

NOAH

3 Months Later

It was dark when we pulled into the gas station. Macey pointed out that the distinct lack of people and absence of light made the scene look like a scary movie. I reminded her that it was midnight, and Sunday was crossing into Monday. Of course there weren't going to be people getting gas at a random station outside of Chicago.

Normally, at this point in the night, we'd be in a hotel somewhere sleeping off the drive or just coming back from a day of exploring. Things were changing now, though.

It reminded me of summers as a kid—how you spent three months straight eating hotdogs and playing games with kids in the neighborhood, only for it to disappear in the span of a weekend. Suddenly, you woke up on Monday and were forced to return to school.

I hadn't felt that way in a long time, yet here I was, on the cusp of returning to classes, homework, and exams.

We'd dropped Daphne off in St. Louis earlier today. She and Macey had teared up when we said our goodbyes, and Daphne made it very clear that if Macey and I ever broke up, she was on

Macey's side. Fair enough. Fortunately, I never intended for anything to get in between Macey and me again.

After three months on the road, Daphne was ready to see her schoolmates and get back into class. I didn't know I felt ready to do something similar until today. It had nothing to do with being prepared—I brought a handful of textbooks and all my old school notes with me to read this summer—but it was more about my mental state.

I wasn't sure if I could ever be ready for change, but this was as close as I got.

And it felt pretty good.

I stepped out of the car, and Macey followed.

"How much longer until Chicago?" she asked as I inserted my card at the pump.

I typed in my zip code. "About an hour. Maybe less, if you're behind the wheel."

She rolled her eyes. The speed at which she drove terrified me, but Daphne found it exhilarating. I loved Macey, but I felt much safer when I stayed behind the wheel. It was inevitable, though, that we needed to trade spots when I was tired.

"Are you excited to be home?" she asked.

"I'm always excited to be with you." I monitored the pump as gas filled the car. "I don't care if it's Aruba, Kansas City, or Chicago."

"Good way to avoid the question," she teased. "You don't miss home, then?"

"No, I do. The change makes me a little nervous, that's all."

Macey stepped closer and rubbed a hand over my bicep. "Yeah. Change is scary. But you've got me."

"I do," I said, running my lips over her hairline.

While Macey's blog thrived this summer—I couldn't keep track of her subscriber count anymore—I hadn't opened social media once. I didn't want to see what people said about me, if they said anything at all. It would be difficult to stay off social media when my girlfriend was a rising travel blogger, but I felt comfortable returning on a part-time basis.

She brought her free hand to my cheek and tugged me down. No effort was needed because I moved eagerly, capturing those sweet lips with mine.

When she started to pull away, I reached forward again. "There's no one here."

"I'm not having sex with you at a gas station." She laughed against my lips.

Sex had been hard to find time for when you were constantly with your sister.

"Of course not," I said, planting a string of kisses down her throat. "A gas station doesn't have everything my plans need."

A small sigh, and then, "Plans?"

"Lots of them."

I slid my hands up the lithe curve of her waist, where the base of her ribs flared with every breath.

"Tell me about them," she demanded.

Suddenly, I was overwhelmed by how far we'd come. This brilliant, beautiful woman was all mine, and we'd never have to fake anything again.

"I can share a preview," was my generous offer.

It was delicious to kiss like this, slowly, lazily, able to enjoy every anticipatory moment. I found myself leaning down, pressing her back against the SUV I had to return tomorrow. When our lips came into play once more, her hands strayed down from my neck to my chest and abdomen.

"I love you," she whispered, and I held onto the words like they were my salvation.

"I love you," I said.

We continued kissing like that, on the cusp of something

new. Just when I was about to pull away and suggest we finish the drive home, I heard a car door slam.

"Macey?" a deep voice asked.

My girlfriend stepped off the car and out of my arms.

Huh. I didn't like that.

She squinted her eyes as she stared at the man who had pulled into the pump next to us. "Landon?"

That name sounded familiar, but I couldn't put my finger on why. Old friend? Ex-boyfriend?

When the man in question, Landon, got closer to us, the light above us illuminated his features. Tall dude, about my height, around our age too. He had short dark hair that I couldn't find a word to describe other than *curly*, and based on the muscles on him, he lifted a lot of heavy weights.

"It's so great to see you again!" He pulled Macey into a tight hug as she gave her nervous laugh.

That laugh was worse than the ones she had around Jennifer in Aruba. This was DEFCON 1. Who the fuck was this guy?

Macey stepped back after the hug, an all-teeth smile frozen on her face. I wrapped an arm around her shoulders, trying to launch her back to the present with a squeeze of a hand on her shoulder.

"Landon," she gritted through her teeth, "this is my boyfriend, Noah."

The male pride in me roared. *Take that, stupid lifter.*

But Landon was unbothered, offering me a hand to shake. "Nice to meet you, man."

Okay, ex-boyfriend was out of the realm of possibilities.

"So," Macey stuttered, her usual confidence momentarily faltering. "What are you doing here?"

Landon blinked, his brown-as-soil eyes squinting in confusion. "Getting gas?"

Idiot.

Macey let out that nervous laugh again, high-pitched and rickety. "Obviously. But I thought you lived in some other state."

"Oh!" Landon adjusted, and I took a moment to glance at his car. It was an SUV, like my rental, filled with boxes. "I did for a bit, yeah. I'm moving back to Chicago, though."

"What?" Macey shrieked, her voice rising higher than intended before she caught herself and calmed down. "I mean, uh, why are you moving back to Chicago?"

"It was time," he said, deflecting.

The words hung in the air between them for a second, begging for the addition of *this is why...*

It never came.

"Oh, right," she said. "Funny how there are so many cities in the world, and yet you're moving to Chicago."

I didn't need to be good at reading people to pick up on the annoyance in Macey's tone and stance. Almost defensive. For the life of me, I couldn't figure out why she felt the need to be like that.

Landon tensed, his laid-back vibe replaced by something more guarded. "Life is funny sometimes."

"Sometimes," Macey repeated dryly.

Okay. This was getting out of hand.

I decided to step in before things got worse. "It was great to meet you," I said, my voice cutting through the moment. "But Macey and I are about to head out."

Landon's eyes, previously focused on the sour expression on Macey's face, darted over to me, surprised. If it weren't for Macey's reaction, I might've thought he was a perfectly average, easygoing guy. Clearly, there was more to this than I had expected.

"No problem," he said, forcing a smile. "It was nice to meet you." His gaze shifted back to Macey. "Maybe I'll see you back home."

Home?

Once he turned his back, Macey whispered, "We'll see about that."

As if the string of events couldn't get any weirder, Macey nudged me out of the way to get to the driver's seat. She signaled for me to go round to the passenger seat.

"I cannot believe this." Macey seethed as she adjusted the seat to fit her shorter legs.

"Me neither," I said. "Mostly because I don't know what I'm supposed to not be believing."

She took a deep breath and checked the mirrors before pulling out.

"Landon is a jerk," she said, like that explained everything.

The hair on my arm pricked. Maybe I had misunderstood the situation earlier. "Did he do something to you?"

"No." She shook her head. "Not to me."

I glanced at the speedometer. "Holy shit, slow down."

"Can't." She glanced at me apologetically. "We have to beat Landon to Chicago."

The seriousness in her tone caught me off guard. I had a feeling that whatever came next was something we all couldn't come back from. "Why?"

"Because I need to warn Kira that the man who broke her heart is on his way home."

AUTHOR'S NOTE

Thank you for reading!

Thanks for joining Macey and Noah on their journey. I hope you enjoyed it.

Please consider leaving a review on Amazon or Goodreads. I cannot emphasize how much they mean to us authors, and you would have my eternal gratitude.

ABOUT THE AUTHOR

Becca Fall is a romance author and coffee enthusiast. Having grown up on a steady diet of contemporary and fantasy romance, she now writes sweet and steamy stories with a side of humor.

Becca lives in the United States with the house plants that she works hard to keep alive. When she's not reading or writing, she can usually be found planning her next trip, baking chocolate chip cookies, or rewatching the same show she's watched a million times.

To get in touch, visit beccafallbooks.com or follow @beccafallbooks on Instagram and TikTok.

www.ingramcontent.com/pod-product-compliance
Lightning Source LLC
Chambersburg PA
CBHW050013120726
47903CB00006B/1751